I Won't Cry

Jaylen and Jessica Series

Shaquanda Dalton

I Won't Cry
Copyright © 2013 by Shaquanda Dalton

ISBN ISBN-13:
978-1491224700

ISBN-10:
1491224703

Printed in USA

Acknowledgements

I want to first thank God for all of my accomplishments, my life, and my ambitions. I also want to thank my mother Ellean and my cousin Lakausha for her ongoing support and encouragement.

I want to give a great thank you to my editor Susanne Lakin and my cover designer Derek Murphy.

Last, but not least, I want to thank my fans for all of their support. I want to dedicate this book to them. Thank you.

Part One:

Jessica

Chapter One

I flinch seconds before his fist connects with my neck. I reach up to grasp my neck, gasping for air. I find myself on all fours on the living room floor trying to remain calm, but the panic rises in my chest and out of my mouth as I scream. He kicks me over and over again, and my body pulses up and down, and I wish it would stop, but it doesn't.

I sit up straight, panting as I look around my room. The same bare lonely walls stare back at me, and I lean back against my pillows and blow out a breath. It was just a nightmare, and Chris can't hurt me now.

Even though I know it was a dream, I can't help myself from lifting up the covers to see if any of the bruises are still there from last summer. I can't see anything past my enormous stomach sticking straight up like a bunny hill, so I thrust the covers down to my ankles and rub my eyes. The clock reads seven thirty a.m., and if I don't get up now, I am going to be late for my first class.

I walk out into the living room and kitchen, finding them empty, then spot a note scribbled on a Hooter's receipt:

Hey Jessica, Had to run in to work early today. Don't worry about me taking you to school. Take a day off. I'll be home around 5. —Malcolm

I take in a short breath. I hate missing school, but I hate taking the bus too, and waiting in twenty-degree February weather isn't a thrill either. I walk through the kitchen and into the living room, stopping right in front of the balcony window. The ground below is completely covered in a white thick one-foot blanket of snow. I inhale deeply before going back to the kitchen and leaving Malcolm a note that I'm will be going to my classes anyway and for him to pick me up.

I close the bathroom door behind me and grab a hand towel from the cabinet under the sink. I stand in front of the mirror, strip my clothes off, and stare at my swollen belly. I know I'm going to love this child more than I've loved anything or anyone in my entire life. This baby will be the only thing I have that's all mine.

Christopher Burguin is the father of my child, and he isn't father material worth shit. I shake my head slowly with disappointment before standing in the tub to let the water from the shower wash over my body taking all my frustration and crankiness away. I can still spot some of the bruises on my arm and legs. Maybe not bruises—more like scars. There's a deep-cut scar going from the top of my left shoulder to the back of my elbow that makes me look like I just got out of surgery. My back has the most scars, but I don't look at those that often. I want to leave the past behind me and move on, and I think it's a blessing that those scars are on my back because I'm not looking behind me. I'm looking forward.

I've been staying with my friend Malcolm for the last seven months ever since I escaped Chris' clutches, and I hate being a burden to him. Malcolm's a playboy and loves having girls around, but my being here, wobbling around pregnant, isn't a real turn-on for the girls who stumble in here late at night. He stopped bringing them around, I think. If not, he's hiding them from me or having his fun when I'm at school or something.

I rinse quickly, then dry off in my room. I don't think I can ever repay Malcolm for letting me stay with him for so long, though. He and his brother, Jaylen, are two of my closest childhood friends from when I lived in Aurora, Illinois, with my grandmother.

I put on sweatpants and then a T-shirt before looking out the window. It's not snowing yet, so I settle on wearing a pink hoodie and my black coat.

Once outside the apartment building I start my journey to the end of the block toward the bus stop. Sometimes Malcolm drops me off at school if the weather's bad, but I told him I need to get my exercise. There are a lot of people at the bus stop this early, and we all stand around looking at nothing in particular. I don't recognize anyone's face, but I do settle my eyes on an old lady sitting on the bus bench fussing with her purse. She reminds me of Grandma Mae.

I let out a sigh and shift my attention again to something else. Anything else. I hate feeling this hurt when I see an old woman who reminds me of the only person who loved me like a mother. My Grandma Mae raised me for as long as I can remember, and she was the most happy, smart-mouthed, fun-loving person I had in my life. Then she was gone.

When the bus arrives, I sit down near the back and stare out the window. I love school, and it makes me feel like I'm doing something productive every time I go. I rest my hands on my stomach as I ride. I have about three more months before I give birth, so I should be able to finish the semester and take the whole summer to bond with my baby before school starts up again in the fall. This will be perfect.

I smile for the first time today, and when I arrive at the school fifteen minutes later and find my friend Kayla arguing with the school's mascot, my smile stretches further.

"Um, what are you doing?" I ask, walking up to Kayla, then giving the panda mascot a sympathetic smile. The school must be having a game, and sure enough the mascot hands me a flyer with all the details of an upcoming basketball game.

She rolls her eyes at the animal, then links arms with me as we enter the school. "Girl, that thing came up behind me, all sneaky and shit, trying to hug me. It took all of me not to beat the shit off that dude. He lucky I settled for cussing him out."

I laughed. Kayla isn't anything if not blunt and smart-mouthed. She's wearing her favorite short Baby Phat coat that covers everything but her legs. Instead she's wearing boots that come up to her thighs, highlighting her curvy legs and ass. Kayla and I share almost every class together, by coincidence, but it's no surprise that we became friends. Well, maybe it was for me since I normally keep to myself, but Kayla told me when we first met that she could not continue walking to class without complimenting the boots I had on. I was wearing black-and-brown leather boots that Jaylen gave me for Christmas last year that I'm still wearing today.

"You shouldn't pick a fight with an endangered species," I say to Kayla as we walk into English class. The room is small and fairly empty except for three other students sprinkled in the back of the room. We settle into our usual seats in the middle of room and take out paper and pens.

She smacks her lips. "Bet you he won't bother me again though." She smiles and I laugh, shaking my head.

I glance at Kayla sitting next to me in our last class of the day and then back up at our instructor. Did he really just say read fifty pages by tomorrow, or did I just imagine that? The look on Kayla's edgy face says it all, and I know she heard him too. I blow out a breath and look down at my desk at the notes in front of me. Oh well. This is what I signed up for when I decided to go back to school. Even though I didn't go back to the University of Chicago because of lack of money, I'm happy with my decision to attend a smaller community college.

The instructor sets his coffee mug down and stares at the blackboard at the words he's just written. He rubs his gray beard, then turns to look at his students, showing a face that's tired and bored. "Okay, that's all I have for you all today, I guess. I was going to say something else, but I guess I . . ."

Kayla and I don't wait around to hear the rest of his words. No one else does, in fact, and we follow the crowd out the door. That man sure can ramble.

"Oh, thank God," Kayla says as soon as we make it out of class. Kayla looks every bit of twenty-five with her black silk weave down her lower back and light-brown contacts that I'm sure she doesn't need. "I thought that man was never going to shut up." We laugh.

"So what are you going to do now?" she asks as we continue down the hallway and toward the exit.

"I don't know," I say. "Do you have something in mind?"

"Eh." Kayla shrugs. "I thought about going to the club tonight, but it's not fun going by myself, you know."

"No, not really," I confess. I had only been to the club one time in my life, and that was with my baby's

11

father, and the night was not a pleasant memory at all. I cringe at the thought of my nightmares.

"Well, it sucks," she confirms. We reach the double doors that lead outside, and she stops walking as soon as we get out. "So you have a ride, right?"

I nod. It's become a routine for Kayla to ask out of courtesy if I need a ride, and I always decline. This is because Malcolm always picks me up from school when he gets off work. "Oh, well. Okay," she says, then reaches over and gives me a hug. "Catch you tomorrow, and don't forget to read!"

I laugh and wave after her. I watch her climb into her small coupe car and drive off waving and smiling.

I'm suddenly pulled away from my thoughts when two loud horns blow out from the street. I turn and see the oh-so-familiar car parked on the street, and I can't stop smiling. What is he doing here? I start walking—or to put it more accurately, wobbling—toward the car, when he gets out and walks toward me with his arms stretched wide

"Hi, Jaylen," I say as he snuggles me in his warmth. "What are you doing here? I thought Malcolm was picking me up." I wasn't complaining. In fact, I couldn't be happier.

Jaylen takes the book bag from my shoulder and helps me get settled in the car. "What, you're not happy to see me?" he asks with a small smile and a raised brow.

"Of course I am."

Jaylen and I have become so close over the years that I consider him my best friend in the world, hands-down. I can talk to him about anything, and I trust him with my life. Yes, we argue sometimes, but even the big argument we had last summer wasn't enough to truly break us. I was in the wrong in that fight, and I regret it to this day because it's the reason my belly is swollen, why I'm single, and why I have no place of my own. He tried to warn me. I just didn't listen.

I reach over and hug Jaylen close. He is shocked at first, but he quickly recovers. He's used to my sudden emotional outbursts since I've been pregnant. He pats my shoulder. "I'm happy to see you too, Jess," he says softly into my hair.

It's not that Jaylen's been away, but he's just been so busy opening up his second sports bar in downtown Chicago that we've hardly had time to see each other. When he's not working on his bars or spending time with his girlfriend, Angela, he comes over to the apartment to hang out with Malcolm and me for a couple of hours a week. But hardly more than that. So seeing him here, at my school on a weekday during heavy traffic hours, is a pleasant surprise.

I break the hug and look up at him with a worried face. "Where's Malcolm? Did something happen?"

Jaylen smiles quickly and starts to pull off. "No. I just wanted to pick you up, that's all."

"Where's Angela?"

There's a pause. "Home."

My mind suddenly goes back to last summer when she and I didn't really get along. She accused me of hanging around Jaylen and Malcolm for their money, and thought I was having sex with both of them— which couldn't have been farther from the truth. I don't see them that way, even if Jaylen and I did—

I stop myself before I finish the thought. I don't want to think about what happened because I'm too embarrassed and ashamed of my actions that I refuse to think what I did with him ever happened. I try my hardest to block out the night we made love every time I come close to him. Yes, it had been a moment of weakness but . . .

I stare out the window so Jaylen can't see my face— or better yet, my blush. We continue driving down the street. However, when we come to our expected turn, he keeps straight.

"Where are we going? You missed the turn."

Jaylen shrugs. "I got to grab a couple things from the mall." He turns to me. "If that's cool with you."

"Yeah, of course."

"Guess what?" he asks, peeking over at me again. "I'm having the grand opening for Miller House next month." Miller House is Jaylen's newest bar located twenty miles from his first one.

"Wow, congratulations."

His mouth curls ups into a smile. "Thank you. You're going to be there, right?"

"I wouldn't miss it for the world."

We continue riding in a nice silence, and I close my eyes to try to get in more sleep. I haven't been able to sleep at night, and it's taking a toll on my body. Most of the time I stay up late crying over Chris. Even though I'm done with him romantically, I can't help wishing he hadn't abandoned me with his baby.

We arrive at the mall, and Jaylen comes around and opens my door for me. I leave my book bag and the rest of my books in the car, and Jaylen and I walk side by side into the entrance.

The mall is crowded inside, but I don't mind at all. I don't get to go to the mall that often, and love window shopping and seeing what they have. I wobble beside Jaylen, who is nice enough to walk my pace. When we walk past a maternity store, Jaylen asks if I want new clothes.

"No, thank you," I say. "I'm about to pop, and hopefully will be able to lose the baby fat soon."

"If you say so. You hungry?" Jaylen asks as we continue walking.

Doesn't he need to buy something? "Not right now," I say. Of course I could eat, but I would hate to waste his money when Malcolm might have something to eat at home.

"You're a weird pregnant woman," Jaylen teases, smiling at my belly. When he first found out I was pregnant with Chris's baby, he was furious and couldn't stop yelling. He hated Chris, and I can't say I blame him for how he felt. Chris was an abusive, possessive asshole, and the only reason he got me pregnant was to trap me so I wouldn't leave him and run to Jaylen or Malcolm's house again. He used my desire to have my own family against me since I never knew my birth parents, and my Grandmother Mae raised me.

I grew up in a small house back in Aurora and Jaylen and Malcolm moved next door to me when I was eight, and when Jaylen was nine and Malcolm eleven. I grew up very tomboyish because of them, but it was cool. I convinced myself that people would have still made fun of me either way. I'm not much of a tomboy now, but I'm still not into makeup, and I don't care too much for perming my hair. My hair is long enough to reach the middle of my back, and I keep it straight with a flat iron and moist with hair spray and lotion. I avoid grease so it doesn't clog my pores.

I stare up at Jaylen and smile, and he smiles back. He has such a handsome smile showing sparkling white teeth that speaks confidence and likability.

"What are you thinking about?" Jaylen asks, walking so close beside me our arms keep brushing against each other. He doesn't notice, or if he does, he doesn't say anything.

"You."

His smile spreads at my honesty. "Good thoughts?"

"Well, I've missed you. It's like I haven't seen you this whole week."

"I've been working on the new bar. You know how it is," Jaylen says with a strained voice like he's unhappy about his work time as well "Angela been bitching about it too."

I freeze. "I'm not bitching to you, am I?"

"No, you're not. But she . . . she says what you're saying in a different way." He pauses. "We argue a lot," he adds so softly I hardly hear him.

We continue walking at a snail's pace, and a lot of people are going around us, but I don't pay them any attention and focus on Jaylen. "Is it bad?"

He shakes his head and I feel relieved. "No, of course not," he says. "Angela says what she has to say. I tell her I'm just trying to get money so she can spend how she wants to spend, and then she shuts up, maybe mumbles a bit more, and goes to bed."

"She's probably just horny," I whisper to myself, but Jaylen hears me.

"Yeah. Most of the time anyway."

We laugh again and start walking a little faster. I don't know what store he wanted to go to, but I'm just enjoying his company. I haven't been able to chill like this with him in months. Since I started going to college again and he started working on a new bar, our time alone has been kind of scarce.

"I want to buy you something," Jaylen says as we pass Forever 21.

"I would like my own mall, please. One with the moving floors just like the airport, so I don't have to walk that much." I say, smiling from ear to ear.

He turns and looks at me with such intensity I think he's going to kiss me. "If I could I would, Jess."

I look down at the floor as I feel the burn surface in my cheeks. "I'll just take an afternoon with you. That will be fine."

"Yeah, sure," he says, taking my hand and directing me inside Foot Locker. "Let's go in here, and let me grab these shoes right quick."

I nod as we go inside, and the place is packed with men and grade-school kids trying on shoes and boots to get them through the snowy weather we're having.

Jaylen picks out a pair of gorgeous gray shoes with dark green strips across the top and side. He grabs a jacket to match, and soon we're standing in line with three people in front of us. "You can go sit down on that bench if you want," Jaylen says, nodding to the brown bench near the kids' shoes.

I nod and sit on the nearest bench, which gives me a chance to rest my feet and ankles and also keep an eye on Jaylen. Not that I should want to, but a part of me just likes to look at him. He's six foot two, with a handsome light-chocolate face, a fresh cut fade, and a stubble. His arms are muscular and big enough to wrap tightly around me in a warm embrace whenever we hug. I shake my head. Why am I thinking about this again? He is taken, for goodness' sake. I wish I had remembered that when ... There I go again. Stop thinking about it.

I shake my head softly and remember that he has a live-in girlfriend. When Jaylen looks my way and shoots me a soft wink my heart flutters in my chest. I shake it off. He can be so silly sometimes.

By the time we leave the mall, I'm hungry and wish I had taken Jaylen up on his offer to buy me food. Oh well. I can just go home and have dinner there. Inside the car Jaylen is quiet—quiet for a guy that has just gotten himself new shoes. I wonder what he's thinking about.

We get in the car and pull off quickly. I want to ask him if anything is wrong, but I don't know what to say exactly. Maybe nothing is wrong. I turn my head facing the window and look at the Chicago skyline as we drive. Just a beautiful-looking city, and part of me wishes I'd been born here and lived here all my life. I came here to Chicago with Jaylen and Malcolm to go to Chicago University, but we all eventually dropped out. Jaylen dropped out to start his own business. Malcolm dropped out because he hated it and now works part-time at Jaylen's bars and part-time as a mechanic at some garage. I dropped out because Chris had convinced me to also start my own business as a professional photographer, but unlike Jaylen's business, mine never took off.

"You okay?" he asks, looking between me and the road.

"Yeah. Just thinking. Why are you so quiet by the way?" I tease, looking over at him.

He shrugs. "Nothing to say, really. I wish you'd let me buy you some new clothes. You wear the same five outfits all the time."

I smirk at him. "I told you. I'm about to pop in a couple more months, so why waste the money? I don't plan on being pregnant again or anytime soon."

"Yeah, that's true," he says softer, almost to himself. We continue to drive, but our silence is interrupted when Jaylen's phone starts ringing.

"Hello?" he answers, one hand on the wheel and the other to his ear. "Yeah, yup. Right now. Yup. All right, bro." And he hangs up.

I want to know who it was, but I don't want to seem in his business. I think he was talking to a man because he said "bro" at the end instead of "bae" or "baby," for Angela. Maybe he was talking to Malcolm, who wanted to make sure I'd gotten picked up safe and sound.

We pull up to Malcolm's apartment building a few minutes later, and I feel disappointed about having to leave Jaylen's company. He's so chilled and relaxed, which makes being with him so comfortable. I reach for the door handle and am about to get out, when Jaylen touches my arm. I turn around, and his face is five inches from mine. My heart starts racing, and before I can stop myself, I run my tongue across my bottom lip. Jaylen smiles and says, "I'm going in here with you for a sec, okay? I want to say what up to Malcolm."

"Okay." I swallow. I start to open the door, but Jaylen walks over and opens it for me. He is a gentleman, and that's one of the many things I like about him. I grin as he takes my hand and pulls me up. I wobble fast beside him, trying to keep up

Inside the apartment building is a grand hallway with a row of apartment numbers displayed on green doors. Malcolm's apartment is on the second floor, to my dismay, and at the end of the hallway. We start climbing the stairs that are conveniently placed right next to the entrance. We continue up the stairs, but when we reached the top, Jaylen drops my hand, and I can't help but feel my heart sink a little. I don't know why, but it kind of hurts. Just a little. I mean, why hold someone's hand if he's just going to drop it later? I take a breath and shake my head. I know it's just my weird moods and raging hormones talking.

When we get a few feet from Malcolm's door, Jaylen slows his pace so that I can catch up. When we reach the door, Jaylen pulls out the key to Malcolm's apartment. The two of them have each other's spare key in case either gets locked out. I've also had a key to Malcolm's apartment since I moved in with him, but it's deep inside my book bag.

It's hot in the apartment, and I exhale deeply, tossing my bag to the floor. I spot Malcolm sitting, boxer shorts only, in the living room, his face glued to the TV and Xbox controller in his hand. He glances over when Jaylen and I enter the room, but his fingers never stop moving. "Took long enough," Malcolm says, giving Jaylen a wink. "I thought you was never gonna bring her back."

My cheeks get hot, and I refuse to look at Jaylen. Instead, I step further into the room and scan the apartment again. "I was only gone half the day. What happened in here?" I ask, trying desperately to change the subject.

Malcolm shrugs.

Jaylen leans against the door with his arms folded. "He was probably waiting for you to clean it up," he says, muffling a laugh.

"Man, shut up." Malcolm pauses the game and looks over at the socks hanging out near the balcony, the plate of what was once a sandwich on the coffee table, and video game cases laid out over the floor. "I'll clean it up in a second. I was waiting until I got up."

I roll my eyes and sit down on the couch too. I look up at Jaylen, and our eyes lock. I wonder why he's still standing. I wish he would sit down. Next to me.

Jaylen nods and turns to open the door. "I'll catch up with y'all later. I have to pick up Angela from work."

Malcolm gets up to clasp Jaylen's hand. "All right, bro. Let me know if you want me working tonight."

"Yeah, most likely I will need you. I thought you was going out with that one girl tonight though?" Jaylen asks, leaning against the door frame.

Malcolm shrugs. "It's not really that serious. If you need me to work, I'll work."

Jaylen smiles. "Oh, good looking out for me, bro. I'll see y'all later." He looks at me, and the corner of his lip curls up. "Stay off your feet for a while, Jess." And just like that, he's gone.

Malcolm turns around and frowns at the stuff scattered around the living room. "See, I'm about to pick it up right now."

"Put some pants on while you're at it too."

He scoops up his plate and goes toward the kitchen. "I don't think I'll ever get used to living with a girl."

I stand up, against Jaylen's order, and follow Malcolm into the kitchen. He places the plate in the sink and turns back toward the living room, leaving the plate unwashed. "What if you wanted to marry one of those girls you be going on dates with?" I ask, going to the refrigerator. "Aren't they nice?"

"I'm never getting married!" he shouts from the living room. I laugh and pull out the ground beef from behind the case of beer. Malcolm steps back into the kitchen a few moments later with pants on, but he frowns when he sees the meat in my hand. He shifts from foot to foot. "I was going to cook tonight, Jess."

"Oh, it's okay. If you're going to clean, I can cook," I say, placing the package on the counter. I reach up in the counter cabinet to fetch a skillet, when Malcolm picks up the meat.

"I'll just order takeout," he says.

"Why? Is something wrong with the meat?" I hold it up to my nose for a quick sniff.

"No." He pauses. "But since I might be working at Jaylen's bar tonight, there's no point in you making a big meal. Besides, didn't Jaylen just say to stay off your feet for a while?"

I smile but keep my voice firm. "Since when do you listen to Jaylen's advice?"

He smiles and scoops the meat from my hand and puts it back in the fridge. "Since it doesn't concern me."

Hmmph. "You know, Malcolm. If you don't trust my cooking, you can say so."

The corner of his lips curl up into a half smile. I guess I hit the mark. "I can show you a few things."

He fishes out a wide pan from the cabinet beside the sink and turns the burner high. "You want to make burgers or tacos?" he asks, leaning against the counter. A handful of his braids fall onto one of his shoulders as he folds his arms across his chest.

"Burgers. Definitely," I answer.

"Good. I think we ran out of shredded cheese for the tacos anyway," he says right before his phone starts ringing.

"Then why did you even suggest—" I stop when I realize he isn't listening. He's talking faster than his lips are moving into his phone, so I turn my attention back to the hot skillet. I wash my hands in the sink before retrieving the ground beef again and scooping up a handful of meat and rolling it into a ball. I flatten it out in my hand the way I'd seen Jaylen do it one time and lay it in the skillet. The burger juice pops at me, and I curse and fling my hand back. "This thing shows no mercy."

Malcolm cups his hand over the mouthpiece of the phone. "You have to season it first, Jess."

"Oh." I turn back to the burger and frown at the lack of pepper, salt, or season salt blended in. Well, late is better than never. I reach up and pull down pepper and salt and sprinkle a little of each onto the burger. I figure I'll wait a few minutes to flip it and do the other side. I face Malcolm again for the next instructions, but he's still knee-deep in conversation.

I'm tempted to just call Jaylen for step-by-step instructions, but it can't be that hard. As long as the inside isn't pink, it's done. I smile when the image of the burnt chicken I made for Jaylen last summer pops into my head. I was staying in his apartment with him when Chris and I broke up, and he didn't mind the chicken at all.

I shake my head and keep my eyes on the beef, when Malcolm nudges my shoulder and hands me a spatula. I flip the meat over and add the seasonings. As hard as I try to focus on the meat, all thoughts of last summer come to mind. My pregnancy—the good. My disastrous fight with Jaylen—the bad. And my homelessness—the horrible. I grimace. All that's behind me now, and I'm allowing myself to move on. Nothing that happened last summer can affect my future if I don't let it. I have to keep thinking that. I'm in control now, and I can handle things. Right?

Chapter Two

Two weeks later, I find myself in yet another mall with Kayla as she holds up a light-blue mid-length dress to my neck and tilts her head to the side. "I think it looks cute," she says, not yet removing the dress. The hanger starts poking my face, and I step back.

"I think it's too short. Let's find a dress that comes down to my knees at least," I stress. This is the third store in the downtown Chicago area that we've been to searching for an outfit for my twenty-fourth birthday party tonight. My actual birthday isn't until Wednesday, but everyone wanted to celebrate it on a Saturday. Even though I'm very excited to spend time with everyone tonight—except for Angela—I don't think Kayla needs to make a big fuss about the outfit. They love me for who I am, so it doesn't matter what I look like. Don't get me wrong—I don't want to walk into Five-Star Lanes looking like I just came out of a cheap chicken coop either.

I smile at Kayla, when I notice her giving me a frowny pout. "You never like dressing up." She groans, putting the dress back on its rack. "What kind of girl are you?"

I shrug. "A simple one?"

She rolls her eyes at me. "Girl, you are far from simple," she says, then takes my wrist in a strong grip and leads me to the back of the maternity store, where they stock the pants.

She holds up a pair of neon-pink pants. "Try this on with the black top I picked out."

I take the pants from her hand and head to the dressing room, taking the all-black top Kayla had picked out earlier. "Also," she calls, "we're supposed to meet up with everyone at the bowling alley in an hour, so these are going to be the last clothes you try on. Try to like them!"

I close the door to the dressing room and remove my boots and pants. I shove one heavy leg in after another until the pants are secure around my waist. The pants fit firm and snug, but they make my ass look bigger than I like. I take a deep breath and remove my own green shirt and replace it with the black blouse with the ruffles on the sleeves that Kayla picked out. I think the shirt looks fancy, while the pants look more wild and spontaneous, but somehow they complement each other nicely. I reach up and finger-comb my hair so I have a few strands hanging over both my shoulders. My hair reaches midway to the curve of my back and has always been my best physical attribute. I look in the mirror and smile at my outfit. This looks nice, and tonight is going to be fun. I smile even harder when thoughts of beating everyone by at least sixty points start playing in my head.

I change back into my street clothes and meet up with Kayla, who's standing not two feet from my door. She frowns after glancing at the clothes I'm wearing. "What the hell, Jess?" she says after scanning me from head to toe. "You didn't even let me see how the clothes looked on you. "

I laugh. "They're fine."

"But what was the point of you trying them on if you wasn't even gonna let me see them on you?"

"You're the one who told me we were in a rush."

"Not that much of a rush. Shit, we have reservations, and it's your party."

I hold the clothes up and smile. "Let's just check out and go have some fun."

I can feel her eyes on my back as I walk away. "What got you so excited?" she asks. The sarcasm drips from her tongue like liquor.

I slide the clothes onto the counter toward the skinny-fingered cashier. "Trying to think more positive in my life."

She gives me a smile and wraps an arm around my shoulders. "Girl, don't we all."

Five-Star Lanes is one of the most popular bowling alleys, and on a Saturday night not even the twenty-degree weather shortens the lines to get a lane. The building has a mature atmosphere with a strict no-children-after-five policy. The entire first-floor lighting is dimmed except for glow spotlights on the lanes. Even the food area and bar in the back keep the lights down low. I inhale deeply when the smell of their famous burgers hits my nose. Ooh, I love this place.

Kayla nudges my arm, turning my attention toward her. She had changed into dark-blue boots to match the blue low-cut dress she's wearing. Even though I'm the one pregnant, her breasts are fully plump and sticking out enough to cause every guy within ten feet to snap his head around for a double take. After we walk inside, she lets her coat fall open and takes off her

31

wool hat. "Let's go find them. They said they'd be on lanes seven and eight."

I scan the lanes until my eyes land on thirty multicolored balloons covering the benches opposite lane eight. "I think I see them," I choke out. I can't even talk. We walk up to the lanes and Jaylen, Malcolm, and Angela are all standing and smiling, bowling shoes on and everything.

"Happy birthday!" they shout as soon as I'm within earshot. Malcolm and Jaylen wrap me in a hug, and Kayla soon joins in. I squeeze them as tightly as I can, and I'm reluctant to pull away.

"You don't have your bowling shoes on," Angela says, breaking off the hug in her annoying high-pitched voice.

I stare down at my boots and roll my eyes. "Oh. Yeah, I know. I'll go get some." Before I can turn, I get a good look at the lane seven seats that hold the balloons. The seats are also filled with gift boxes, cupcakes, a cake, party favors, plastic plates, silverware, and pink and white decorations. "Wow," I breathe.

"I got your shoes right here, Jess," Malcolm says, holding up a pair of torn size eight-and-a-half red-and-blue shoes.

Angela's eyebrows pinch together, and I laugh. "Thanks, Malcolm," I say sweetly as I take the shoes from his hands.

"Yeah, thanks . . . Malcolm, was it?" Kayla says, strolling up close to Malcolm.

Jaylen taps my arm and nods at Malcolm's face, which has frozen in a stare at Kayla's body in that dress. "I think his tongue is about to fall out," Jaylen whispers in my ear. I laugh, and Angela shoots us both a look.

I clear my throat. "Let's just bowl."

"Good idea," Jaylen says, then grabs Malcolm by the collar and drags him to the touch-screen monitor to put our names in. "Do you want to go first, Jessica?"

"Why you asking her? I'm your girlfriend," Angela says, her fists clenched and eyes zoned in on Jaylen's back. Whoa, that was random.

Jaylen turns around with a look so deadly I think he's going to cuss her out or worse, but he takes a deep breath. "Girl, if you don't—"

"'Cause it's her birthday, why you think?" Kayla says, stepping up to Angela fast. I see her ankle start to shake, and I know Kayla is about ready to come out of those heels.

Malcolm's arm snakes around her waist, and he pulls Kayla back a couple of feet. "Slow down, Ma. Don't mess up your hair over that."

Kayla stops struggling and turns to look at him. Then she laughs. "Trust me, I won't." She pats her hair a few times, then mean-mugs Angela before walking over to the chairs and taking a seat.

I turn back to Jaylen, but he's staring a bullet hole through Angela, who's just standing there with her lips tight and her eyes firm.

Malcolm nudges Jaylen out the way. "Well, I guess I'll put the names in," he says, trying to break the tension. "I'll be first. Jess, you're second. Then Kayla, Jaylen, and Angela."

My eyes jerk back to Angela to see if she would object to being last, but she doesn't say a word as her eyes stay locked with Jaylen's. Jaylen walks closer to her and whispers something in her ear. She rolls her eyes, but Jaylen doesn't stop talking. A few minutes pass, and they're still talking. Is he talking about me? About their relationship? Her attitude problem? Malcolm touches my arm, and I jump up a full foot in the air. "Your turn to bowl, Jess," he says.

I give him my hard eyes for scaring me, and he laughs. I pick up a medium-size ball and throw. My arm has grown stronger since my pregnancy, but it hasn't improved my aim, and I gutter the first ball. Oh, well. So much for beating everyone by sixty points.

"You got to watch your feet, girl," Kayla says from the seats. She's sitting next to Malcolm, who has an arm draped behind the back of her chair. Both of them are smiling.

I try to focus on the ten pins, but my eyes sneak back to where Jaylen and Angela are standing. They've stopped talking now, and Angela's looking down at the floor. Jaylen nods at me, and I nod back and face the pins again. This time I manage to knock down six with two pins remaining on both sides.

I turn back to my friends, and Jaylen and Kayla are smiling. Malcolm walks up to me, takes my arm, and swings it toward the lane. "Okay, do it just like this next time. You were so close. I think you got the aim, I just think the way you roll your ball is a little off. It's all about the release," he says, still not letting go of my arm.

"Okay, I think I got it," I say, pulling my arm from his hand.

"Watch me, girl," Kayla says, bouncing up and choosing a small-size ball. "It's all about focusing."

All I hear is a hum because my eyes and ears have gone back to Jaylen and Angela, who are now sitting down talking in a low voice. When Jaylen peeks up at me, I quickly look down pretending to check out my shoes, until I realize I can't see my feet.

"So, Jess," Angela asks, rolling her tongue across her teeth. "How many months along are you again?"

Um. Hmmph. She's actually trying to have a conversation with me now. "Seven months."

"You're big for seven months. Are you sure you're not having twins?" she asks. Jaylen gives her a horrified look, but it's nothing compared to the frozen opened-mouth look I have.

I clear my throat before answering, "I'm sure."

Kayla peeks back at us, rolls her eyes at Angela's comment, then nods toward the monitor. "Your turn, Jaylen," she says, coming over to stand beside me.

"Aren't you scared it's going to hurt?" Angela asks, scrunching up her face with her eyes locked on my belly. Her look makes me squirm, but I try not to let it show. I've also never paid a lot of thought as to how it would feel giving birth to my first child. I figure it's going to hurt, but maybe I can handle the pain.

"Of course not," I say. I hope bad lying isn't hereditary.

Angela gives me her satisfied smirk, and I groan. Jaylen stands up and pats my shoulder as he walks by. "You'll be fine."

"Yeah, girl. You got this," Malcolm says. He's sitting with two empty seats on either side of him and has his arms spread out behind both. Probably waiting for Kayla to come sit down. "Don't believe the hype."

I smile.

"So," Angela says, leaning forward and lacing her hands together. "Are you still claiming Chris as the father?"

Jaylen gutters. Kayla's mouth falls open, and Malcolm's eyes gets wider than his hands. "Okay," Malcolm says, standing up. "Time for gifts."

I don't think anyone would believe the rumor that Chris had spread around all summer about him not really being the father, and I hate to wonder how it got back to Angela. Unless Jaylen had been talking to her about it. I shake my head and look at Jaylen. We lock eyes and he shakes his head. I look Malcolm in the eye, and all he does is shrug. Hmmph.

Kayla's head tilts to the side as she eyes Angela mildly. She leans down to my ear. "What that hoe mean by that?"

"Nothing."

Kayla looks likes she wants to say more but doesn't when Jaylen come back over. He looks at Angela sharply. "Bowl."

Angela tosses her hands in the air like a guilty child proclaiming innocence and stands up. "It was just a question."

Malcolm stands up and goes to the lane seven seats and picks up a long, wide box wrapped in pink-and-white paper. "Here you go, Jess. This is from me."

He hands me the box, and I sit down in the seat he had previously occupied. Jaylen had stepped from the lane and stands a few feet away watching as I open the box. A blue cotton robe with matching house shoes. I smile. "Thank you, Malcolm. I really appreciate it."

Malcolm nods. "Your old one was pretty rough-looking, so yeah." He laughs.

"Open mine!" Kayla says, picking up two small boxes. "It's a necklace-and-earring set. Open it and see if you like it."

Everyone around gives her a curious glance. Probably wondering, like me, why she told me the surprise. "Oh, whatever. It's not like she can't tell what it is from the long slender box and the small short one," Kayla says.

I open the boxes and nod in approval at the blue and silver set. "Sexy and classy."

"Just like me," Kayla says, laughing and fanning herself.

"Open mine," Jaylen says, smiling down at me.

"Ours," Angela stresses, going over and retrieving the biggest box in the room. Whoa. She plops it down at my feet and smiles. "I picked these out. Open it."

I look at Jaylen for reassurance. It's not that I think something evil is going to crawl out of the box just because she claims she picked out my gift, but, um . . . one can never be too careful of one's enemy. Well, she's not my main enemy. Chris is and I know that. It's just—I eye the box again—weird of her.

Jaylen's chuckle is so soft that if it wasn't for his eyes shining with humor I would think I imagined it. He places a hand on Angela's shoulder and nods. "Go ahead."

I tear the gold-and-white wrapper off and pull out the baby bag hidden beneath. It's heavy and obviously full of more stuff. I tug the zipper back, exposing baby bottles, pacifiers, diapers, and toys. "Thank you both," I say, meaning every word.

"You're welcome," Jaylen says.

Angela's face lights up. "I picked everything out. Jaylen paid for it, of course. But I picked out everything you would need. I figured since you're going to be a single mother, you'll need all the help you can get."

"Ang—"

"What? We all know Chris isn't going to lift a finger to help."

"Just leave it alone, Ang," Jaylen says, all traces of humor gone.

Angela sighs heavily. "It's not like everybody's not aware of her situation." She nods toward me. "She doesn't have an apartment, no job, and she's living off of Malcolm, for crying out loud."

Malcolm snaps his head toward her. "Um . . . excuse me?"

Kayla leans into Malcolm, not even trying to whisper. "This bitch is really about to make me fight tonight."

"Just because I don't have a job doesn't mean I'm not trying," I find myself saying. The anger of her words keeps thumping in my ear. "And another thing—I appreciate everything that's been given to me, and I'm not some stuck-up woman who takes everything in her life for granted like you, so learn some manners, 'cause you never know what situation you may be in one day."

"Damn," Malcolm and Kayla say at the same time.

"Well. Whatever," Angela says, shrugging and walking away, closer to the lanes.

Jaylen doesn't follow her but remains staring at me with admiration in his eyes. Well, at least I think it's admiration.

"Sorry," I say low enough so only he can hear. "I didn't mean to lash out like that. I just got so angry."

He shakes his head. "You good, Jess." Then the corner of his mouth curls up. "I got another gift for you."

Angela's head snaps back in our direction with a fresh redness on her face. "What do you mean you got her another gift? You didn't tell me about it?"

"'Cause it didn't cost money to buy. Well, not that much money."

A staff worker walks up to our lane and gives us a sympathetic smile. "I'm sorry," she says. "But my boss says that you have to continue your game because of the wait list. You've gone past the twenty-minute standstill."

"A twenty-minute what?" Malcolm asks, looking at her with his famous Kevin Hart face.

The woman swallows hard. "It's a rule we have here that requires active bowlers to be, um . . . actively bowling."

"Oh, no—that's fine," Kayla says, then turns to Angela and waves her off. "Your turn."

"What's the second gift?" Angela says, completely ignoring Kayla's comment.

Malcolm walks over to the lane and picks up a ball. "I'll bowl her turn. It's going to be my turn next anyway."

The worker smiles politely and walks away, and Angela never takes her eyes off Jaylen. "Well?" she asks.

Jaylen smiles at her. "Let me get it." He walks over to the pile of gifts and picks up something hidden beneath his coat. It's a thick box the size of a notebook but larger in height. He walks it over to me and motions for me to sit down. Everyone walks closer as

Jaylen takes a seat beside me. "I'm not going to take all the credit on this one. Malcolm helped me decide what it should be, but everything else, well . . . just open it." He's smiling proudly, and part of me doesn't want to look away from his handsome face, but the pull of curiosity overtakes me.

I glance down at the purple and white ties sealing the box and slide a hand across it. No wrapping paper this time, just a beautiful ribbon. I untie the ribbon and open the box. A cream-colored baby photo album faces me, and I pick it up and trace the pink and white loose-fitting swirls that cover the trim of the book with my finger. Oh my God, he made this. He made this for me.

I turn to face him but can't see him through blurry eyes. He reaches up and wipes a tear from my eye. "Don't cry, Jess. It's not that great."

"I love it. I love it so much, Jaylen. Thank you," I say, clenching the book to my chest.

"That's sweet," Kayla coos. "You're going to put all the pictures of the baby in there, right?"

"Duh," Malcolm says, playfully nudging her.

"Figured since you're a photographer that you'd be taking a lot of pictures of your baby and needed a place to put them in," Jaylen says.

I'm about to respond and say thank you again, but an irritated groan from Angela's direction stops me. I turn to catch her roll her eyes, groan again, and march straight toward the exit sign. I look back to Jaylen and see him watching her. "You better go talk to her."

Jaylen doesn't say anything as he stands up, shoves on his coat, and follows her.

Chapter Three

I walk fully into my bedroom after our long evening out and sit on the end of the bed. I take a deep breath and begin the long process of getting undressed. My shoes are already off, but by the time I get down to my underwear, I'm tired again. I walk over to the dresser and grab a huge T-shirt to sleep in, like I do every night.

I slide the shirt on just as Malcolm knocks on the door. "Come in!"

Malcolm peeks his head through. "Jaylen just texted me. He said he'll be taking you to school on Monday."

"Oh." That's different. "What made him want to do that?" I ask, starting to get excited.

Malcolm smiles. "He wants to give you something. That's all I'm saying," he says, then closes the door.

I'm really excited now, and my mind starts racing with the possibilities. What does he want to give me, and why didn't he want to give it to me tonight? Is it so big that he couldn't fit it in the car or have it delivered? Did he forget to give it to me tonight?

I pull out the book I'm supposed to read and roll under the covers. Even though I stare at the words in front of me, I can't keep my mind off Jaylen. Mostly because he's going to take me to school Monday, and he plans to give me something that he didn't want to give me around Angela. Hmm. The more I lay still, the more my thoughts drift off to more naughty places than they should. I shake my head and scowl at myself.

I turn and face the wall next to my bed and try to read with the book lying in front of me, but I can't focus. How is it that I can't get someone else's man out of my mind? He's Angela's man, and I shouldn't be lying up at night excited about seeing him again— gift or no gift.

Eventually I fall asleep and dream about my life back with Chris, and as expected I wake up screaming and crying. Malcolm rushes in and wraps his arms around me, rocking me gently. "Jesus, Jess. Almost a year later, and you're still having nightmares?" he asks.

I can't help what I dream about, but I wish I didn't dream at all. I stay in Malcolm's arms and rest my head on his shoulder. "You know, when I was younger I could never get away with telling my mom I was too sick to go to school," Malcolm says. He tells me a story every time I have a nightmare as if I'm a little kid, but secretly I love when he tells me stories. It keeps my mind off Chris and the painful memories. "That was because my mom used to work as a part-time nurse. You remember, don't you? So, yeah, I had perfect attendance growing up. Jaylen too. If there was something wrong with us, Mom would give us the medicine, and we'd be on our way to class."

I smile beside him, not saying anything, and listen quietly to his words. Yes, I remember his mom Sheri being a nurse a long time ago, but she had retired before I entered high school. His mom was always kind to me, inviting me over for hot chocolate and snacks. Sheri still lives in Aurora, Illinois, in the same house Malcolm and Jaylen grew up in.

I take a deep breath and relive the memories of all three of us playing around in the front yard between my house and Malcolm's house. Malcolm continues to talk, but my mind half-listens and half-thinks about my Grandmother Mae, who sat in a chair on the porch and watched us all play.

Grandma Mae.

I miss her so much. She had died on my graduation day when I was eighteen. She'd had a full-blown heart attack, and I was too busy walking across the stage to realize she wasn't in the audience. I had to be at the school early for the ceremony, and she still had a few chores to do at home and said she'd meet me there. There'd been no one around to call 911.

I shake the memory out of my head and take another deep breath. I have to learn to let go of my past. But how can I when it's a part of my present, even my future? I reach my hand around and rub my baby. My baby. It's nobody else's baby but mine.

Eventually I stop crying, and Malcolm stops talking. He gives me a peck on the forehead, when his phone starts ringing and gets up and leaves the room. I lie back down and try to focus on sleeping, but I can't. I fling the covers aside and walk over to the desk in the corner. I pull out my journal from the drawer and start writing. At first it's just scribble-scrabble about nothing much. I really just want to clear my head.

As I continue to write, I notice my writing veers toward thoughts of anger. Why did Chris have to hit me? Where was he now? Does he still think this baby isn't his? Does he know where I am? All these months of being pregnant and living with Malcolm—it's been over seven months since the last time I saw him. I used to love him, and the more I scribble, the more I realize how fake our love was.

I think back to the time when he led me into a local bar not too far away from our apartment. We were going to celebrate my pregnancy and also our engagement. He went in all smiles, showing me off like I was the prize he found in the cereal box, and he was the happy kid. That was before one of his friends accusingly said he slept with me, even though I don't know any of Chris's friends personally. He believed his friend instead of me, and before I knew anything that was going on, Chris had dragged me out of the bar. He beat me until I couldn't think straight, but I just curled up in a ball and tried my best to protect my womb.

Thankfully, for the baby's sake, Chris focused on my head and chest and back. He didn't try to uncurl me, and I think part of him didn't want to be a murderer. If he killed the baby, he knew he'd have to kill me too. There would be no way I wouldn't go to the police and tell them what happened even if he did threaten to kill me. I never knew how little my life meant to me compared to my child's. That was a feeling I never expected when I got pregnant, and I guess it made me grow up fast.

It's Monday morning, and I pull my pink-and-white maternity shirt over my swelled breasts and stomach as I get ready for school. I smile to myself as I look in the mirror, placing one hand on my stomach. "You'll be here soon, little one."

I find Malcolm in the kitchen chewing on double-sided buttered toast, and he salutes me "what's up" with a nod. I laugh. "This is what you do with your extra time since you're not taking me to class today?"

"Yup."

"No work?" I'm referring to his job at the garage or his job as the manager of Jaylen's new bar.

"Not until later tonight," he says, talking with his mouth full. I can't say anything since it's his place, so I scan the room for my book bag and purse to be ready to go when Jaylen texts me that he's outside.

I sit down and awkwardly maneuver into my winter boots. I hate bending over, and I hate standing back up after sitting down. Just too much sideways motion. When I get the expected text from Jaylen, I throw on a hat and scarf, heave my bag over one shoulder, and wave Malcolm good-bye.

Jaylen's standing outside his car not wearing gloves or a hat despite the February weather. He smiles and takes my bag. "Happy birthday," he says, steering me past the icy patches that the landlord of the building apparently missed.

"Thanks, Jay, but it's not till Wednesday," I say, smiling up at him. His eyes are soft and inviting, and I want to ask him what he's thinking, but he speaks first.

"I know. I just like the smile it puts on your face."

I'm burning red as I slide into the car, but thankfully he doesn't see it.

I try to flush out my mind by thinking about the classes I have today. Photography, math, science, and English. Only about four and a half hours, and I should make it without boring myself to tears in science or burning my brains cells too much in math. Maybe if I sit close enough to the teacher, the volume of his voice will keep me awake.

"You're not going to ask what your gift is?" Jaylen asks after driving for five minutes.

I had forgotten all about the gift and smile in anticipation. "Sure. Um . . . what did you get me?"

He's quiet for second. "I'll show it to you when we get there."

I'm about to object, but I don't want to seem too impatient. Inside I am burning to know what he got me, and thoughts from cameras to journals all come flying into my head. When we arrive at the school, I turn to face him, and he smiles and arches his eyebrows. "Yes?" he says.

Was he teasing me? "Um . . . you said I can have my gift now."

He nods and smiles as he reaches into the backseat and pulls forth a black plastic bag. "Close your eyes." I close my eyes and then feel something like a cube that's rough in my hands. "Okay, you can look."

I open my eyes and look down to see a red velvet jewelry box. Oh my God. I glance at Jaylen's face, but he just nods for me to open it. I open the lid and a gold locket, the size of my palm, stares back at me.

"It's a locket—so that you can have a picture of your baby in it and keep it close to your heart."

I trace my fingers along the edges of the locket, then press the latch on the side, causing the heart to pop open. The inside is empty for now, but my mind starts swimming with ideas of baby pictures to put in them. I suck in a quick breath. This really is the sweetest thing anyone has ever done for me.

I reach over and wrap my arms around Jaylen's body. He's shocked at first, but soon hugs me back.

"Why didn't you give this to me last night?" I ask with a squeaky voice.

"Well, you saw how Angela reacted to me giving you a photo album. I was going to wait till Christmas to give this necklace to you, but then I thought now was as good a time as any, so—"

I cut him off mid-speech to give him another hug. "I love it."

"You're welcome. Now get to class. I have some errands to run," he says, grinning down at me.

I get out of his car, but not without engulfing him in another hug and giving him a peck on the cheek. My day is starting off great, and if school goes well, I'll be on cloud nine for sure.

Chapter Four

The rest of the month goes by fast, and before I know it, it's the second week in March and I'm sitting in Malcolm's car going to Jaylen's grand opening for his new bar, Miller House. The snowy roads, freezing temperatures, and harsh winds have become a routine even in March, and I wonder how many people are going to show up tonight. It's already six o'clock, and I find myself yawning against my will as I lean back in the passenger seat. I look over at Malcolm, and he's quiet, driving with one hand on the steering wheel and the other leaning on the door's sill.

"Did you hear from Jaylen?" I ask, rubbing my hands together and bringing them to my mouth. Malcolm has the heat on, but it's taking time to warm up the car.

"Yeah. He said for us to just come on in and find a seat at the bar. He'll find us."

"Okay, cool."

"Angela's going to be there, but he told me she's not going to say anything to you that will come off offensive."

"Hmmph."

"I know. I told him she probably shouldn't say anything at all then."

"Why do you think he . . . ? I mean, I know he loves her, but what else does she give him?" I ask this question because I'm genuinely curious as to what makes him cling to Angela all this time, no matter what they go through.

Malcolm shrugs. "That's his ride-or-die chick. He's going to always stay by her side."

"Oh."

"Unless she fucks up."

Hmmph. I doubt that. "It has to be something else though. Something we're not seeing." Or something I missed completed that went straight over my head.

"Well. Angela loves the shit out of Jaylen, and he knows this. It's hard not to love someone who loves you so much. Also, they have a lot of things in common, and Jaylen always liked strong, independent women. I'm sure there're more reasons why they've stayed together that only the two of them know about, but those are just some of my observations."

Oh. I think back to first time Jaylen introduced me to Angela. She had just gotten off work at the mall and still had her uniform on. She smiled politely and asked how Jaylen and I knew each other. When I told her Jaylen and I had grown up together and had moved from Aurora to Chicago together, her demeanor changed. Or at least I saw that it had. She narrowed her eyes at me and asked if I had a boyfriend. This was before I met Chris, so my telling her I was single and had a good friendship with her boyfriend didn't really get us going with a good start. She'd eyed me with suspicion ever since.

"Here we are," Malcolm says, snapping me back to the present.

I look out the window and inspect the building. Balloons and banisters populate the entrance, and a huge neon sign announces MILLER HOUSE right above the arc of the door. The building's windows are huge, and I can see a crowd of people both at the bar and the nearby pool table. I can't spot Jaylen through the window, but I'm so proud of him at his point that I open the door to get out before Malcolm has a chance to finish parking.

The inside is far more impressive. The second I walk in, the sound of laughter, high fives, and pool games ring in my ear. The bar has a large spacious area with tables and chairs on the left side, games and TV screens on the right side, and the bar straight in the middle. The smell of beer and burgers overpowers my nose, but I like it. I step in fully, and Malcolm closes the door behind us, trapping in the warmth of the bar and keeping out the cold of the night.

"There's the bar," I say, pointing straight ahead. "Jaylen should be around here somewhere."

"You got the card?" he asks.

I smile brightly and hold up Jaylen's congratulations card I picked up the night before. It came as a blank card on which you write your own words, so I took the time and wrote him something really special to express how proud we were and how far he's come over the years. He started out with nothing three years ago, still in college with me and sharing an apartment with Malcolm while I stayed in a dormitory. He dropped out after a year and opened his own bar with no business degree—only his innate common sense, business sense, and determination. His first bar, Miller, was a success, and now, two years after the fact, he's opening up his second bar. I know he didn't succeed all by himself, and a lot of his help came from Malcolm and the bank that loaned him the money, but man. I couldn't be more proud of him.

Malcolm and I walk up to the bar and find a couple of seats near the rear.

"Don't you think you're too far along to be drinking tonight, ma'am?" the bartender asks, drying a beer glass with a rag.

"Oh, no. I'm not here to drink. I'm meeting up with my friend. Have you seen Jaylen?" I ask, smiling.

"You know Jaylen?" the man asks, giving my stomach a once-over with his eyes. "Is he expecting you?"

"Yeah, man. Go get my brother," Malcolm says, tapping the bar with his fingers.

"Oh, Malcolm! I didn't see you there, sir. I'll be back right away!" The man rushes off, leaving the beer glass and the rag behind.

"I see he knows you," I say, nudging Malcolm with my arm.

"That's Mort. He's working as manager at the moment."

"You're not the manager right now?"

"Not tonight. It's the grand opening, so we're all just trying to have a good time. Me and Jaylen will probably stay here all night though. I mean, once I drop you back at home I'll come back."

A hand touches my shoulder, and I swirl around in my chair. My eyes soften and my heart beats faster when I see Jaylen. He's wearing a white button down with khaki pants and a pair of new white and silver shoes. Jaylen smiles at me, then shakes hands with Malcolm. "Glad y'all came. Where's Kayla?" Jaylen asks me, giving the bar area a quick scan.

"She had to work tonight but congratulates you on your bar, and she wishes you all the best," I say smiling up at him.

"She's fucking hot," Malcolm says, nodding his head.

Jaylen and I laugh until our eyes lock. He smiles gently and nods toward the bar. "Is that card for me?"

"Huh?" I say, still lost in his stare. "Oh, right. Yeah, here." I hand it to him, but just before he takes it I pull it back to my chest. "Wait, I mean. It's not your traditional card, so don't be expecting anything witty or funny. It's one of those cards that let you write whatever you want to say in it."

"Oh," Jaylen says, still eyeing the card with the same excitement, if not more. "No money then?"

I laugh for a second and then stop. Maybe money in a card would have been a better idea.

"I'm joking, Jess." I look up, and the corners of his lips are pulled back.

"Oh, thank God!" I laugh.

Malcolm shifts in his seat, staring at us with his eyes slightly squinted, like he's trying to figure out a puzzle. "You guys are acting weird."

I keep laughing and laughing and don't stop until a sharp pain slams into my abdomen, and a pool of water runs into my boots. "Oh!"

"Jess, what's wrong?" Jaylen asks, rubbing my back and caressing my hair as I hunch over.

"Oh, shit! Did your water just break?" Malcolm says, standing up. He pushes a few chairs aside and waves his hands in the air. "Everybody clear out! I think she's going into labor."

Jaylen cups my face in the palms of his hands, forcing eye contact. But I can't talk. I can't say anything as this pain ripples through my body. I just want it to stop. What's happening?

"Jessica, focus. It's going to be okay. Do you want to go to the hospital?" Jaylen asks, his face two inches from mine. His eyes bore into mine, and for the first time in my life I see something I've never seen before in them. Fear.

I nod.

"Are you asking her? She's scaring me half to death. She doesn't have a choice!" Malcolm shouts, sweat building on his forehead. Everyone had cleared out, and a big area of space appears around all three of us. Not everyone in the bar knows what's going on, and the loud noises evaporates some of Malcolm's shouting. I'm betting Angela's on the other side of the bar, not even knowing what's going on. I don't even know what's going on.

"Go pull the car up, Malcolm, so we can go," Jaylen says, cradling me in his arms. The pain has calmed down a notch, and I find myself able to talk.

"You stay here and find Angela and meet us at the hospital," I say between breaths.

"No."

"You have to stay and tell her what's going on. She'll want to come too." Maybe. "But if you're gone, she won't have a clue, and even she does, she wouldn't have a ride," I explain. Even if it hurts not having Jaylen at my side, I don't want him to disappear on Angela. Besides, maybe I am okay. Maybe that was just a random—

"Ouch!" I scream as another pain stabs me.

Jaylen stares at me hard, slowly shaking his head. "We need to get you to a hospital. Now."

Malcolm comes out from the crowd and stands in front of us. "I got the car running. Let's go."

"Okay, but Jaylen's going to find Angela and meet up with us there," I say.

"Jessica, I don't care! Just get in the car so we can go!" Malcolm dips a shoulder under my arm and helps me walk till we reach the door. Jaylen's on my other side and stays with us until we get inside the car. He stays out, however, and leans his face against the window while Malcolm walks to the other side.

"I'll be okay," I promise him.

I swear he's about to say something, when Malcolm honks his horn and waves for Jaylen to step back. We pull off into the night, and in the side mirror I see Jaylen stand on the street for two seconds before running back into the bar to fetch Angela.

I ride the whole way to the hospital muffling my screams. Malcolm uses his cell phone to call ahead to the hospital and also alert Jaylen and Angela of what's going on. They promise to meet us there. If I'm going into labor, then the baby will be premature and could die. I can't think about that happening and push the D word out of my head.

Why did this have to happen to me? My heart rate won't slow down, and I am really starting to panic. I can't get hysterical. That can't be good for the baby either. I don't know what to do, I don't know what's going on with me, and I feel totally helpless and at the mercy of my body. And my body could be killing me.

I'm biting my lip so hard when we arrive at the hospital that it starts to bleed. A nurse with blond hair and heavy makeup is waiting for us outside with a wheelchair. The pain in my lower abdomen hasn't subsided, and I'm afraid to look down in case I see blood. I probably still wouldn't know what that means. How can I be so uninformed? I should have been like other responsible mothers and done research on what was happening to my body instead of just winging it. In fact, I planned on looking up information. I just thought I had more time. A lot more time.

Malcolm parks the car in front of the emergency doors and jumps out. He is over to my door in an instant, helping me out of the car and into the awaiting wheelchair. "Do you want me to go in there with you until you get settled? I have to come back and park the car," Malcolm says.

I shake my head. Of course, I don't want him to leave my side, but I don't want his car to get towed either. I don't have time to think, and his car is not the most important thing right now. The baby is. "Just go," I say between breaths. I can't even talk; I'm trying so hard not to scream in pain.

Malcolm gives me a hard look before dashing off to park his car. The nurse wheels me into the hospital quickly and then into an elevator. I don't get a good look at the hospital's lobby, but I'm sure it's clean and sanitized. I'm whisked up to a higher floor of the hospital, and the smell of bedpans and sanitizer floods my nose. I hate hospitals because of the smell. It's like they try to cover the smell of death with unscented soap and expect no one to notice.

They put me in a small room with only a bed, some machinery, and a big grand window on the far wall. I love the fact that I have the room to myself, but something happens to me when she pushes me into the room and I see that I am actually in the hospital. Like it's for real and I am really here. I can't explain it, but for a second I experience a moment of relief. I made it safely into a hospital, in a room where I'm going to give birth, and everything will be okay. I hope.

The second I realize this I let out the biggest scream I can possibly stand to hear. Everything that I was holding in while at home and during the car ride unleashes, and I can't stop screaming. The nurse has called the doctor because two people's hands are on me trying to take my pants off. I still don't stop screaming because I know the baby is coming. This baby has a mind and motive of its own, and it doesn't matter what I think or what the doctors think. This baby is coming now.

I am lying on the bed fully when Malcolm comes into the room looking at me in horror. My eyes are blurry because of my tears, and I hope his facial expression is due to my going into unexpected labor as opposed to there being something totally wrong with me and he doesn't know how to say it.

At some point during this whole ordeal, my pants get taken off, and the doctor is telling me to push. Malcolm stays in the corner. I try pushing, on the doctor's order, but I can't. Every time I lean forward, I feel my body ripping apart. I can't do it. I'll kill myself.

I start to feel lightheaded, when someone touches my shoulder. I look over, and Jaylen is standing beside my bed with Angela right beside him looking like she's seen a ghost. I guess my screaming is affecting more people than I thought. Malcolm has stepped a lot closer since the two of them arrived, but the doctor ignores them. He keeps encouraging me, and I keep screaming to the skies. I don't want the baby to come out anyway. Let it stay inside me for a couple more months or so. I don't know. I'd rather the baby be inside too long and be overdone than come out early and risk dying.

"Come on, Jess," Jaylen says softly into my ear. "Just push, so it can be over."

He says it like all I was doing was ripping a bandage off. Doesn't he know the risks? I shake my head and continue to scream. Jaylen holds my hand and my shoulder and leans me forward, to my dismay. I want to move from underneath his hand and get away from the pain, but I can't. Every way I turn I am inadvertently forced to push, no matter what I want. Why is Jaylen doing this to me? What did I do to him?

I close my eyes and pray that the pain will stop and everyone will let me fall asleep, but that doesn't happen. I feel a gush below my stomach and then pressure like the weight of a cat on my chest. I open my eyes and drop my mouth open.

Oh my God. It's my daughter.

Chapter Five

I stare at my baby girl cradled in my arms and become speechless. She just came out of me. She was freaking inside me and was walking around with me all this time. She had gone to bed, showered, ate, and slept with me all those months, and I hadn't even seen her face until now. I see her.

She is tiny in my arms, but she is mine. I smile. Jaylen leans down and kisses my temple, and I remembered where I am. I am in a hospital, and I just gave birth to a baby girl. What should I name her?

I suck my lip as I try to think, but just as I'm trying to pin a name to her face, the doctor reaches up and scoops her out of my arms. I'm left with my arms wide open, and my eyes start brimming up again. What's going on now?

Jaylen leans down. "He's just going to clean her up and make sure she's okay. He'll bring her back."

I stare up at him to read his face. I can tell when he's just saying things to make me feel better and when he is really telling the truth. Why didn't the doctor tell me that himself? What kind of hospital is this?

Malcolm steps forward and stands between Jaylen and Angela, who, to my surprise, isn't saying anything. "She'll be all right, Jess. I promise," Malcolm says.

"But she's so small. Isn't she early? Why did she come out so soon?" I have so many questions, and I know none of my friends have the answers. I close my eyes, lean back against the headboard, and shed silent tears. To my surprise, moments later, I feel smooth arms warm around me. I open my eyes, and Angela is hugging me with tears in her eyes too. Why is she crying?

"She'll be all right, girl. Just keep your faith," Angela says softly in my ear. I start to relax a little bit if even Angela is telling me to calm down, but I don't know. I just don't want to let my guard down completely.

The doctor comes in with my daughter a few moments later, and I realize how hard I was breathing because when she is placed back into my arms again, it feels like the world has resettled and I can breathe again.

My daughter's face is light brown, small, and round. Her lips are pouty, and her black hair is scattered all over her head. Her eyes are closed so I can't see them, but her nose is as small as my thumbnail, and I just love looking at her perfect skin.

"What you gonna name her?" Jaylen asks, standing with one hand around Angela like he can't wait for the day she'll be pregnant as well.

"I don't know. What do you think, Malcolm?" He is standing near the foot of the bed, and he just shrugs. I can tell he's tired, and I have no idea what time it is now.

I look down at my daughter and then up at Jaylen, and he smiles gently. I think about all I've been through in the last twenty-four hours, and I can't believe it. So much has happened in so little time. Everyone is here for me too. I am so thankful.

"I'll call her Jaslene," I say after a while.

Everyone nods approvingly, and it makes me smile hard.

"Pretty. Classy. What made you think of that?" Jaylen asks.

I think about it for a while, but I know the reason. I want her name to be something similar to Jaylen. Jaylen's the one who pushed her out of me when I didn't even want to move. It's more like he gave birth to her. Without him I would still be screaming to get her out.

"Just 'cause," I decide to say instead. No need to tell all the details of her name now. I just want to get her home.

Suddenly, the doctor tells me I have to deliver the placenta, and everyone leaves the room. That whole process is really weird, but eventually it's over.

"Why is Jaslene early?" I ask the doctor once I get situated on the bed again. "She's not supposed to be here for another two months."

The doctor who has strong Spanish accent and narrow beard gives me a contorted face like he's studying me. "Your daughter is not early. According to her size and weight, which is seven pounds and sixteen inches, she is full term. You have nothing to worry about."

Full term? Not early? That's weird. "Are you sure?"

He straightens out his glasses as he looks down at my chart that was placed at the foot of my bed. Then he looks up. "Why did you only have one appointment to see us before the birth, ma'am?"

"Huh? Oh, I don't really have good medical coverage, and all I really needed was a checkup and prenatal pills. I've been reading books and taking care of myself by eating right and exercising."

He scowls at me, and my upbeat explanation sounds like a childish excuse. "I'm just glad she's healthy," I conclude, ready to end the conversation and just spend time with my daughter. The doctor leaves shaking his head, and after a while everyone starts piling back into the room. Everyone but . . .

Then I remember something. "Chris," I whisper, not expecting anyone to hear, but everyone in the room does.

Jaylen's eyes narrow, like he knows what I was about to say. Or ask.

"No."

Both he and Malcolm are wearing the same stubborn faces.

"Just let me call him and tell him the baby's born. It's his daughter. He should at least—"

"No, Jess. It's over. I don't give a shit if you want to talk to him. It's done," Jaylen says, keeping straight eye contact with me.

I don't know what to say, but I know it isn't fair to keep someone out the loop about something as important as the birth of a child. I look over at Malcolm for sympathy. He is sitting on the edge of my hospital bed, but his eyes say he fully agrees with Jaylen. I sigh and take a seat on the other side of the bed.

Angela stares at me from where she sits in the chair against the wall. "Maybe we should call him," she says, shrugging her shoulders. "I mean, it's not like she'll be talking to him. Maybe we can even get him to start paying child support," she continues. Malcolm and Jaylen just stare at her. " Look, Jaylen, you can call him, tell him the baby's born, and hang up. It's that's simple. So when he gets the news about her suing him for child support, he'll know it's for real."

"What's the point of even calling him then if we're just going to notify him of the child support?" Malcolm asks, sounding annoyed. "We ain't got to tell him shit."

"That's what I'm saying," Jaylen says, pacing the room. "Fuck Chris."

Jaylen had told me about the time he and Malcolm went searching for me when Chris threw me out of the house. They stopped by Chris's house and beat the holy crap out of him. I didn't want to hear much of the details, but I guess the beating was enough to keep Chris from ever contacting me again. A large part of me is thankful for that, but there's a tiny part of me that wants to contact him for the sake of this baby. It's not right to keep Chris out of the loop.

"Can't you just have him see the baby? It's his daughter, and he has the right—"

I don't even get a chance to finish my sentence before both Jaylen and Malcolm cut me off. They both start yelling at me at once, and I can't separate whose curse words belonged to whom.

"You guys, just shut up!" Angela shouts suddenly. I feel grateful for her loud and obnoxious voice because I really feel smaller than a mouse with the stares Malcolm and Jaylen give me as they shout. "God, it's no big deal. You know Chris is going to see her again at some point 'cause they got to go to court. Stop babying her like she can't make a decision on her own. If she wants to tell the nigga the baby is here, let her do it. It's not like you guys can really stop her."

Malcolm remains silent, and Jaylen just stares at me. He takes a deep breath and reaches into his back pocket. "I'll call him. I'd rather you not talk to him. Especially in the late hours of the night when he can tell you more bullshit."

I don't disagree with Jaylen but keep quiet. I look over at Jaslene, who is miraculous still sleeping through all the loud yelling going on in the room. She looks so beautiful and peaceful that my mind suddenly drifts off to thoughts of her, and I forget all about

Chris for the moment. Jaylen follows my eyes, sighs, then leaves the room. Malcolm pats me on the shoulder before joining Jaylen in the hallway. I don't look up as they leave, but I hear Angela get up from her chair and join me on the bed. "Men can be jerks," she says. Her voice is impassive, and for a while I wonder if she is talking about Jaylen and Malcolm as well as Chris, or just Chris. I don't consider Malcolm and Jaylen jerks. They are just looking out for me.

"They mean well," I say, still staring down at Jaslene as she lies all bundled up.

Angela huffs and shrugs. "Well, anyway, you're welcome. I just didn't want to hear Jaylen's mouth all night about how stupid he thinks you are for even suggesting calling Chris." After she says that I wonder if Jaylen really talks about me behind my back. Or more interestingly, does he think about me enough to bring me up to his girlfriend while the two of them lie in bed? That just sounds weird.

Jaylen and Malcolm return to the room a few minutes later with blank faces. "He doesn't care, Jess," Jaylen says carefully, watching the expression on my face slowly sink. He doesn't care? My heart bangs in my chest, and I feel close to throwing myself face-first on the bed and crying my heart out. He doesn't care about Jaslene? She's his daughter. He doesn't want to see her?

I can't stop the tears from falling and wish I'd never gone back to Chris the second time we broke up. He got me pregnant, I believe, to keep me from leaving him again when it was he who'd dumped me. He got me pregnant, asked me to marry him, and then dumped me and beat the shit out of me because of false rumors about me cheating. How does that make any sense? He believes that I cheated and believes the baby isn't his. "What did he say exactly?" I cried.

Jaylen's face looks pained, and I can tell he doesn't want to say anything, but I have to know. What exactly were his words that caused me to hurt so much? I could tell by Jaylen saying Chris doesn't care that he summed up the words Chris said. "Just tell me," I say.

Malcolm says, "It doesn't matter, Jess. He ain't no good anyway. What could he give Jaslene? Nothing. Forget him."

I look over at Angela, and her face says the same thing Malcolm said. Forget him. I take a deep breath. I am going to have to move on with my life without Chris, but it seems Jaslene has to too. I close my eyes to take a much-needed rest. I'm not sure what tomorrow has planned for me, but as long as I have my daughter I will be fine.

I open my eyes later and realize I'm still in the hospital bed. I turn around and find Jaylen and

Malcolm engrossed in the TV. I look around for Jaslene and spot her in her own miniature bed the nurse had put her in right next to my bed.

When I sit up fully, Jaylen turns around. "How do you feel?" he asks.

I start to say "awful" because of Chris, but I just gave birth to a beautiful healthy baby, so I can't be doing all that bad. So I shrug. "The good outweighs the bad." I look around, but I don't find Angela anywhere in the room. "Where's Angela?"

"She went outside for a while. She complained her cell phone connection was bad," Jaylen says with a shrug.

"What does she need to have access to anything online right now or her phone? It's too early in the morning, isn't it?" I look toward the window, but the blinds are closed.

"Not that much later," Malcolm says. "You've only been asleep for thirty minutes."

I yawn deeply and snuggle into the bed a bit more. Just as I'm about to relax again, Chris pops into my head. My chest tightens, and I wish I had stayed asleep. It hurts too much to think about him, and I feel like an idiot every time he comes to my mind. Why did I even give that loser a second chance with me?

"What are you thinking about?" Jaylen asks, studying my frowning lips and narrowed eyes.

Malcolm's looking at me too, and his face is blank and waiting.

"I can't get my mind off Chris," I blurt out. "I feel like he abandoned—no, he did abandon my daughter, and I can't wrap my mind around it." I pause to see if their faces give away any indication that I'm overreacting, but they're both quiet, looking at me.

"He has no right to make a child with me and then decide he doesn't want to be a part of her life," I continue. "I feel used, and I feel like he rejected my family."

I lean over slightly and nod toward Jaslene. "There is nothing wrong with Jaslene, and I just don't understand why he doesn't want . . . why doesn't he want his daughter?"

Tears of anger start falling, and Malcolm and Jaylen surround me. I can feel Malcolm patting my lower leg, and Jaylen's right beside me caressing his hands through my hair. He leans down and whispers, "It doesn't matter what Chris thinks."

I shake my head. "It hurts, Jaylen. It hurts. You don't know how much I love Jaslene. I carried her in my belly with me all these months, and even though you guys just met her, I've been sleeping with her, eating with her, and feeling her move inside me every day, so it hurts to have someone to openly claim they want nothing to do with her. I feel the rejection, and

Jaslene doesn't deserve rejection. She deserves a family."

My tears don't stop streaming down my face, and at some point I catch Malcolm and Jaylen exchange a worried glance. I know I'm an emotional wreck right now, but I can't help it. "I've tried. I've been trying so hard to rebuild my life. I went back to school, I'm staying on top of my homework, I ate the right foods and did the right exercises so that Jaslene could come into the world the healthiest, and now her father, her own father, doesn't even want to see her on the day she's born."

I take a deep breath and catch eye contact with Malcolm. It's a strong stare, as if he's trying to give me mental strength with his look. After a few seconds I break the stare and look down until I feel the stroke of Jaylen's hand on my back. It feels so good, like a massage. I turn around and look at him, and he's giving me the same intense stare as Malcolm.

"I never discounted me having to raise Jaslene on my own. I expected that. I just thought that Chris was madder at me than he was at his daughter. I guess I also thought that once he saw her he would fall in love with her and want to be a part of her life." Jaylen stops rubbing me when he considers Chris coming anywhere near me and this baby. I shake my head though. "He acts like he doesn't care if I'm alive or not."

Jaylen comes around from behind me and engulfs me in a hug. It's tight, firm, and secure, and I've never felt more comfortable. His Armani cologne smells fresh, and I take a deep breath. My favorite scent.

I pull away from Jaylen slowly, only to be hugged by Malcolm. I am about to thank them both for making me feel better, when Angela comes back into the room looking tired and pissed off.

She squints her eyes at me, and Malcolm then shrugs. "You ready to go, bae?" she asks, coming over to stand in front of Jaylen, who's still hanging out by my headboard.

Jaylen looks down at me for a second, then at Malcolm. The two of them hold eye contact, then nod. Jaylen reaches down and gives me a peck on the temple. "Ang and I'll be back to see you tomorrow. Get a lot of rest. Malcolm's staying with you."

After a few words of good-byes, he leaves with Angela right in tow. I shake my head and smile. She is so lucky to have him. He's lucky too.

Chapter Six

Two days later I'm finally able to take Jaslene home. Malcolm's spare bedroom/my room had been turned into a baby's room while I was gone. There is a crib where the desk used to be, and the desk has been moved under the window. The crib is pink and white, and I admire the soft mattress on the bottom. The bars are sturdy and that's good. The main thing I want is for Jaslene to be safe.

Jaylen and Angela sit in the living room chatting with Malcolm as I explore the new room. The three of them had gone out and bought me the crib and changing table that I know must have run them around five hundred dollars. I take a deep breath and sit down on the edge of my bed with Jaslene wrapped in my arms. I look around the room and feel grateful for friends like Jaylen, Malcolm, and even Angela. When she wants to act like a friend anyway.

Jaslene yawns, and I stand up and place her in the crib. I lay her on her back just like the doctor said. I have a lot to learn about babies, but I can tell I lucked out with Jaslene. She's so calm and relaxed, and she hardly cries unless she needs milk. I stand watching her from above the crib until her eyes close and her breathing smoothes out. I smile and walk to the living room to join my friends.

Jaylen smiles when I enter, and I feel my face get warm. It isn't like I'm doing anything wrong, but the way he smiles at me makes me feel special, like I'm wanted. This probably has a lot to do with Chris refusing to come see Jaslene at the hospital and how I spent the better part of that night crying into the uncomfortable pillow the hospital gave me. Jaylen stayed with me for most of last night in the hospital, and we talked about what happened last year over the summer. I had forgiven Chris and went back to him, like the idiot I was. Chris laid his hands on me, something he'd never done before, so I thought it was a onetime thing. I forgave Chris, against Jaylen's advice that I shouldn't. Chris didn't change however, and after three months back in the relationship we got into another bloody fight.

I don't exactly know how Jaylen and I got to talking about last summer, but I do feel a little better afterward. He made me feel that Chris not showing up at the hospital was a blessing instead of a curse. It's better for Jaslene not to know her real father because her father is not even worth being called one.

I smile back at Jaylen and take a seat next to him on the couch. Angela is on his other side, and Malcolm is in the kitchen taking food out of the refrigerator. "She's asleep already?" Jaylen asks, looking over his shoulder at me. I nod. "She's a good sleeper," he says.

I nod again. "Yeah, but she'll probably be up in, like, two hours wanting some milk." I nod to my chest and am glad I decided to breast-feed Jaslene. The doctor said it was better than giving the baby formula, and since I don't drink or smoke, breast-feeding is okay for me.

Angela leans over Jaylen's lap and says, "Doesn't breast-feeding hurt?"

I smile again and blush. "No, not really. I mean, not once you get the hang of it."

Angela and I go back and forth for a while with her asking questions about breast-feeding and pregnancy and me answering them like the expert I'm not. I start to wonder why she is so curious about pregnancy. Maybe it's just a woman thing, because Jaylen and Malcolm aren't asking any questions. Well, at least we are talking, and she's trying to be a lot nicer to me considering my hard breakup with the baby's father. It's like ever since she found out about him hitting me she's become a lot nicer and stopped accusing me of trying to steal Jaylen away from her or sleeping with Malcolm just for the hell of it.

By the time Angela has finished asking all her questions, Malcolm and Jaylen entered halftime on NBA Live. I had watched them play the whole time I answered her questions. Jaslene is still asleep, and she's been asleep for almost an hour. I went to check on her twice already, but I now have the itch to check again. If it wasn't so loud in the living room with the boys being animated with their game, I would bring Jaslene in here and have her sleep in my arms.

I get up, and Malcolm's eyes follow me. "Checking on her again?" he asks, leaning over and taking a sip from one of the beer bottles he got for him and Jaylen.

"Yeah," I say, pausing before I leave the room. "You know how new moms are."

Jaslene is peacefully asleep, but I have a feeling she is going to wake up soon and start crying for food. I want to just wait in the room, but I don't want to miss out on too much excitement from the living room.

Jaylen is winning, and it's fun watching Malcolm get animated with his words of encouragement as he struggles to catch up to Jaylen. Sometimes he manages to, and this game is a close one.

I sit down on the edge of my bed and lean back. I can't believe I'm a mother. I don't even really feel like one. I still feel like me, except I'm taking care of a little baby. She doesn't really feel like mine. I'm expecting some woman to walk through the door and thank me for watching her child. That's a heartbreaking thought, but it's like I'm in a surreal state. I wasn't expecting her to come for another two months, and now she's already here, and I'm already a mother.

I close my eyes and think about my own mother. I didn't have a chance to know her or my father since the two of them ran away together and only came back home to drop me off with my grandmother. I don't know what was wrong with them or why neither of them stayed to raise me, but as I grew older I did feel abandoned. How could I not feel that way? They didn't even know me, and they didn't want me. Now with Jaslene here and Chris not here, it's like he's doing the same thing to Jaslene that my parents did to me. They didn't want me. They didn't care.

I wake up the next morning to give Jaslene her six a.m. feeding. Last night, I had stayed in the room until

Jaylen and Angela left. I had fell asleep thinking about my parents, which is not something I do often. At least I didn't have a nightmare with Chris in it again.

Today is Tuesday, and it's raining in Chicago. I hold Jaslene in my arms and put my breast in her mouth as I stare out my bedroom window that is hovering over my desk. I love the sound of rain and the saltwater smell rain gives to the air. Watching the rain is like taking a dry shower for me. I get thoughtful, thinking about things I normally wouldn't. I take my time doing things, and time sits still.

After Jaslene finishes, I walk to the kitchen to start preparing my own breakfast. Passing the living room, I notice my book bag still lying next to the door on the floor. Oh, school. Am I giving that up now too? I've only missed one day, since I gave birth to my baby over the weekend, and I came home Monday. I wonder what Kayla is thinking. My class doesn't actually start till eleven a.m., but I can't leave Jaslene. I'm still breast-feeding her. Well, that's the excuse I'm going with.

I turn away from the door and snuggle Jaslene against my chest as I open the refrigerator. I know deep down I'm not going to go back to school for a while. I can't believe I was so close to finishing the semester. I only have a month and a half to go, I think.

Jaslene wasn't due for two months. It was working out so perfectly.

After I finish getting out the ingredients for breakfast, I go to get Jaslene's snuggly so I can cook and have her against my chest at the same time. Malcolm isn't going to wake up for another hour and a half to work at Jaylen's bar, and I always make breakfast. Then he usually drops me off at school, works a shift, and picks me up. Now I'm not going to school, but Jaslene has me up already, so I might as well continue my routine.

I'm halfway through frying the eggs, my favorite, when Jaslene needs to be changed. Stopping midway through whatever I'm doing to give Jaslene my undivided attention is something I am still getting used to. But deep down I don't mind. I love Jaslene, and I love staying busy and being needed.

Malcolm comes into the kitchen just as I finish the bacon and sausage. It's his favorite. He looks at me with tired eyes, and I can tell he stayed up all night with Jaylen, playing the game. "Are you going to school?" he asks, taking a seat next to the plate of bacon and eggs.

"No. I have to take care of Jaslene. I don't think I can finish the semester," I say.

"Why not?" he asks, chewing a slice of thick maple bacon.

I rub Jaslene's back. "I can't do both. I have to be with her for the first three months, and I have no one to watch her. I can't afford child care. And I'm breast-feeding her."

He stares at us with soft eyes for a while. I come closer and take a seat opposite him. I grab a slice of bacon for myself. Jaslene has fallen asleep again. Malcolm doesn't say anything for a while, and I wonder what he's thinking. We continue to eat in silence, but I look up from my plate and catch him staring at me with his mouth slightly open and his chest filled with air like he's about to say something. When I raise my eyebrows, however, his chest deflates and he shakes his head. It's like he doesn't know how to word whatever he wants to say because I know he wants to say something.

"What is it?" I ask. Malcolm leans back, still thoughtful. "Can't you just say it already?"

He looks up at me. "When are we going to get child support from Chris?"

As soon as he says Chris's name, my face falls. It hurts like a knife stab, and I didn't realized how much I hate that name. I know I shouldn't hate anyone, but that man . . . he deserted me and our daughter. He doesn't deserve my respect. "I'm not," I said.

Malcolm takes a deep breath. "I thought you might say that."

"I don't want his help. I can do this on my own," I say with my voice low and even.

"I know you can, Jaslene, but . . . a baby is expensive and—"

"I know, Malcolm. I never said it was going to be easy. I just know I can do it. I've been trying all these months to find a job, but school's been taking up so much time. I don't want to make excuses but—"

"You don't have to be so prideful either, Jess. Let the man take responsibility. You letting him off with a clean slate with no money to pay monthly while you struggle. Tell me that ain't right," he says, his voice getting deeper.

I think about Chris walking down the street acting carefree while I stay here with Jaslene struggling as a single mother to make ends meet. It isn't fair, I know. It's just something about me taking anything from him. It'd be like I needed him, and I don't want to be dependent on Chris ever again. It never got me anywhere.

"I still don't want his help, Malcolm. Not his. I do realize I need help taking care of Jaslene because I have to come up with money for diapers, clothes, and toys for her. I just don't want the help coming from him. I just . . . I hate that man for what he did to me. I don't want to need him. I want to do this on my own."

Malcolm nods slowly, but I can tell by his hard face that he still wants Chris to pay up. I don't blame him at all, but Malcolm wasn't with me the day Chris pushed me into the entertainment center and gave blow after merciless blow to my body just because I accused him of sleeping around. What kind of man is that? What kind of woman would I be if I went to him asking for money now?

After Malcolm leaves for work, I straighten up the house between diaper changes and feeding Jaslene. It is a slow day, but around noon I get a phone call from Kayla asking why I wasn't in school. She doesn't know I had my baby and I'm already back home. She also doesn't know I'm not returning to school.

"Hello," I say.

"Hi, stranger. Where you been at?" Kayla asks. The background noise of people talking makes her raised voice more understandable. She must still be on campus.

"Um . . . well, I . . . don't panic when I say this, but I went into labor Friday night."

"Oh my God. Are you all right? Are you still in the hospital?" Kayla asks, her voice raised a couple of notches.

"Yeah. I'm fine. I'm home actually," I say, walking into my bedroom. Jaslene is sleeping in her crib breathing normally, which I have a tendency to check. "It was a quick birth."

"Oh my God, girl. You didn't tell me. I'm coming over now!"

"No, Kayla, you have class. You can just stop by to see her when you're done with classes," I say.

"Oh! It's a girl! I can't believe it! What's her name? Did you speak to Chris? OMG, I have so many questions! Did it hurt?" Kayla asks with her voice peaking at an eardrum-busting level. "What's her name?"

I smile. "Jaslene."

"Oh! So cute!" Kayla says, then gets quiet for a second. "Okay. I got one more class today, and I'm only going to go 'cause we have this quiz I've been studying for, but after that I'm coming over to see my goddaughter. Talk to you later, okay?"

After we hang up, I sit on the bed and take a deep breath. Man, that girl can scream. I am about to start some dinner for when Malcolm comes back, but my phone starts ringing again. I run out of the room because I want to cook baby-free, so I need Jaslene not to be woken up for a while. "Hello?" I say.

"Hey. How are you?" Jaylen says.

My heart rate increases despite myself, and I suddenly became excited. "I'm good. How are you?" I answer, sitting down on the couch. The time on the TV reads two o'clock, and dinner should be ready around three, when Malcolm gets off. Or maybe I should call him to bring takeout.

"Straight." His voice says he wants to say more, but I don't want to push it. "I told Mom you had your baby."

"Oh. Yeah, I got to send her some pictures." He meant his mom, not mine. Jaylen and I aren't related. We are far from related.

We are quiet for a while, and I get the feeling he wants to say something a lot more important than what he is saying, but I can't figure it out. "Do you need anything from the store?" Jaylen asks, his voice gentle.

"Not right now. You and Malcolm supplied me enough to get me going for the first month. I really appreciate that, by the way," I say.

"No problem," Jaylen says, then grows quiet again. I am about to say something to fill in the quiet gap, but he continues. "Have you been thinking about Chris?"

So this is what he wanted to ask. "No, I mean not really. I mean, how can I not? I don't want to, but I find myself hating him and thinking about him at the same time. I wish I could just forget him but . . . I don't know why, but I can't."

There is silence over the phone again, and I wonder what Jaylen is thinking. I wish I was a mind reader, and if I became an outcast because of it, at least that would be my only problem. I can hear Jaylen take a deep breath, and I take a seat in the kitchen chair. I know when a lecture's coming.

"I called to talk to you about getting child support. I know you don't want to do it because you want to be independent and everything, and that's fine, but you really need to think about what's at stake here. You can't be too proud to the point where you're being selfish—"

I have to stop him here. "How am I being selfish? I want to take care of my daughter on my own. If he's not going to be in her life, I don't want to take his money for something he doesn't want to be a part of."

"I understand what you're saying, Jess, but just listen to my side, please. I don't want to take away your independence of being a single mom, but getting child support doesn't do that. It helps you. I know you don't want his help because I know what he did to you. But I'm telling you as a friend, you are being selfish—"

Before he can continue, the front door cracks open, and Malcolm walks in holding a bag with a box of Popeye's Chicken inside. His eyes scan my irritated face, and I know he knows something is wrong. Yeah, his brother. I look over at the time. "Oh, Jaylen, hold on. Malcolm just walked in with food."

"Jess—"

"I'll call you back when I'm done eating, okay?" I say, grateful to have an excuse to get off the phone. Selfish? How dare he call me selfish.

I set the phone down and look at Malcolm. "Are you all right?" he asks. I shrug. "What was Jaylen saying?"

"He thinks I'm selfish because I don't want to have Chris pay child support."

Malcolm's quiet, and after a few seconds I realize he agrees with Jaylen. "How can I be selfish? It doesn't make any sense."

Malcolm shrugs, and I go into the kitchen and sit down. I don't say anything else to Malcolm as I shove chicken down my throat. I hate being frustrated, but I just wish these two would understand where I'm coming from. After spending so much time with someone who didn't give a damn about me, how can I go asking for money? I don't want anything from that bastard.

Malcolm keeps looking at me from time to time as he eats, and sometimes he opens his mouth to say something but doesn't. Eventually, as we're placing our plates in the sink, he asks about Jaslene, and I tell him she's asleep. He nods and goes to the living room. "Come take a seat next to me, Jess."

We both sit on the couch, and he looks at me with his soft brown eyes. His eyes are darker than Jaylen's, but I can still see my reflection in them. "I think we need to call a judge, or a lawyer or something, to get Chris to pay child support," he says finally. "Now, before you start telling all about your reasons why you shouldn't, I want you to really consider the benefits."

I listen to him as he says the things he's already told me. Just as he is wrapping up, the doorknob turns and Jaylen walks in like he owns the place. Jaylen stares at us sitting on the couch but mostly at me. He's wearing basketball shorts and a blue T-shirt with matching shoes. His hair is cut into a fade, and even though his face is frowning he looks handsome. I look down and scowl at myself for staring.

"Hey," Jaylen says. Malcolm moves beside me to stand up. I hear them clasp hands. I look up and catch Malcolm nodding his head before walking back to his room. Jaylen's staring at me, and I look down at my hands. He comes and sits next to me.

"I wanted to finish our talk," he says slowly. "I don't want it to seem like I'm calling you selfish on purpose."

I look at him then. "What did you want to call me? Selfish on accident?"

He shakes his head and pats my knee, and I ignore the weird sensation in my stomach. "You're not a selfish person, Jess. I didn't mean your personality. I meant your actions. With this whole Chris thing, I just thought you were acting selfish by not letting Chris take some of the responsibilities for having a child."

"I'm sure he wants no part of any responsibilities."

"I know, but when it comes to child support, he doesn't have a choice."

"Why can't I just take care of things on my own? I'm doing my best to move forward. I'm heading in the right direction, and I don't want any of his help."

He's quiet, looking at my mouth. Then he speaks up. "How is it any different from taking help from my brother?"

It's like his words slam into my chest, and it takes me a moment to recover. I look around the apartment and instantly become reminded of Malcolm's selfless gratitude. Since I've been staying here, he hasn't asked me for a dime. I, however, have needed money since the day I got here.

"He's letting you stay here, and he's helping you take care of Jaslene like it was his job. He shouldn't have to be taking up Chris's slack. Look, just because you don't want Chris doing his part to help out doesn't mean the workload is getting any smaller. Why should Malcolm have to come in where Chris should already be? That's why I said not wanting Chris to financially take care of the baby is selfish of you because it means that responsibility is being put on someone else." He pauses. "I know you don't mean for it to be that way, but you can't raise a baby all by yourself. You'll need help at some point, especially if you plan on getting a job and a place of your own."

I don't say anything. I never wanted my situation to affect Malcolm's personal life. Never. I guess taking child support from Chris can be a way of paying him back, by helping out around here more. If I can do anything to pay Malcolm back for his generosity, I will.

I turn my head toward Malcolm's bedroom. I should go in there right now and apologize, but what would I say? I don't want to seem selfish, but I don't want Chris giving me money either. I was so sure of my decision to be independent, and now I'm not so sure.

I turn my head back to Jaylen. He looks at me with my favorite brown eyes. "You don't have to worry about anything, Jess. Me and Malcolm will take care of everything with the child support if you want us to."

"I don't want to see him, but I don't want Malcolm taking care of me and Jaslene forever."

"You don't have to worry about seeing him, Jess. All four of us will go down to the courthouse in front of the judge. Do what we have to do, and then walk out of there together. When that's done, it's all about the checks coming in."

"Are you sure there isn't anything else? I mean, will I have to talk to Chris or look at him?"

"No. They'll just need a paternity test, but after that we're good. Chris should agree to take one since he's so confident he's not the father."

I take a deep breath. I don't want to have to deal with it, but I guess my choices are gone. I don't want Malcolm feeling like he has to take care of a close friend and her baby like it was his job, and I don't want to be selfish.

"Okay," I say. I trust Jaylen to know what he's doing. I just hope to get it over with so I can move on.

Chapter Seven

Two weeks later, I walk out of the hospital after giving them a DNA sample of my daughter's cheek cells. Chris would be at the hospital later to give his DNA sample for the paternity test, which I thankfully don't have to be around for. The hospital will be informing us of the results by paperwork mailing and a phone call in about seventy-two hours. At this point, however, I'm just glad I made it through without seeing that man. I hope I go forever without seeing him.

Malcolm smiles as he walks beside me. "Now that wasn't so bad, was it?"

I look down at Jaslene, who is looking up at me from the snuggly. "Yeah. I guess not."

Malcolm drops me off at his place before going to work, and I sing to Jaslene for a while until she drifts off to sleep. I would normally take this opportunity to get some chores done, but for some reason I'm too tired and decide to take a light nap instead.

Two hours later I wake up to Jaslene crying and a wet diaper, feeling more tired than when I laid my head down. I change her diaper slowly, and I think about having a good night's sleep. I haven't had one since Jaslene came home, and I need a break. The other thing I realize is that Jaylen was right. I do need help taking care of Jaslene.

I look around the empty apartment and listen to the dripping faucet in the sink. It's so quiet right now. I'm sitting on the couch staring at the TV as I breast-feed Jaslene. When she finishes, I spend the rest of the night watching old movies until Malcolm strolls in around six o'clock. By this time Jaslene has fallen asleep in my arms, and I'm about to nod off too.

Malcolm closes the door and holds up a bag of Chinese food. My stomach growls in greeting, and I get up. "Thank you so much."

"Yup."

Malcolm sets the food on the table and I put Jaslene down. "Can I talk to you about what Jaylen told me?" I ask Malcolm as we sit down to eat. He nods, so I keep going. "I didn't mean to come off as selfish. I know it's a big deal for you to have kept me living here all this time, with a baby, nonetheless. I know you don't always like going out to the girls' house for fun because you can't do it here, but I just wanted to tell you that I really appreciate your sacrifices."

He smiles and a soft laugh escapes. "I fuck here too, you know."

My mouth hangs open. "When?" And where was I?

"Mostly around one a.m. when you two are asleep. Girls come over and we chill in my room."

"But doesn't she see all the toys and baby stuff lying around?"

"Yeah. I tell them that my sister has a baby. Which is true in an extended-family sort of way."

"And they believe you?"

He shrugs. "Why shouldn't they? They're not my girlfriends, nor are they trying to be. If they ask question, I give them an answer."

I know we veered off-topic here, but I'm just shocked that this man still gets his groove on while me and Jaslene are here. Leave it to Malcolm to find some sort of way to get the goodies. "Anyway," I say, "I just wanted to say sorry for making you feel responsible for Jaslene and me. You shouldn't have to finance us when Chris should be doing it."

He nods and smiles. "That's what I've been trying to tell you. At least we getting it all worked out now. Think about it this way too, Jess. The extra money could also help find you a nice place for you and Jaslene."

"Yeah, that's true. Since Chris has a full time job at the grocery store, I should be able to get child support." I pause before adding, "I'm not sure how long finding a place of my own might take though."

He waves me off. "Don't worry about that for now. I told you last year when you left that bastard that you can stay here for as long as you need to. Just remember, when you do move out one day, I'll be here for you. Even if that is about six months from now."

We laugh. "Oh, Jess. I forgot to tell you. Mom is coming up here next week to see the baby. I'm not sure how long she's staying, so she'll be sleeping in my room, and I'll have the couch."

I nod. "You better clean out your room then. I'm scared to go in there. I hate to think what toy—I mean, things, she might find."

"Shut up." He laughs, taking a bite of his food.

The next morning, I smile in triumph as I slide the bright-yellow eggs and brown link sausages onto the plate. Malcolm's been helping out with my culinary skills, and I haven't burned any food in almost two weeks. I take a seat at the table and prepare to dive right in. I have just laid Jaslene down for her late-morning nap, and with Malcolm already gone to work, it's just going to be me and her for the whole day, and that's perfectly fine with me.

The phone rings, and I just up to fetch it off the couch. I would hate for that phone to be the reason my Jaslene wakes up when it took me thirty minutes to get her quiet enough to sleep. I cradle the phone in my hands, not even looking at the caller ID before punching the green button. "Hello?"

I walk back to my bedroom to check on Jaslene as I listen to Kayla's greetings over the phone. I find myself checking on Jaslene a lot, not knowing which particular sounds will wake her up and which sounds will go undetected.

"Let's go do something," Kayla says, her words bouncing through the phone. "I know you must be tired of being stuck in that house."

"Eh. Not really. It's not so bad. And look at the weather outside," I say, shaking my head and looking out of Malcolm's balcony window. Blinding white snow covers not only the lawns, streets, and sidewalks but the cars and trucks parked in the compacted parking lot. I place a hand on the window, then drop it as soon as the cold bites it.

"It's March in Chicago. What do you expect?" Kayla says, laughing. "Look, let's just go out and have some fun. I'm off work today, and it's Saturday. Let's just enjoy ourselves."

"Um . . ." I go back to the kitchen table to finish my food. By now it's a tad colder, but I eat it anyway without hesitation. I will never waste food because of the temperature. A lot of that reasoning has to do with Grandma Mae's refusal to buy a microwave and strong belief in the fact that food is food whether it's cold or not.

"Let's have lunch. Let's go the Cheesecake Factory." I can practically see Kayla smiling through the phone, but I almost choke on my food.

"I can't afford to eat there," I say after a fit of coughs.

"Well, let's go somewhere. Shit, we can eat at the mall for all I care. Oh, let's go pick out some baby clothes for Jaslene."

I smile at her enthusiasm, and I wonder why she's so excited to hang out, and then I remember that she hasn't met Jaslene yet, and we haven't seen each other since the last time I was in school. "What time?" I ask.

"Let's go around two o'clock. It's eleven now, so I'll take a nap, shower, and get ready and be there at two. I can't wait to meet the baby!" Kayla says.

"Okay, see you then."

By the time we hang up, I'm done with my eggs. Before Jaslene wakes up, I clean as much of the apartment as I can. I have gotten a lot messier since Jaslene came home. I kind of want the place to look nice when Malcolm's mom, Sheri, comes to visit. I haven't seen her in a few years, but she treats me like a daughter, and for that I appreciate her more than she knows.

When Kayla shows up outside, Jaslene and I are already standing and waiting bundled up in hats, scarves, and coats. I'm glad it's not snowing because I would hate to slip on freshly fallen slush.

Kayla's car is a hot-pink Camaro, and she waves as she pulls up close to the sidewalk. To my surprise, she jumps out of the car and starts walking toward me with her arms spread wide. "Oh, look at you, Mom!"

I blush as I glance down at Jaslene in her car seat. Kayla scoops me into a bear hug, and I smile. She pulls away and gives me a look like a proud parent. "You look great."

"Thank you. I didn't really do anything yet. I still have the baby fat," I say, placing a hand on my still-protruding stomach.

Kayla rolls her eyes and wraps an arm around me. "Don't be so raving with positivity," she says with as much sarcasm as she can muster.

I smile and then shrug. "I'm not really in a position to be too positive."

"Why not? Is anything wrong?"

I don't want to talk about Chris not caring about Jaslene enough to see her on the day she was born and the fact that I was for sure destined to be a single parent. It's not like we are going someplace private, but I would like to take this day to enjoy myself and get some fresh air.

I need a distraction. "Let's get in the car so you can see Jaslene." Jaslene's face is currently protected with a flap over the car seat to block the cold air.

Kayla grins. "Yes," she says, leading the way back to the car.

Once I strap Jaslene in the car seat correctly, it takes us another ten minutes to pull off, because Kayla has to get her fill of playing with Jaslene's toes, blabbing baby talk, and making the most funny faces she can muster. After we take off in the direction of what I hope is either the mall or a nice affordable restaurant, Kayla's forced to shift her focus to the road. I'm glad she hasn't brought up Chris, because, frankly, I'm trying to forget about him.

We pull up to a Mexican restaurant, and before we even walk in, the aroma of the days' meals seep through the doors. I inhale the cold, but good-tasting air as I step out of the car.

It takes us twenty minutes to get a table, but Kayla just sits beside me chatting her tongue off about her male friend she brought home last night. In the time it takes for the hostess to call us to our table, I feel like I know more about that man than I think I need to know. Especially his performance capability in the bedroom.

The hostess directs us to a booth overlooking the parking lot. I smile. I love sitting by a window, but I keep my coat on because of the chilled air that seeps through.

"So," Kayla says as soon as our waiter leaves to fill our drink order. "Tell me the scoop. Did you take the paternity test yet?"

I nod as I unwrap Jaslene from her blanket but leaving her in her coat. After a thought, I unzip the coat but keep Jaslene on my right side—the side that's not close to the window. "Yeah, we went to take it yesterday," I say.

Now that I am situated, I look around the dining area of the restaurant more closely. The tables are black oak, and there are no tablecloths. The crowd ranges from dinner-timing elders to lunchtime teenagers. The babies are mild-tempered and pacified by the chips and salsa dip decorating each tabletop. I turn back to Kayla and notice how fast her lips are moving, but her voice is really just one of the many loud buzzes of the crowd.

"How was it?" she asks, leaning forward. Her voice is slightly raised, so she's probably repeating the question.

"It was . . ." I shrug. "What I expected, for the most part. Chris gave his DNA at a later time yesterday, so I'm thinking we'll hear of the results in a couple of days."

"Oh. Cool. So are you getting a letter or something? Phone call? Maury? I mean how does this all work?" Kayla asks, digging her fingers into the tortilla chips. She eats them plain without dipping them in the sauce. The waiter comes and brings us our drinks. Kayla had ordered a lemon-and-strawberry margarita, and I sip my water.

"We did our test a little differently. We're both going to get separate notification of the test by either phone or mail. I asked for both. I think the phone call might come first because it takes the results a couple of days to come through the mail."

"Can't wait to get the answer, huh?" Kayla asks before taking a deep pull of her liquor. I hope she doesn't get too drunk. I think about Jaylen and how he's told me a thousand times to get my driver's

106

license. I bite my lips. If she's too drunk, I'll call him to get us.

"I already know what the results will be. I just want Chris to see them and know the truth. He thinks I slept with his best friend. Someone I've never met or even heard of," I say, letting the words spit out as if they're distasteful cigarettes.

"Oh, he's that kind of guy, huh? Let me ask you something. Did he ever cheat on you?"

"Yes."

"Yeah, I'm thinking his guilt of cheating makes it easier to believe that you fucked his best friend. He probably thought you did it to get back at him for his cheating."

I nod my head and then shrug, looking down at Jaslene. "I don't care what he thinks. I just want him to take care of his baby."

"I mean, why do you need him to take care of her? Why can't you be an awesome single mom and raise her yourself? You're stronger than you think, and you don't need a man to help you when you can help yo' damn self. Look at me. My momma raised me by herself since the age of sixteen, and she still got herself an education, so I know you are no different. You just need to get a job.

"Look," she continued. "Put it like this. Chris doesn't want this baby. If he's in her life, it's just going to be forced, and he's not really going to care—"

"I thought that once he saw her face he would change his mind. I just can't believe he doesn't want her."

Kayla pauses as she scans my face. I refuse to cry though. I hate crying and am sick of crying in front of people. I'm not pregnant anymore, and I should have my emotions under control.

Kayla opens her mouth, and her words come out crisp. "Any man that doesn't want a beautiful and perfect daughter like Jaslene is clearly not mentally stable enough to be raising kids in the first place."

I stare at Kayla's eyes and then smile. She's right, of course. He doesn't deserve Jaslene, and I need to step up and be more to my daughter than I ever thought possible. I nod, and a few moments pass until our waiter comes back requesting our orders.

Throughout the rest of the meal the conversation stays light—or at least not on the subject of Jaslene and Chris. I tell Kayla how much baby décor we have at Malcolm's apartment. I really appreciate what he and Jaylen have done for me since I gave birth. I even think Angela helped out a little, even if she did just want to going through a baby-craving phase.

108

We split the bill and gather up our things. Kayla tosses three dollars on the table, and we leave. Inside the parking garage the snow and cold blow in, eliminating any shelter it should have provided. I move slower than when I first walked in, feeling the pounds added to my stomach. Kayla walks two feet ahead of me, looking back every once in a while, but continues to hold a striking conversation about her date with a lawyer after work tomorrow. I nod my head and grunt when appropriate while staring down and dodging ice patches that someone neglected to salt over.

Kayla's talking nonstop, and even though I nod and give the occasional grunt, my mind is far from listening to her fully. I just can't pull my thoughts away from the idea of being a single mother and handling everything, for the most part, on my own. But Kayla's right about that. I can't depend on Chris.

Kayla stops at a red light, and I catch something out of the corner of my eye. I grit my teeth and my fists clench up. Chris is leaning against a building talking to two rough-looking men. I can't hear their voices, but one side view of Chris is all I need to identify him. Part of me wants Kayla to speed off and get as far away from that abusive, heartless man as I can. But part of me wants to confront him and make him look his daughter in the eyes and tell her he doesn't want her. I know he wouldn't be able to do it.

At least, I don't think so. I glance quickly at Jaslene, who is breathing deeply with her eyes closed in peaceful sleep. The next second I look up at her father. I don't know if it's due to my evil stare or whether it's just chance that he glances over, but we make eye contact in one brief, sharp second. In next second the light turns green, and Kayla speeds off, and I realize that Chris had winked at me.

The second I get home I put Jaslene in her crib. She's asleep now anyway, and I don't want to disturb her. I look around my room and decide to pick up a few loose clothes from the floor and toss them into my dirty clothes laundry basket. I want to keep my mind as far away from Chris as I can. Seeing him brought up so much anger inside me that I feel like killing him. Maybe it's my mother's instincts, but I don't like people who don't like my child.

I make up my bed, but I move slowly. If I want to keep my mind off Chris, I actually have to think about something pleasant. Of course, Jaslene comes to mind. I glance over my shoulder in the direction of her crib in the corner of the room. I smile, and then my face goes stern. I have to be a good mother for her. Since she doesn't have a father, she's going to need me twice as much. Kayla is right. I need to put any feelings I have for Chris—no matter how hateful and deserving—aside and keep Jaslene as my number-one priority. Because not only am I all that she has; she's the only real blood family I have left.

Chapter Eight

I put Jaslene on my other arm as I answer the phone. It's been three weeks since I brought her home from the hospital, but it's little things, like always taking her with me when I do the simplest tasks, that I'm still getting used to.

"Hello?" It's eight o'clock in the morning, and Malcolm left for work a few hours ago. I'm about to start the chores, when Jaslene needs to be changed.

The voice on the other end is soft, feminine, and chirpy. "Hello. Am I speaking with a Ms. Jessica Smith?"

"Yes, you are. May I ask who's calling?" I take a seat on the couch with Jaslene.

"This is Amy Brown from St. Mary's Hospital. You had requested a paternity test with us a few days back, is that correct?"

"Oh. Yes, good. How are you?" I answer, feeling relieved. I don't know why I thought it was a bill collector.

"I'm doing just fine, thank you. Now, Ms. Smith— is your daughter's name Jaslene Smith?"

"Yes."

"Great. Thank you. Now would you like me to tell you the results or wait for them to come in the mail, or both?"

"Both. That's what I agreed to when I left the hospital."

"Okay. Well, it looks like Christopher Burguin is not the biological father of Jaslene Smith, according to our test results. I'm suppose to tell you that if you want them to retake the test, you can come down to do it again, but you will be charged more, and the results are not likely to change. We will be sending out informative information about the test in the mail in the next three-to-five business days. Okay? Ma'am, are you there?"

I set the phone down and listen to her call my name again and again, but I don't care. I can't think. I just cannot think right now. Eventually the dial tone sounds, and I click the phone off. I sit and wait for her to call me back to tell me she made some sort of mistake, but she doesn't, and I'm still sitting on the couch with my daughter, waiting like some idiot.

That can't be right. I must have misheard her. Yeah, that was it. She was talking so fast. She must have been waiting to go on break. I can't go off of what she said. I'll just wait for the results to come in the mail. That will confirm everything. I clench and unclench my fists repeatedly, and as the time goes by and as Jaslene drifts off to sleep, I find my mind growing irrational.

Chris isn't the father, my mind is saying. My mind is stupid. Maybe he cheated on the test. Or maybe he paid someone to show up for him and take his spot. He would be low enough to do something like that.

But the hospital checks ID. And Chris has been begging to prove he isn't the father, so he probably didn't think he had to tamper with the sample he gave.

I shake my head as I walk to my room and lay Jaslene down in her crib. I don't look at her too long. It hurts to. I cannot focus right now while my heart is beating out of my chest, and I can't sit down. Why would the woman on the phone lie to me? I've done nothing to her, and she pays me back with lying? How could Chris not be the father? What she said just wasn't true.

I pace the entire room back and forth. I wish I wasn't alone, and I wish I had someone to talk to. I think about Kayla from school, but she's so disconnected with everything I've been through that she wouldn't understand. At least I don't think she would. Especially when I think about . . .

Oh my God.

Jaylen.

I collapse on the bed and bury my face in my hands. I'm a sinner. I deserve to burn for this one. Oh my God. I got pregnant by . . . oh my God.

I can't think it. It's not true. I have to be making this up. Why won't anyone slap some sense into me? I can't let myself think back to the time, nearly a year ago, when I had left Chris and moved in with Jaylen for a while. One night. One night that had been so wonderful. So shockingly wonderful and sinful that both of us vowed to never breathe a word about it again—not even to each other. So beautiful of a night that is so stuck in my mind and one I sinfully relive sometimes late at night when I find myself constantly thinking about him.

I hold my fingers in the air and count down the months. I gave birth in March, so March, February, January . . . I had sex with Jaylen in July right before I moved back in with Chris a few days later. I found out I was pregnant in September and was maybe a month along. But if Jaylen's the father, then I would have already been two months pregnant by September, not one. And If I had gotten pregnant by Jaylen in July and gave birth in March, then that would mean Jaslene was born full term and was not a preemie.

I stare down at Jaslene and marvel at her seven pounds. She was not born premature. My mind goes back to the doctor in the hospital when he told me she was fully term. I just thought it was weird or that maybe she was a fast-growing baby. I was wrong. She came out right on time.

I swallow deeply. Of course if Jaslene isn't Chris's, she's Jaylen's.

My heart starts pounding in my chest as I take in what this mean. Jaylen and I have a child together. Our own little family. I smile as I feel my face get warmer in blush. Wow. I never thought that would ever . . . wait. What am I saying?

I bite my lip and taste the tears that fall across it as realization kicks in. I can't have Jaylen's baby. What about Angela? Oh, I screwed him so bad. I deserve all the criticism, all the hateful remarks, all the bashing. I feel lower than dirt, and I don't even want a shovel. I feel like I'm drowning in guilt, and Jaslene is the only reason I'm hanging on to the life raft. I could lose my mind, but Jaslene needs me to stay sane. She needs me for everything.

After two hours of crying I walk over to the crib and make sure Jaslene is still asleep. I walk out of the room and take a quick shower. I don't want to be alone right now, but I can't be with anyone until I can clear my head. What am I going to do if this is true? Who would I tell? Am I going to tell?

Of course I have to tell Jaylen. It's going to be hard to, but I know I have to if Jaslene is indeed his and not Chris's. I don't want to ruin Jaylen's life. All hell will break loose if I have to tell him the truth—and hell's first name is Angela.

I hug myself in the shower at the sheer thought of Angela banging on Malcolm's door at two a.m. begging to kick my ass. I don't want that confrontation. I don't want any confrontation.

I get out of the shower in ten minutes. It's only noon, and Malcolm won't be home till much later. I go back to the room and slip on some clothes. Maybe I should go up to the hospital and talk to that nurse face-to-face. Just to make sure I heard her right. I brush off the idea a moment later though, and just settle for waiting for the paper results in the mail.

What if Jaylen truly is the father? I don't know what to do. If I tell Jaylen, he'll have to tell Angela, and they'll break up. If I tell them the results prove that Chris is the father, then they'll want to take the whole child-support thing to the next step and get in front of a judge. But Chris knows the results too, and he would never show up. And if he did, it would be to embarrass me and claim how much of a hoe I am.

Then a lightbulb goes off in my head. Chris thought I cheated on him with one of his friends back when we were still together right before he broke up with me. What if I keep that lie going with Malcolm and Jaylen? What if I tell them that Chris isn't the father, but that I don't know who the real father is, so there'd be no need to get another paternity test or child support?

That would solve the problem of my having to tell Jaylen that he fathered my child. It would also solve the problem of seeing Chris and dealing with his ass. But Jaylen won't believe my lie. Neither he nor Malcolm would. They both can read me like a book, and if either of them gets even a hint that I'm lying, I'd never be able to prove to them I'm not. Especially Jaylen. He knows we slept together, and if he thinks for one second that Chris is not the father, it's going to be a big hit to him that it is his, and I can't let that happen. For his own sake.

I think about the choice I'm going to make, and I realize it's not an easy one. I'm not going to tell Jaylen that he's the father. I'm not even going to tell him that the test results came back. I just can't ruin Jaylen's relationship like that. Just because I can't have a good one doesn't mean he can't. I close my eyes and think of my deceased grandmother. What would she do in my situation? I have no idea.

Malcolm comes home around six forty-five with food. As we sit at the table and eat, he rambles on about his time working at Jaylen's new bar. Malcolm sometimes gets such interesting customers that he has to come home and tell me about them. I listen and smile and laugh when he says something funny. He doesn't notice right away until he pauses and looks at me. He asks, "You all right?"

"Yeah. Just tired," I say, taking a bite of the wings.

"No, you look sad," he says, then pats my shoulder. "What's wrong?"

"Nothing. I'm just . . . tired."

"Tired from what?" he asks, releasing my shoulder and taking another bite of his food. "Taking care of Jaslene?"

"No, just—"

"Oh, I know. You anxious to get this whole child-support thing over with, huh? I am too. I can't wait for that nigga to start pulling some weight with his own daughter. I mean, that man ain't done shit," Malcolm says.

How do I even begin to tell the truth when Malcolm doesn't even know I slept with someone other than Chris—not to mention his brother? He doesn't even know that Jaylen took my virginity when I was twelve, and for all Malcolm knows, Chris popped my cherry. How can I blurt out, "Well, Chris is not the father. Jaylen is. Oh, I didn't tell you? Me and your brother had unprotected sex two nights before I went back with Chris"?

I nod my head to Malcolm's comment instead and continue eating. I don't know where I would start off telling the truth, so for right now, until I can confirm what I heard over the phone with the paper results, Chris is still Jaslene's father, and I have not received any notification of the results yet. Yeah, that will help me get a good fifteen minutes of sleep tonight.

"Hey, Jess, come here. My mom wants to talk to you," Malcolm shouts from the living room. I come out of the bedroom still half asleep. Less than half, actually. I've gotten no sleep after finding out Chris wasn't Jaslene's father yesterday. I rub my eyes as I step out into the brightly lit hallway and into the living room.

I let out a yawn before taking Malcolm's cell phone from his hand and putting it to my ear. "Yes ma'am?"

"How you doing, baby?" Sheri's voice is nice and sweet just like I remembered.

"I'm fine. I'm just so tired."

"Lawd, I bet you are. I'm coming up there to see the baby, did they tell you?"

"Yes ma'am. Malcolm told me. I can't wait till you come," I say, actually managing to smile at the thought of seeing the woman who's been like a mother to me.

"Yes, well. I do want to see my grandbaby," she says. I freeze. Did she say her grandchild? With this being Jaylen's daughter, Sheri is Jaslene's grandmother. My mind goes immediately to Grandma Mae, and I wish she was here to see Jaslene and be in her life. Sheri would love to have grandchildren too, and my heart warms just thinking about Jaslene having a loving grandmother in her life.

"Um . . . uh . . ." What do I say, what do I say?

"How's that baby's father of yours? Did he come around yet?" Sheri asks, and I exhale. She must have said "her grandbaby" as a figure of speech since she thinks of me as a daughter and not because I sexed her son. She doesn't even know I did, nor does she know that Jaslene may not belong to Chris.

"He's still denying her. I haven't spoken to him in a long time, and I'm not planning to."

"Oh. Well, I'm going to be coming up there soon, and I was thinking that if you needed help with all this baby stuff that you are more than welcome to move down here with me."

I smile. She is so thoughtful and caring. "Thanks, Sheri, but I'm fine right here."

"I'm serious, Jess. You need help raising that child, and I'm retired now, so I spend all my time at home. I mean, that child just a baby now, but she gon' grow up, and you'll need a lot of help watching her in her terrible twos. I can also watch her while you go to school—that way you can continue your education." She pauses before continuing. "And what good is you and Jaslene staying in that one bedroom? I have three bedrooms in this house, and I'm only using one. If you and Jaslene move down here, y'all each have your own room. I mean, what you gon' do—have a teenager sleeping in the same bed as you? There's just more room here."

Of course I would love for Jaslene to have an official baby room, but there's so much going on in my life right now that moving is the last thing I want to do. And how can I leave knowing that there is probably a slim chance that Jaylen might be Jaslene's father? Shouldn't they be close? Oh wait. I wasn't going to tell anyone. Yet. I think. I don't know what my plan is, but moving is not one of them.

I take a quick breath. "Thanks, Sheri. I appreciate that. I really do, but I'm just not into moving right now, and I'm happy where I am." For now. "I'm going to try to get my own place up here and continue going to school here."

"Oh . . . well. I mean, you know it would be a ton easier to do that here. Free rent. I won't be lonely. I can help you raise your child, and you can have a life again. A social life. Don't give me an answer now. I know you dealing with Chris and the whole child-support thing, so maybe when that all blows over you can feel a lot better about moving down here."

"Okay."

"Okay, baby. I'll talk to you later."

"Love you," I say. After I hear her return the love, I hang up. Malcolm's staring at me with confused eyes, and I explain to him his mother's offer. He nods thoughtfully.

"I'm glad you're staying, though. I would never see you anymore if you went back home," he says, taking his phone back and pushing it into his pocket.

I sigh, and thoughts of Jaylen not seeing his daughter and Malcolm not seeing his niece pop into my head and punch my heart. "Yeah. I don't want to be that far away either."

It's crazy that even though Jaylen isn't here, I still think about him. I wonder what he's doing and if he's thinking about me and Jaslene. After we made love so long ago, we just went back to being friends. Not close

close friends, but we did the normal things we used to do and interacted with each other. We never are alone for long periods of time. I think it's because we both know that at some point we'd talk about what we did that night, and we don't want to make each other feel uncomfortable. Besides, what good would it do? He has a girlfriend that he loves, and I have a baby from a previous relationship, according to him, so it's not like we could be together or something crazy like that.

I blow out a breath of frustration and go back to my room. I stay there in bed with Jaslene until I fall back asleep.

Chapter Nine

Later the same day I find myself staring at the baby bottles on the shelf in aisle seventeen. It feels so tempting to stop breast-feeding and put Jaslene on formula, but I know breast milk is better. I sigh and decide to deal with tender nipples. I continue to push Jaslene and the shopping cart down the aisle. I stop when I spot Angela and Jaylen standing in the checkout line.

Jaylen looks so handsome leaning over the cart looking carefree. He has on blue jean shorts and long black-and-red tube socks. He has on a NBA Bulls' throwback with the matching snapback. I smile in his direction. He doesn't see though and continues to talk to Angela, who's standing in front of him dressed in suede boots and a tight turtleneck sweater. Her hand-sized earrings falls to her neck, and her naturally cut hair tops off her whole attire.

I look down at my baby bump that is shrinking but still present. I sigh and make my way over to them to say hi. I haven't seen them in so long.

As I approach their cart, Jaylen sees me and stops talking. His smile broadens and makes my own face smile. "Hey," he says, giving me a tight squeeze. "What you doing here by yourself? Where's Malcolm?"

"I just had to come here and pick up a few things. I walked." Jaylen frowns and I bite my tongue, literally. "It was just a quick run, and I do need my exercise. I mean, I been in that house for so long I had to get out and stretch my legs, you know? And Jaslene needs fresh air."

With Jaylen being so close to Jaslene, I take a second to do a comparison between the two of them. I don't think they look too much alike at first. She mostly looks like me. Then I see it. I see it and I wonder how I didn't notice it before. They have the same hairline. I glance at Jaylen again and notice that Jaslene also has his chin. Oh no—his ears too. How could I have missed this before? Maybe because I wasn't looking. Jaslene's other features on her face are mine. The nose is mine, and so is her hair, eyes, and mouth, but everything else is Jaylen's.

At the mention of Jaslene, Jaylen smiles down at her. He leans over and kisses her several times on her cheeks. I swallow and think about the consequences of him staring at her for too long. What if he notices their resemblance?

"You okay? What's wrong?" Jaylen asks, straightening up.

"Uh. Nothing. You guys better move up. You don't want to hold up the line," I say. Angela had come over and was now giving Jaslene plenty of kisses too. I've never felt more like a home-wrecker than I do now.

"Are you ready to check out?" Jaylen asks, eyeing my cart of fruits, meats, and diapers.

"No, not quite yet, so I better keep at it. It was nice seeing you guys," I say, turning my cart in the other direction.

"Hold on," Jaylen says. "We can wait till you done too. That way I can drop you off at home. Ain't no point in y'all walking back alone."

"Oh, I'll be fine." I say, brushing off his remark with my hand.

He stares at me with a stern face, and I know he wants to argue with me, but since our last big fight that almost ended our friendship, we try to avoid as many fights as possible.

I take a deep breath. I guess the least I can do is not argue in public. "Okay. Fine. Um . . . You guys check out and wait for me. I'll grab two more things and meet you at the car."

"We'll just all check out together. Come on—we'll shop with you," Jaylen says, pulling his cart out of line and steering both our carts in some random direction.

"But I just need milk and butter."

"Cool," Jaylen says, directing his cart to the refrigerated section. Angela walks besides me, texting on her phone, not looking like she cares one way or the other.

She and I are walking side by side like we're girlfriends, and I'm feeling like the Grinch after he stole Christmas—sad, guilty, and ashamed.

After we get the milk and butter, we head back to the register. When we walk through the toys aisle, I spot a small baby swing. It's priced at fifty bucks, and I've stared long enough at it that Jaylen notices my secret desire. "You want that for Jaslene?" he asks softly.

I smile as I turn to face him. "It's cute, but I think it's a little out of my price range at the moment. Um . . . maybe next time or Christmas." I shrug off the urge to get my daughter the gift and start walking again, but Jaylen stays, still eyeing the swing.

"I'll get it for you," he says after a few seconds.

My heart warms at the thought of giving Jaslene the swing, but he doesn't have to do that. "Thank you," I say with a genuine smile. "But that's okay."

"No, for real. I will. My gift to her. From Uncle Jay. Besides, I know you're going to keep thinking about it, and I know Chris ain't gon' buy it, so why should Jaslene have to miss out?"

I groan inwardly. It hurts to hear him bash Chris when Chris isn't her father. Wait, I mean, of course Chris is the father. Nothing's changed, and I'm going off my decision that I never received that phone call. For now.

I smile despite the pain in my heart. "Okay. Only if you want to."

He looks kindly into my eyes. "It's my pleasure. It's not her fault who her father is."

"Mmm . . ." I nod.

Jaylen puts the swing on the bottom of my cart. "I'll drop my groceries off at home, then come back to your place to set it up."

"Oh, Malcolm can set it up."

"We both can. That way we can all chill together too. Ain't did that since your birthday."

I nod, thinking about the days when I thought my world was pretty straightforward for the most part and not in total chaos.

We get to the register, and I'm about to put the black divider bar between my stuff and theirs, when Jaylen takes my hand. My hearts stops, and I swallow while looking up at him. He smiles back and says, "I got all your stuff today, Jess. Just relax."

I think about the grocery money Malcolm keeps above his fridge for food and how I take it to buy food and my own baby stuff, like toys and diapers. That isn't fair to Malcolm or his money, but here is Jaylen buying it for me, and this isn't fair to him either. Well, it is fair since it's his daughter, but he doesn't know it, so to him he's just doing me a kind favor.

I nod, wanting Malcolm's wallet to take a break from supporting a child that isn't his. At least since Jaylen's paying, I can return the money back to the spot above the fridge. "Thank you," I say softly.

We reach Jaylen's car parked outside near the east side of the parking lot. I put my things in the left side of the truck while Jaylen puts theirs on the right. Angela hangs back and plays with our baby. I mean with Jaslene. It's too weird right now to think of her as "our" baby with Jaylen. So weird and new that I don't even want to explore that feeling. Not right now anyway.

We get in the car and start riding in silence. I'm in the backseat cradling Jaslene, and Jaylen and Angela are in the front being quiet. As we near Malcolm's apartment building Jaylen speaks up. "Do you want me to help you carry that stuff in?"

"Sure."

We all exit the car after parking, and I grab one bag and Jaslene. Jaylen grabs the swing, and Angela grabs my groceries. I smile, getting excited walking to Malcolm's apartment. I never played with a baby swing before, and I can't wait till Malcolm gets off so they can put it together.

After I get in the apartment, Jaylen lays the swing on the floor near the couch. Angela places my groceries on the table. I thank them both sincerely, and they reply back sweetly. After they leave I sit down on the couch and rock Jaslene to sleep.

That wasn't so bad. I can do this. I can pretend that Jaslene is Chris's and that he's such a deadbeat that he doesn't want to be a part of her life. I just have to keep this secret. I can never breathe a word about this to anyone, and if the mail results prove without a shadow of a doubt that she's not Chris's, then I guess I'll just have to burn the letter and pretend it never came. I don't know how long I can keep Jaylen and Malcolm believing that the letter didn't come because they might call over there. However, if I can prove to

131

Jaylen and Malcolm that I can take care of myself and Jaslene without help from anyone, then maybe they won't bother me about it. It's worth a shot.

All I have to do is find a job. Then an apartment. Then a car. This is going to take a long time to do, but maybe my progress alone will be enough to convince them that I can take care of Jaslene on my own without anyone's help.

As soon as Malcolm gets home, my phone rings. It's Jaylen saying that he's on his way to help build the swing set. "Cool," I say.

"Did Malcolm bring home food?"

"No. I'm going to make dinner tonight with the food I got from the store today. I was going to invite the two of you since y'all are coming to fix the swing anyway."

"How about all four of us go out to dinner? My treat," Jaylen offers. Why is he being so nice? I mean, he's nice normally, but this is going above and beyond regular.

"That sounds great too. Thanks," I say. We say good-bye and hang up. After I tell Malcolm the plan, I can't get my mind off Jaylen and Jaslene. I wonder if they'll look more alike when Jaslene grows up. I wonder if she's going to act like him. I wonder what Jaylen traits she has lying beneath her skin and in her genes.

Malcolm sees me smiling on the couch and walks over laughing. "What you so happy for? That Jaylen bought you a swing?"

My smile broadens. "Yup." Malcolm hooks up his 360 in anticipation of Jaylen's arrival. Suddenly I can't wait till he comes here too. I don't know what I'll say or do, but just him being here will make me feel excited.

Then I think about how ever-changing Jaslene is and how Jaylen might notice facial similarities if he keeps hanging around her. I slump down into the couch as I watch Malcolm play his game. I take a breath low enough that Malcolm doesn't hear me. I want to have Jaylen here all the time, but I don't want him getting suspicious.

Just as Malcolm has five minutes left in the first quarter, Jaylen knocks on the door before turning his key in the lock and pushing the door open. My smile returns as he comes in and greets us. He takes a seat between me and Malcolm and watches Malcolm play the game. Angela comes in behind him and takes a seat on the floor right between Jaylen's legs.

Jaylen joins Malcolm's game, and Angela and I sit back and watch the men play. Eventually I get up to check on Jaslene in her crib and come back periodically to watch. They haven't set up the swing yet, but it's okay. I'm in no rush.

As the final seconds of the game tick to zero, Jaylen pumps his fist in the air. Angela turns around and pats his thigh as she smiles. "Good game, baby."

Malcolm stands, crosses his arms, and glares down at Jaylen. He nods toward the door. "You ain't gon' beat me in real life though."

We all start laughing and Malcolm smirks. "You lucky we got to build this swing set though," Malcolm says, walking around to the box in the corner.

Jaylen nudges Angela to move over so he can stand up. He joins Malcolm in the corner, and both of them empty out the contents of the box. "We can always go after we eat," Jaylen says.

"Aw, that's a bet then," Malcolm says, and they clasp hands.

I watch them put the swing together. Angela's quietly watching 106 & Park on BET. Jaylen and Malcolm do more talking than concentrating, so I think it takes them longer than needed to finish. In about ten minutes the swing's up and ready, and I smile at it. It's pink and white and has an automatic rocker setting. I want to have Jaslene try it this very second.

"I guess you like it, huh?" Malcolm asks, staring at my face. I nod, grinning from ear to ear. She's going to love it.

"Well, let's go eat," Angela says, standing up and smoothing out her blouse. "Been waiting too long. A bitch starving." Jaylen rolls his eyes and stands up too.

We decide to take Jaylen's car since the backseat has more space than Malcolm's. I place Jaslene in the car seat in the back between me and Malcolm. Jaylen keeps the music down low, and the sound of Tupac's voice is deep and rhythmic and gives the car a low vibration as we drive. No one's saying much, and I'm hoping it's because they don't want to wake up Jaslene and not because of something else. I catch eye contact with Jaylen through the rearview mirror, and he gives me a quick smile. I lean back in my seat and spend the next fifteen minutes with my eyes closed.

I open my eyes when the smell of burgers and steaks spills into the car. I look up at the red-and-gold building through my window and can't wait to get inside and devour one thick burger. The parking lot's crowded, and after waiting for an elderly couple to stop holding hands long enough to get in their car and pull out, we are able to get a parking spot and get out.

"I thought you were just joking when you said you wanted to come here." Angela tries to whisper to Jaylen, but of course all three of us hear her. I'm walking a few feet behind Jaylen and Angela, while Malcolm falls a foot behind me with his phone five inches from his face.

Jaylen only shrugs and reaches out to hold the door open for all of us to enter. The place smells even better than the outside. I take a deep breath and inhale smoked sausages, sirloin steaks, and burgers. I look over at Angela, and her face and her lower lip are sticking out.

"This place is disgusting," Angela says, sucking her teeth.

Malcolm peeks up from his phone. "Hey, yo, Ang. Why you gotta be such a bit—"

"It's a nice place, Ang," Jaylen cuts in before Malcolm can finish. I look around the interior at the cherry-red seat cushions, oak tables minus tablecloths, and dim lighting only showcasing each booth and individual table. The low music gives off a calm, chill mood. If Angela wanted some place hype, this definitely isn't it.

"You only came here because she likes it," Angela says, nodding in my direction. I suck in a breath and take a defensive stance. I did not tell Jaylen to take me anywhere.

A short blond hostess approaches us carrying menus and a smile. "Table for four?"

We nod, and she leads us to a table near the bar and places our menus in front of us. I'm sitting across from Malcolm, and Jaslene is placed in the chair between me and Angela. Jaylen's sitting across from her. I skim over the menu and see Angela from the corner of my eye making silly faces at Jaslene. It's interesting how she doesn't like me but adores my baby.

Soon we're greeted by our waitress, who has several strands of hair that escaped from her ponytail and blocks of ketchup stains on her white apron. "Can I start anyone out with something?"

Jaylen and Malcolm ask for a beer, while Angela and I order water. When the waitress leaves to give us time to look over our menus, Angela leans forward to Jaylen, and he nods and clears his throat.

"Okay, we've got an announcement to make," Jaylen says suddenly, and my eyes pop up. He smiles at me and Malcolm, and I can literally feel my heart starting to fall out of my chest. "Angela and I are engaged."

My mouth drops open, and I'm sitting bug-eyed. I stare at Angela's hand, which I hadn't looked at before, and sure enough there is a nice-size diamond rock on her left ring finger. I swallow my heart down to keep it from beating so loudly in my chest. Engaged. They're engaged. Jaylen's engaged, and he's starting a new life, but I have . . .

I look at Jaslene and feel pity. She can never know her true father now. Not after this. Not now that he's engaged and is going to get married. How can I tell him and have it destroy his world? How can I tell him and have him break Angela's heart? I know what it feels like firsthand to have the person you love tell you that they've been unfaithful, and I don't want Angela going through the same thing.

I shake my head and smile. "Congrats, you two. I . . . um . . . I honestly can't believe it." My voice trails off with my last word, and I fumble to say something else, when I get a peek at Malcolm, and his mouth is open so wide I can see traces of his food.

"Married? Married, bro?" He switches his gaze back and forth from Angela to Jaylen. "You didn't talk to me about . . . I mean, congratulations. That was fast, though."

Angela smiles and folds her hands on the table in front of her. "Well, when you know what you want, you go get it. He knew what he wanted," she says, giving Malcolm a preppy girl's smile.

Malcolm's eyes narrow slightly, and I turn to Jaylen to change the subject before Malcolm can get another word in. "When did you propose, Jaylen?"

"Earlier today. I would have done it here at dinner, but I wasn't sure if y'all wanted to go out or if y'all was cooking, so I just did it not too long after we got home. In privacy."

For one split second I see disappointment in Angela's eyes, but she quickly recovers and turns over a smile. I nod at both of them. "Congrats, you two. I wish you all the best in the world."

I can't wait to get out of that restaurant and go home. I haven't even eaten, and already I've lost my appetite. I sneak glances at Jaylen when the waitress comes to take our order. He gives me a small smile, and I tighten my fists under the table. It's so frustrating to know I have this secret and that I can never tell him now. He'll lose everything, especially Angela, and I know he doesn't want that. I can't have him break her heart. I can't be the cause for that. I've already caused too much trouble.

After Jaylen and Malcolm split the bill, we all stand up to leave. I scoop up Jaslene and go to the bathroom for a quick diaper change. I squeeze between chairs and tables and around waitresses until I reach the far corner of the restaurant. The bathroom smells like fresh cotton, and I take a second to suck in a deep breath. Okay, this isn't so bad. I can handle this. Nothing has changed, and I'm still raising my child. I'm her mother, and I'm going to take care of her like I'm supposed to. Jaylen is going to live his life with his wife and have a family of his own and . . .

I can't think anymore as I feel the threat of tears stinging the back of my eyes. I close my eyes shut and lean against the bathroom wall. I feel like I'm sacrificing so much so Jaylen can go on with his life, and he doesn't even know I'm doing this for him. But he can't know I'm sacrificing for him. He'd never approve of that.

I change Jaslene and head back to the table. Everyone's standing and waiting for me. I nod and follow them out to the car. I trail behind everyone, and Malcolm peeks back a few times and tilts his head in a questioning fashion. I nod, and he shrugs and keeps walking. I'm quiet the whole ride back, but Angela's talking her ass off about wedding plans and how many bridesmaids she's going to have. I think I liked her better before I knew she was engaged. At least on the ride to the restaurant she was quiet

"Have a good night," Jaylen says softly, looking from me to Jaslene as we stand outside his car window. My heart starts pounding as I think about how close he's been to Jaslene all night. He didn't sit next to her at the restaurant, and he didn't get a good look at her in the house since she'd been in a crib in the back room. I don't want to take any chances, so I hurry out a good-bye and start walking toward the apartment building.

I hear Malcolm and Jaylen clasp hands, and a few seconds later Malcolm's walking beside me giving me weird looks. "What?" I ask, after his stares become more constant and annoying.

"Do you believe that shit?" he asks, nodding his head back in the direction of Jaylen's car. "He didn't even tell me he was proposing."

I let out a sigh. At least he isn't interrogating me about my mood change. Yet. I shrug. "He really loves her, Malcolm."

"I can kind of see why he loves her. I mean, she fine as hell, and she's not a pushover, but damn, her attitude sometimes make her seem like a bitch."

The corner of my mouth turns up, but I shake my head as I climb the stairs to the second floor. "Jaylen knows what he's doing and—"

"I didn't say he doesn't know what he's doing, and I'm not saying I don't approve of Angela. Frankly, my opinion of her don't really matter. It's the whole getting married thing and how random it is. I mean, that was random as hell."

"Yeah, it was," I say as we reach the landing of the stairs and start walking toward his apartment. I can't help thinking about Angela and Jaylen being married. Why did he propose all of a sudden? Did Angela make him? No, Jaylen would never do anything he didn't agree with. Not if he could help it. But what if he couldn't help it? What if she's hanging something over him so that he'll marry her?

My fists clench tightly again, but I know I'm getting ahead of myself. Jaylen would never let anyone manipulate him. I have to believe that.

Chapter Ten

For the next few days I walk around the apartment like a zombie, waiting for the mail to arrive. The letter should have the results of Chris's paternity in it since I asked for the results to be mailed and also for them to notified me over the phone.

I found out last night that Sheri isn't able to come up to visit after all since she's fallen ill and doesn't want to get Jaslene sick. I understand her on that one and appreciate her concern.

I haven't spoken to Jaylen since we left the restaurant that night, but I sent them both a text message to congratulate them again. It seems the only thing I can say is congrats. I pound my fist as I continue to wait for any deliveryman. Maybe the mailman dropped the letter in the mailbox downstairs. I would go down there, but that would make it my fifth time today. I sigh, but I can't sit down.

Jaslene's being rocked softly in her new swing, and I can tell she's about to fall asleep. I feel so many things when I look at her now. I feel pride and admiration. I feel relief knowing that her father isn't Chris but tremendous guilt from forcing Jaylen into infidelity because I was too horny. I guess she's a reminder of the sinful things Jaylen and I did, but somehow I just don't want to think of her like that. I mean, I just want her to be Jaslene. My daughter. Not the symbol for this or that but just my daughter Jaslene. Is that too much to ask?

I sit down on the floor next to the swing. Standing up pacing is not going to make the time go faster, but I have to know if Chris is Jaslene's father or not. Yeah, I see similarities between them, but I could be making them up by psyching myself out about the whole thing. Maybe I did mishear the lady, and this whole episode is a waste of time.

I watch Jaslene as she starts to drift off to sleep, and I suppress a yawn. I haven't been getting much sleep lately, and under the circumstances, it's no wonder to me. It's almost ten a.m. now, but the mail still hasn't arrived. Just as I'm about to give up for the day and hope for tomorrow, I decide to take one more look downstairs at the mailbox. I scoop up Jaslene, and we both walk out of the apartment quietly. She stays asleep in my arms, and I try not to be too noisy.

I reach the mailbox and spot a white envelope. I insert Malcolm's apartment key and pull out the form. It's from the hospital, and my heart thumps in my chest. It's the mail verification that I was waiting for containing Jaslene's paternity test results. All written out so there will be no chance I'll mishear a person over the phone. It has all the details, so I can look and see what I agree with or don't.

I clutch the envelope and go back to the room. Once inside I set Jaslene back down in the swing. I look at the letter and hesitate. What if this letter does nothing but cause me more pain. And Jaylen. Should I open it? What if I threw it away and pretended I never got it? I could just say that the hospital never gave me the information. That would buy me some time. But then I think about Chris, who also got a copy of the paternity test. If they ever heard from Chris, they would find out that I was lying, and I don't want to risk that embarrassment.

I open the letter quickly, thinking that if I don't like what I see, then I can just throw it away. I prepare for the worst. I open the letter, scan it, and lo and behold! Big shock. Chris is not the father. I exhale and collapse next to Jaslene. I can't believe my life has turned into such turmoil. How do I get out of this situation? Why did I put myself in this situation in the first place? I don't know what to do, but I feel like I just screwed up big-time. I can't believe I gave in to temptation and had sex with Jaylen. I mean my best friend. How could we have done this? How can we hurt the people we love with this information?

I ball up the letter and toss it in the trash. No one is ever going to know that truth as long as I can help it. As I let those words sink in, I know it's not true. I have nothing, and there is nothing but love that I can give my daughter.

Then I think about Sheri and the offer she gave me about a week ago, and I know what I must do. I must move back home to Aurora.

I'm sitting at the kitchen table later that night with a cup of hot chocolate, when Malcolm opens the door. His face is dazed, and I can tell he's been working too hard. I smile softly in his direction, and he nods and kicks off his boots and slouches in his chair. I know he's not going to like what I have to say, but I have to tell him at some point.

"What's wrong with you?" Malcolm asks, eyebrows frowning.

I let out the air I had built up and shake my head. "Nothing. I wanted to talk to you."

"Is it about that girl that kept calling here last night? I told that chick she's too clingy."

"No," I say, shaking my head again. "It's about your mom's offer for me to come live with her. I think I'm going to do it. I mean, I am going to do it. It's just better this way."

I watch Malcolm's face go from tired and sluggish to alert and pissed off.

"Are you crazy?" Malcolm says.

I don't see what's so crazy about it, and the more I thought about it earlier, the more sense it made. "No, I'm serious. Don't you want your own place back?" I ask.

His eyes widen. "I ain't had it to myself in almost a year, and now you saying I should be craving it back?"

"Well, you can move another girl in here once I leave so you won't get lonely. I just want to move out."

"But why, is all I'm asking," Malcolm says, rolling his eyes like I missed my one big cue.

"Your mom offered, and I've been thinking about it, and I think that it'll be best for me."

"My mom will say anything to get what she wants. She just wants to help take care of your baby so she'll feel like a mom again. That can be taken care of in one visit. You don't have to move in with her."

"Why shouldn't I move in with your mom?" I ask with my chest poked out.

"No reason. I'm just saying that you're making so much progress living here and that moving back would be like giving up and starting over."

"I've given up on a lot of things, and I do need to start over. I left school and a relationship, and I need help raising my child."

"You can get help from Chris whenever we hear back from the hospital about those results. Just be patient."

"I don't want support from him. I can take care of her myself. Me and your mom anyway."

"So you want my mom to have the financial burden?"

I stop cold when he says that, and guilt washes over me again, but then I remember that Sheri was the one who offered to help me in the first place.

"I'll be fine, Malcolm, thank you."

"What? You'll be fine. So you really just gon' move out just like that? No notice. Not even try to talk it out? What about this child support case? We can't do it if you're not here."

"Forget the case. Just forget I even asked for the paternity test."

"Are you serious? What's wrong with you? You're acting weird."

I shrug. "I have to do what I have to do, Malcolm."

"And what's that?"

"I don't want to stay in Chicago anymore. I want to go back home. There's nothing for me here."

"What about me, Jay, and Angela? What about that chick from your school you used to talk to? You got friends here, Jess."

"Yeah, and some enemies. I don't want to live in the same city as Chris. I want to stay in your mom's house with her three bedrooms. I want to have my own space again, and I haven't had that in a long time. I just want to move. This city has so many bad memories attached to it that—"

"And Aurora hasn't? Your Grandma Mae died in the house next door. Why would you want to go anywhere near that place?" His words stab my heart, but I won't let him use my grandmother in a cheap shot to get me to stay here. I hunch my shoulders back.

"I'm not avoiding it, and besides—when I'm there, I can visit her tombstone anytime I want. I can show it to Jaslene."

"Jessica, I think you're making a rash decision. How about you take the next couple of weeks and just think about it without doing anything?"

"I can't. I want to move out as soon as possible." His face looks hurt, but I don't want to stay.

"Just stay here."

I shake my head and fight back tears. "I don't want to have to run into Chris."

"Don't worry about Chris. He won't bother you, I swear. Is this about the paternity thing, because we're forcing you to do it? And that if you move to Aurora you won't have to feel pressured by us?"

It sounds like the perfect excuse, and I kind of want to say yes just so he can stop arguing with me, but I shake my head. "Not even half of it."

"Well, what's the half?" he asks, staring at me so hard I get nervous.

I take a deep breath, and decide to tell him half the truth. "It's Jaylen and Angela. They just got engaged, and I feel jealous because I was once engaged to Chris before it all went downhill. I don't want to be around them all lovey-dovey as a reminder that I'm still single. I want to leave."

"Okay. How about this? I'll call Jay right now and tell him to not act like that with Angela in front of you. I'll tell him why."

"No! Don't call Jaylen!"

He stares at me for a few seconds, and I realize how I must look to him. "Why not?"

"I don't want him having to change his behavior for me. That's not fair."

"So your leaving the city to avoid something he can prevent is fair?" he asks slowly so I'll seem stupid.

I take a deep breath. "No, I don't want you to tell him because I don't want to him to have to act differently just because of me. This is their time, and I don't want to be around for it."

"You know that's stupid, right?"

"It's not stupid. Look, I'm leaving, and there's no reason we're discussing it anyway."

"We're discussing it because you're leaving for a stupid reason."

"It's not stupid! It's very important!"

"Why? How the hell is being away from Jaylen doing his engagement to Angela so important? Why do you want to leave because of that? It has nothing to do with you."

"Yes it does, Malcolm. It does. You just don't understand!"

"Well, make me understand then, because you're speaking in riddles. Just come out and tell me why."

I open my mouth and am about to shout it out at him, but then I close it. I can never ever tell anyone this secret, and Malcolm isn't even directly involved in

151

it, so he definitely doesn't need to know. "It just is, okay? Let's just leave it at that. Forget I mentioned it in the first place. I'm leaving, and I don't really have to explain why."

He looks hurt again, but his face stays firm. "Then you don't mind me telling Jaylen that you're leaving because of him and Angela?"

"Don't do that. Please."

"Then tell me the truth."

"I just don't like it here anymore, okay? I told you why. I don't want to be reminded of Chris. There's more space at your mom's house than in your apartment, and I don't have to be around the love birds while they're engaged. I also don't want to be a burden to you. Needing money and everything. You've helped out enough already. What's so complicated about that?" I ask, getting frustrated again.

"What about the paternity results?" he asks softly. "Don't you want to stay around until they come in?"

"Not really."

"I think you're leaving because of the results." My heart stops when he says this. Does he know? "Because you don't want to deal with seeing Chris in court, is that right?"

"No." Or maybe I should have said yes. I shrug to make it a little more even.

"Then what is it, Jessica? I know it's something big, because all this information my mom told you last week, and you didn't want to go then, so why now? I mean, the only thing different was that Jay and Ang got engaged. Is it really because of that? You can't put your feelings aside and just be happy for them?'

"I am happy for them—why do you think I'm leaving?" I say, and as soon as the words slip out of my mouth I regret it.

"You're leaving to keep them happy? Or make them happy?"

"No."

"Why?" he asks, like I didn't interrupt.

"I . . . he . . . um . . ."

"Does this have to do with Angela? Do you not like her marrying Jay?"

"She's not the problem."

"Who's the problem then?"

"I am." I say finally. "I'm just jealous."

He looks at me weird, and I realize he thinks I'm talking about the other kind of jealous, like "I wish I was in her place" jealous. I just meant engagement jealous. "Not like that," I say. This conversation isn't getting anywhere.

"And why is your jealousy the main reason you're leaving?"

"I told you."

"If they weren't engaged, would you still leave?" I think about Malcolm's question and realize that I wouldn't be leaving if they weren't engaged. It just seems like there's a lot more at stake with me staying, and I don't want to get in their way. If Jaylen ever finds out the truth about Jaslene, their relationship would be over. All because of me.

I don't know how to answer Malcolm's question, and I guess my silence is answer enough. "You have to be strong, Jess, and not let other people's situations affect your life. You shouldn't feel like you have to move because of them."

"You just don't understand, Malcolm."

"God, Jess, then help me understand. There's something you're not telling me. Your reasons don't make any sense."

I feel the urge to tell him and just get this weight off my shoulders. I haven't told anyone. I hardly like to admit it to myself. "I can't be around them. I need to get away."

He's quiet and listens to me. He just sits there and waits patiently for me to continue, and even though I feel no pressure, I keep talking against my better instincts. "I don't want to interfere with anything they have going on. I want their relationship to stay pure and carefree. I don't want to mess that up."

I can tell by his face that he's begging to ask why. I don't say anything for a long time, and I think he's gonna ask me to continue, but he doesn't. He just still sits there patiently, nodding occasionally as if I was still talking. Then I say, "I made a mistake, and I don't want Angela getting hurt."

His eyes pop open wider, and I look down at the floor. My shame is just too bright. "We had sex, Malcolm."

I hear him let out a breath, and finally he talks. "I can understand that being a reason you want to leave, but, um . . . everyone makes mistakes, Jess, and I don't think that's reason enough for you to leave. Look— he's engaged now, so apparently y'all's sex didn't cause much harm. Just stay here, and he can be with Angela without you feeling guilty. Just keep it hush-hush from here on out. Don't even talk to Jaylen about it."

"I haven't talked to him about it."

"Oh? How long ago did y'all do it?" he asks.

I look up at him now, and my words come out faster than I can stop them. "About the time Jaslene was conceived."

He stares at me, and I see his face slowly understand. "Are you saying . . . that there's a chance Jaslene is Jaylen's?"

"No," I say. Malcolm breathes a sigh of relief.

"I'm saying that Jaylen is the father. I got the phone call from the hospital a few days ago, and the mail report came in today. Chris isn't her father. And that only leaves Jaylen."

I feel a ton of weight fall off my shoulders when the truth finally slips from my lips. I never thought it would feel so good to let it out instead of keeping it bottled up inside.

I watch Malcolm's face go from stunned to energetic as he jumps up and storms into Jaslene's room, where's she's sleeping in her crib. I follow him into her room and catch him staring down at her like he's trying to figure out a puzzle. Eventually he turns away and walks back out quietly. He stares at me with confusion. "Why didn't you tell me? Does Jaylen know? I'm an uncle? Oh my God."

I shake my head. "No, he doesn't know. That's why I have to leave. I can't be around him, raising his daughter, because he might notice some similarity or find out. And if he finds out, he'll have to tell Angela, and they'll have to break up. That's why I'm leaving. I have to save their relationship. If I'm in Aurora, I don't have to see them or Chris, and it can be just me and my daughter."

Malcolm runs a hand down his face. He leans against the hallway wall, and I do the same across from him. "You have to tell him."

156

I shake my head. I already went against my rule of telling no one by telling Malcolm in the first place, and the only reason I did was so he would get off my back about my reason for moving out. I just need him to keep this secret between us. Who am I kidding? There's no way he's going to have more loyalty to me than to his brother. "I don't want them to break up. Look, I'll be fine. We'll both will be fine. We just need to get out of this city and move back home."

"No," he says slowly. "You need to tell my brother what's up, and you need to do that instead of focusing on trying to leave."

"I'm still leaving."

"No, the hell you ain't," he says, and I swear he reminds me of Chris right now, and that's not a good thing. "How you gon' take my brother's baby—my niece—and just move without him even knowing it's his? That's some low-down shit right there."

"I'm not leaving to hurt him. I'm leaving to help him," I say, trying to get him to understand.

"Help him? Jess, he's a grown-ass man. He doesn't need you to cover for him. He laid down with you, so he gon' have to stand up to his responsibilities as a father, but you're not even giving him the chance."

"I can raise her without him having to do anything," I hiss. I am so tired of repeating the same information. Why can't he understand me?

"Are you really gone rob Jaylen out of a daughter? What about Jaslene? She's only four weeks old. You just going to deprive her of her father because you think he shouldn't have to deal with the consequences of his actions? Tell me now—how is that fair?"

"Jaslene . . . she . . ." I stop. I don't want to deprive my daughter of anything, but I don't want to cause anymore problems to Jaylen's relationship than I already have.

"Okay, look—put it like this," Malcolm says, clasping his hands together. "What if Jay and Angela break up for something totally irrelevant to this issue? Then you got Jaslene without a father, Jaylen broken up with Angela, and you still not getting any added help.

"What I'm saying, Jess, is you can't not tell Jaylen just because you think it's going to ruin his relationship. Honestly, that's not your problem. He knew he had a girlfriend when he slept with you, and who knows if he's even going to tell Angela? The point is still the same. You have to tell Jaylen, because if you don't, I'm going to tell him for you. And trust me—it's going to sound worse coming from me no matter how nice I try to put it. He needs to hear this from you."

I stare at him, but I don't want to say anything. I knew he would insist on telling Jaylen, and I kick myself for telling him the truth. Why did I do it in the first place? Did I want this secret out?

When I don't say anything, Malcolm continues. "Trust me, Jess. The longer you put off telling him, the worse it's gon' be. How you gon' explain to Jaylen later that your five-year-old daughter is his? How can you rob Jay of years of his daughter's life, quality time that he would have spent with her? This baby is not just yours, Jessica. It's his too." He pauses and stares at me hard. "It is his, right? There's no other possibility?"

I sigh. "If there was anyone other than Jaylen that I could claim Jaslene with, I would have done so. I never wanted this to happen. Not to him. I feel like I've ruined his life with this."

I start getting choked up at the thought and Malcolm comes over and lets me lean on his arm. "Well, if it's his, Jess, you have to tell him. There's no getting around it. You can't put this off, and nobody is better to do it than you. Trust me. I think Jaylen's going to be fine with it. Well, once he wakes up from passing out he'll be fine with it. You know he's got your back. We both do. You just need to tell him."

I think long and hard. I don't want Jaylen's relationship to crumble, but I don't want Jaslene to lose out on a father. I never got the chance to know my father, and if someone had stopped me from getting to know him, no matter what the situation was, I'd be pretty pissed at them. I don't want Jaslene pissed at me one day if she ever found out the truth. What was I going to tell her a few years from now anyway? That her father died? And I never want to lie to my daughter.

I nod at Malcolm. "I'll tell him on the way to Aurora."

"You're still going to go? He needs to spend time with his daughter."

"He can come see her anytime he wants. Look, I agree to tell him, but I still think Aurora is a better place for me and Jaslene right now. Away from Chris—and Angela, in case she tries to hunt me down. Also I'll have more room and someone to help me raise Jaslene 24/7. 'Cause I know you be at work, and babysitting isn't really your thing. This way you can have your own space back."

"Fuck my space. I'll be lonely," he says, opening his arms wide and looking over his whole apartment in a glance.

I laugh and roll my eyes. "I'm sure you'll come up with a way to not be lonely." I give a wink just in case he missed my hint.

He thinks for a second, and after a long time he nods. "Can't argue with that logic." We laugh.

"Look, Jess. If you're going to live with my mom you should be aware of a few things," he says, his voice growing serious again.

Is he coming around to me moving out? I hope so. I nod for him to continue. "My mom loves to cook and clean, but she loves it even more when someone helps out, so don't be surprised when you find yourself doing chores all over the house as well as schoolwork. You are planning on going to school, right?"

I nod my head fast. "Of course, I'm going to transfer as soon as can. I'm just taking a break to bond with my daughter. Even if I have to start when a new semester begins, I will. I'm staying in school."

"Good. Another thing, Mom is crankiest late at night and in the early morning, so be careful."

I laugh. "Thanks, Malcolm. Anything else?"

"No," he says, then thinks longer. "Can I ask you something?"

I nod.

"You care a lot about Jaylen's relationship with Angela, right? So, I mean are you—"

"Jealous? Oh no! I'm happy for them."

"Um . . . I wasn't going to ask that. I was going to ask about you and Jay and if you're . . . um . . . never mind."

"What?" I ask, squinting my eyes in confusion.

Malcolm laughs softly and shakes his head. "Never mind. I think deep down I know the answer to that question." He gives a flirty wink, and I blush as I think of all the thoughts that could be going to through his mind about me and Jaylen. It was only one night. Just sex. We're still just friends, just like before. We don't have any feelings for each other, other than that. Right?

One look at Malcolm's teasing face tells me I might be wrong.

The next morning I squint my eyes at Malcolm's laptop as I try to read about another school listed near the Aurora area. I took the conversation I had with Malcolm last night very serious, and I'm planning to have a great future back home. I've been searching for the last two hours ever since I told Malcolm the truth about Jaslene last night. This college is the third one I've written down, and the only one I found interesting is the community college. I lean back in the computer chair and rub my eyes. I've been staring at the screen too long, and it's giving me a headache.

I look around the living room and notice how the apartment is quiet for a Tuesday, with Jaslene asleep in her swing by my feet and Malcolm at work. I had told Malcolm I was going to get out of the house and go somewhere, but I've decided that staying in and finding another school to transfer to would be better. I don't want to drop out again, and I want to be able to provide for my child.

I keep the windows closed and locked but pull the blinds up. I love watching it snow, especially when it's snowing soft and slow like it is now. I pull the blanket further up my arms, feeling the cold seep through the glass. I'm about to write down the school's name on my notepad, when I hear a knock at the door followed by the knob turning. I suck in a breath and look at the clock. Three p.m. Malcolm shouldn't be back yet.

The door flings open, and Jaylen's face appears. I let out a breath I didn't know I was holding. "What are you doing here?" I ask, then pick up my cell phone that has no missed calls or text messages. "You didn't call."

Jaylen closes the door behind him and shrugs off his heavy coat, revealing a nice blue-and-black sweater that hugs his abs in all the right spots. He walks over to me and peers at the computer. "I just got off work. Just wanted to stop in and say what up." He looks down at Jaslene and then back at me, and my stomach tightens.

"She likes that swing?" he asks, standing less than a foot away with one hand on the desk.

"Yeah," I blurt out, glad that's the only observation he's making. "She likes it a lot." I look down at

Jaslene to keep from looking at Jaylen. He can read my face like a book, and he can tell when I'm nervous.

"You all right?" he asks, tugging my chin so that I'm in his line of view again.

I force a smile. I still haven't told him the truth about Jaslene. "Of course. Why?"

He doesn't answer me but cocks his head to the side as if he's deciding whether to believe me or not. I hold eye contact with him and give him my best stern confident stare, but his eyes only narrow more. I try changing the subject. "Malcolm went to work already, but he should be back in another hour or two if you want to wait for him."

He continues to stare at me, but then sighs and shakes his head. "I came to see you."

"Oh?" I say.

"Yeah, I was . . ." His voice trails off, and I look to where he is now facing. My computer screen with the list of schools in the Aurora area shows brightly and proudly on the screen. If his eyes were narrowed before, they're slits now. I quickly shift my body so that it'll block whatever view he has of the screen, but I know it's too late. "Why you looking at schools in Aurora?"

"Um . . ." I sigh. I didn't want to tell him like this. I wanted to have Malcolm with me and go over to Jaylen's house and tell him there. That way the two of us wouldn't be alone, and that way I wouldn't have to tell him by myself because Malcolm would be there to back up my reasons. Oh well. Jaylen was going to find out at some point. "I'm moving back home."

Jaylen rolls his eyes as if he could sense the drama coming, then slides a hand down his face. "Why?"

I take a deep breath and mull over all the things I had planned to say—all my logical reasons that were going to sound great when I marched into his house to tell him. But now, right now when I need those reasons, those answers, I can't think of a single one. "Um. I just need a new start." There, that's good.

At least I thought so. Jaylen folds his arms across his chest as he waits for me to continue. "I want to start over in a place where I don't have a bad reputation."

"Bad reputation? For what?"

"Chris has been telling everyone that I slept with one of his friends while he and I were engaged, and I would hate to run into any of his friends and have them all—"

"Have you ever run into one of his friends before?"

"Er, no."

"So you can't leave just because of something that might happen. Did you fuck one of his friends?" he asks.

165

"No, of course not. I was never introduced to any of his friends."

"So why are you afraid of running into them? What Chris said wasn't true, and you need to ignore all the people that say shit that don't apply."

I take a deep breath and turn around to face the computer. "I know that, Jay, but that's not the only thing." I try to come up with something off the top of my head, but I can't think of any good reasons anymore. How come I can think so clearly around Malcolm, but when Jaylen comes around I get so caught up? I decide to think about Sheri. "Your mom offered to let me move in with her, and I know she can help me raise Jaslene."

I turn back around to catch him raise an eyebrow, but he doesn't interrupt. "I'm new to this parenting thing, and it'll be nice to have someone constantly there to help me. Since Sheri doesn't work, she'd be there to help me all day if she wants to. This will give me a lot of time to study and go to classes without worrying about a babysitter, and I wouldn't have to worry about anything but my grades and my child." Minus Jaylen finding out it's his child too, of course, but I'll worry about that another day. I'll tell him soon enough. I think about Malcolm's promise that he'll tell Jaylen himself if I don't do it, and shudder. "And you know I need a go to school to get a good job."

Jaylen watches me closely, his eyes burying into mine. I realize this is the first moment we've had alone since he and Angela announced their engagement. Maybe if I change the subject he'll let my decision be. "How's Angela? That's crazy how you two are engaged now."

He grunts, then shakes his head softly. "Nice try."

I smile innocently up at him, and he chuckles and leans a hand on my desk. The veins in his arms bulge out like he's just finished lifting weights, and I ignore the slamming of my heart against my chest and pull my view to his eyes. He leans down until he's within an inch of my face. "I don't want you to move," he says so softly that I think I imagined it.

I open my mouth, about to tell him I'm going to miss him, but the sound of the door bursting open stops me. Jaylen springs around at the sound, standing directly in front of me, blocking me and Jaslene from whoever is barging in. Jaylen's shoulders tense up, and his fists are tighter than I've ever seen them before. If I thought his veins were bulging a while ago, they are at attention now.

It all happens so quickly, and just as soon as Jaylen tenses up, he relaxes. He still doesn't move from in front of me, and from my view I can't see what's going on. I stand up and peek around Jaylen's arm. Then roll my eyes. "Malcolm . . ."

"My bad, y'all," Malcolm says, stumbling in with a clearly intoxicated woman on his arm. The woman was tall and lanky, almost towering over Malcolm if she stood up straight. Her makeup is smeared like it's been raining, and her smile has a lopsided snare to it. Malcolm wraps an arm around her waist. "Jess, I thought you was gone."

"Um, no, I . . ." My voice trails off as I watch the woman lean her head against Malcolm's shoulders and close her eyes. This is the type of woman he brings home? How could I have missed this?

"Sorry," Malcolm says. "This is my friend Katie, and she—"

"Hi, I'm Katie," Katie says popping her eyes back open.

Malcolm frowns at her and leans her over so she's standing more on her own. "This is my brother, Jaylen, and our friend Jessica."

"Oh, you're Jaylen?" Katie smiles wider, and her eyes goes back and forth between Jaylen and me. "Congratulations, Jay! Malcolm just told me you just became a—"

'Engaged man!" Malcolm says while simultaneously clasping a hand over the girl's mouth. "I just told her you and Angela was engaged. Nothing else."

"But I thought you told me that he—"

"Oh, I need to take you home. You're imagining things," Malcolm says, guiding his lady friend back through the door. I feel my blood rush to my face with irritated frustration and mortified horror. Did that chick really almost tell my secret? Why the hell did Malcolm tell her? Who is she? Oh, he's going to get it.

We hear the woman grumble a few words, but Malcolm shushes her as he closes the door behind them.

When the door clanks shut, I quickly neutralize my facial expression before looking at Jaylen, who smiles and shakes his head, still eyeing the door. "That's another reason I think moving in with Sheri would be a good idea. Malcolm needs his space. His whole apartment back. It was never the plan for me to stay here forever, especially once the baby was born."

Jaylen stares at me for a while and then sighs. I know I've won the argument when he doesn't say anything else. I know at the end of the day he just wants me to be happy. He comes close again and wraps an arm around my waist and scoops me into his chest. I feel like I'm hugging a rock, and I ignore the fact that I like it.

"Are we still going to court when the results of the test come back?" he asks.

The blood drains from my face, and I look straight ahead at his shoulder instead of his face. "Of course," I say. I hate lying to him, but for now that's all he can know.

Chapter Eleven

I stack the last of the remaining dishes in the cabinet above the sink. It only took me a few minutes to wash four plates and a couple of glasses. I've cleaned the whole apartment except for Malcolm's room and the balcony I've been working on since Jaylen left earlier today. Most of the cleaning was done with Jaslene asleep in her crib, but after her nap she wanted to be held while I did easier things, like picking up trash off the floor and wiping the kitchen table and counters.

I walk into the living room, when I hear the sound of Malcolm returning home. He staggers in and lets out a loud breath. "You still up?" he asks, looking at me through squinted eyes.

I nod and point to the clock above the entertainment center. "It's only eleven," I say, shifting Jaslene to my other arm. "By the way, what was up with that girl you brought over here?"

Malcolm laughs, then plops down on the couch. "Don't worry about Katie. She's . . . different."

"She was drunk," I say firmly with a hand on my hip. Malcolm looks me over, then laughs.

"She was. I'm not gon' lie. I swear I didn't think you was home. I brought her here 'cause she was into babies, and I told her I have a niece at home. I was just going to show her the crib and stuff, then take her home. I thought you went to look for a job or college or something."

"Yeah, on the Internet."

"Yeah, see, that's where we misunderstood each other," he says, and we both laugh.

"So, you use my daughter as a pickup line to strangers? And then have those same strangers almost tell my secret?" I ask.

"Naw. I mentioned Jaslene as a conversation starter," he says, giving me a Kool-Aid smile. "And Katie almost saying Jaylen was the father wasn't my fault because it shouldn't be a secret. Anyway, what was Jay doing here? Don't think I forgot," Malcolm asks, looking at me with a smirky grin, clearly trying to change the subject.

"Um . . . he just came to say what's up. To talk. That's it."

Malcolm nods a few times. "Oh. Cool. Did you tell him about Jaslene?"

I can feel my face get hotter, but I manage to control my blush. "No. Not yet."

Malcolm twists his fist in a why-not gesture, and I sigh. "I don't know. I just don't know how to say it. We were too caught up on the subject of me leaving anyway."

"You can tell him you're leaving the city, but you can't tell him he's a father?"

"Two very different topics."

Malcolm chuckles, then stands up and claps his hands together. "Okay. I'm going to help you out." My eyebrow raises and he continues. "I'm going to be Jaylen, and you're going to tell me I'm the father of Jaslene."

I smile brightly, which quickly turns into a fit of laughter.

"What, girl? I'm for real. Look, look." He goes to sit back on the couch and stares straight at the TV screen, unmoving. "I'm Jaylen. Go. Tell me, and I'll react how Jaylen would react."

173

I'm flabbergasted. He's serious. I stare at the side of Malcolm's face as he continues to stare at the TV. He really is serious. I bite back a smile. "Jaylen doesn't sit like that."

Malcolm turns around and gives me a death stare.

"Oh! Oh! He does look at me like that sometimes!" I say, pointing directly at Malcolm. He rolls his eyes.

"Girl, just start. Put Jaslene down."

I roll my eyes and set Jaslene down in her swing next to the couch. "What do you want me to do exactly?"

"Just tell me about Jaslene."

"Just say it?" I ask, stepping closer to him. How exactly am I supposed to do this?

"Yeah, like you would in real life."

I sigh. "Um . . . okay. Jaylen?"

He turns his head slightly, completely in Jaylen mode. "What up, Jess?" I laugh. "Come on, Jess, be for real!"

I laugh harder. "I can't take you seriously, Malcolm. You cannot be Jaylen."

"All right, all right. But you do need to tell him for real though, before you leave." He's half smiling, but I know he's 100 percent serious, so I nod.

"I know, Malcolm. I know. I'll tell him. Soon."

"Jaylen actually called me a few hours ago telling me that you planned to move. He said he saw you lookin' at schools on the computer."

I nod. "I didn't want to tell him like that, but I guess he found out."

Malcolm pauses and stares at me hard. "I told him you got the paternity test results."

My voice catches in my throat. What? Why did he tell him that? What did Jaylen say? Malcolm reads the panic on my face and shakes his head. "I didn't tell him Chris wasn't the father, but I had to tell him the results came because it's been days since you did the test, and he would have figured out on his own that you had the results. I told him that you won't do the whole court case thing until after you get settled in Aurora with Mom. That way you won't have to be worried about two things at once."

"Okay." I nod, breathing better.

"But you have to tell him before you move to Aurora. You can't keep lying to him, Jess."

"I know."

"Do you know? For real? Because I told you before that I will not hesitate to tell my brother if you choose not to, and it's not going to sound good coming from me," Malcolm says, his voice firm.

I nod and walk over to pick up Jaslene from her swing. "I know, Malcolm. I know. I don't want to keep Jaslene away from her father."

"When are you going to tell him exactly?" he asks, staring at Jaslene in my arms.

I think about the time I have left in Chicago. I want to move as soon as possible, and I guess the sooner I move, the sooner I have to talk to Jaylen. "I plan on moving in three days, so at the very least the day of."

Malcolm's eyes narrow at the mention of me moving so soon. "When?"

I think about it for a second. "If we can arrange it so Jaylen is the one driving me to Aurora alone, I'll tell him then. That way no one will be around, and we'll have the whole hour-and-a-half trip just talking it out." Unless he gets so shocked he gets in an accident. I bite my lip.

Malcolm nods and stands. He pats me on the shoulder. "Good. I'll let Jaylen know the plan." He lets go of my shoulder, then looks around the room. He stares at the polished kitchen table then down at the vacuumed floor. "Yeah, I'm going to miss your cleaning frenzies."

I smile sadly. "I'll only be a short drive away."

Over the course of the next three days I pack most of my stuff, but I still have a few extra things to pack. Today is moving day and also the day I'm going to tell Jaylen the truth about Jaslene. I talked to Sheri a few days back, and she's satisfied that I changed my mind and decided to come live with her after all. I plan on looking at the colleges down there firsthand and picking one that I like. I want to tell her she has a granddaughter after I tell the truth to Jaylen. I want us to tell her once we move my stuff into her house. That's the plan anyway.

I am nervous though. Well, that is an understatement. I'm scared out of my freaking mind. After I told Malcolm who Jaslene's true father was, he agreed not to tell Jaylen—but only if I agreed to tell Jaylen on the way to Aurora, which I plan to do. But even though it's now three days later, I'm still scared.

So now I'm in my room packing as much stuff in suitcases as I can find. Malcolm said he'll bring down anything I forget, but I'd rather do it all in one trip.

Just the thought of Jaylen makes my heart warm. We're still just very good friends. So what if we have a one-month-old baby? A lot of friends have babies and still stay friends. Jaylen has his life, and I have mine. I don't know what's going to happen after I tell him the truth, but I guess I have no choice but to just find out when I do.

I watch Jaslene play in her swing and think about the trip we had at the grocery store with Jaylen. He's so sweet, nice, and generous, and I know he'll make an excellent father when I tell him. I don't know why I'm so scared to. I just need to say it and get it over with. The way I say it is not going to change any DNA status, and I know he'll love Jaslene and accept her as his daughter. Not that he will reject her, but some guys don't want to claim their child even if they know it's theirs. My mind flashes back to Chris for a second, but I quickly shake my head, erasing him from my life fully. I have no reason to think about him anymore.

I know Jaylen's not that type of guy, but all these negative thoughts are spinning through my head, and nothing seems too crazy. Malcolm only said I had to tell him, but I can't force him to be a part of her life if he doesn't want to. But wouldn't he want to? My mind goes to Angela, and I think that she might be the only reason he would ever want to keep secret that he is Jaslene's father.

After I gather as many clothes and materials as I can, I go fetch another suitcase. I'm already on the third one. I take my time packing, daydreaming about my life in Aurora and how I hope it will be different from here. I know deep down I'm thinking about Chris. Leaving this city for good means that I'm leaving the place where I met that boy. Now I can move on and not look back. The only reason I'd come back to this city now is for Jaslene to visit her dad and Uncle Malcolm. That's it and then we out again. I look at Jaslene, and I think I see her nod in approval.

I hear footsteps coming in through the door and realize Malcolm must be home. He's come home early to help me pack before I move out tonight. He volunteered not to accompany me and Jaylen down to Aurora so the two of us can have our private talk in the car. Jaylen doesn't know this though, but we're not going to say anything until the last minute. We were able to talk him into leaving Angela at home, claiming that the extra seat in the car would be needed to hold my things. It sounds mean now that I think about it, but Jaylen didn't have to use the excuse, as it turns out that she has to work late tonight anyway.

"Hey," I say. I look down and notice he didn't bring back food. "I'm hungry—you didn't stop for grub?"

He shrugs. "I figured I'd keep you hungry in case you and Jaylen wanted to stop by a restaurant and eat on the way to Aurora."

"What? Why? It's only about an hour and a half away."

"Just giving you extra time to tell him about Jaslene." He winks, and I know he's talking about me telling my news.

I sigh. "Whatever you say."

Jaylen arrives about an hour later, and the two of them carry my luggage out to Jaylen's car. I stay in the house with Jaslene and continue to pack. As I gather all my belongings I've collected since my moving here, I can't help but worry about the trip. How will I start off the conversation? How soon on the trip should I tell him, and how will I go about explaining her birth date matching up with the month in which she was conceived? I don't want to just blurt it out, but then again, I don't want to beat around the bush.

I think about our friendship over the years and all we've been through. My very best friend is now the father of my child. What will happen to our friendship? Will we just become acquaintances, only talking when it concerns our child? Will he think of me different? How will he even react to this news?

I decide to push back negative thoughts about the awaited conversation and continue to pack Jaslene's bottles. Around five o'clock I'm moved out and into the car. I didn't have too much to bring, so the truck and entire backseat is mostly filled up with my clothes and Jaslene's baby things. I wasn't able to pack the crib, but Jaylen promised to bring it down to me later this week.

Before I get in the car with Jaylen, I turn around and give Malcolm a huge hug. I'm going to miss him.

"Visit soon, okay? And no late-night partying or coming in late and drunk. Pretend that Jaslene and I are still living here."

He chuckles and releases me from his grip. "I'll try my best." He pulls me into a tighter hug and whispers, "It's all going to be okay." He releases me, and I'm staring at him with teary eyes. Why did he have to go and say that? Why did he have to remind me that this whole ride to Sheri's house is going to be filled with shock, confusion, arguing, and just plain depression?

I sigh and nod. I pick up Jaslene and carry her in her car seat to the car. I sit down and place her on the floor between my legs. Jaylen looks over at her and smiles. I smile too. I turn my head one last time and wave to Malcolm as Jaylen and I pull off. I'm going to miss this apartment, but I'll be back to visit. Someday.

Jaylen and I had just gotten on the freeway, when right away we run into traffic. I glance at Jaylen's gas gauge and feel relieved that he has a full tank. "I guess we'll be getting there sometime later tonight if this keeps up," Jaylen says, leaning further into his seat.

"Yeah, I know this sucks," I say.

"Well, it's not all bad. I was actually planning on talking to you during this ride, and I'm glad Malcolm decided to stay home," he says nervously, thumbing the steering wheel.

"Oh?" Yes—a distraction from what I have to say. "What did you want to talk about?"

"Um . . . us," he says, staring straight ahead. "More specifically about the event that we never talked about."

I know what he means. The "why we had sex" talk.

"Jay, it was just a moment of weakness purely on my part. I just gave in to temptation and, um, made a bad choice."

A smile reaches the corner of his mouth. "Yeah, I can understand that, Jess, but what about me? Why did I do it? I didn't have to submit to your seduction."

"I don't know if I'd call it seduction. I just kissed you. I was just horny. Yeah, that's all it was. Sex. I mean I knew you had a girlfriend, and I had just broken up with Chris, so you know it was nothing more."

"I know this, Jess. I just want to see if you knew . . . I mean, I wanted to see where your head was at through all this."

I nod. "My head is where your head is. I think we should just keep moving forward and move past that part of our lives. That weak moment."

"Do you think about it sometimes?"

Oh my God. Yes! "Uh, sometimes. Maybe once or twice," I say, shrugging and looking out the window. I try to ignore the heat rising in my face.

"Me too," he says. My heart gives a giant jolt. He thinks about the time we had sex? How many times? How often? I want to ask him these questions, but I just sit there dumbfounded. I never knew that.

We don't say anything for a while, and I know this is the perfect time to mention Jaslene's paternity, but I don't know how to say it. I just can't say, "Hey, speaking of our having sex, guess who's really Jaslene's father?" I look down at Jaslene as she wiggles around a little. She's looking up at me, and I feel so much love in my heart I can't help but smile. My heart warms with satisfaction that Jaslene has Jaylen's genes and will have his qualities instead of Chris's. Through it all I feel like I dodged a bullet.

"You really love her, don't you?" Jaylen says. I look over at him, and he's staring at me and her with admiration. "Can I ask you something?"

"Yeah, sure," I say, choking out my words a bit.

"Do you think I'll make a good father?" he asks.

I'm so shocked at his question, I don't know what to say. How do I answer that? "Oh, you'll make a great father. In fact, here's your daughter right here"?

"It's just that Angela wants a baby," he continues. "She wants one bad. She keeps asking about you. How you're doing and how's Jaslene. At first I thought it was because she genuinely wanted to know how you guys were doing, which is partly true. The main information she wanted was how your day-to-day life is going with the baby. Like, has raising her gotten any easier so far, and how many feedings you have to do a night. Just weird questions."

He takes a breath, then continues. "I think she's using your life as an example of how her life will be once she—I mean, we—have a baby."

I pause and take it all in. "To answer your question, I think you'll make a great father, Jay. I mean, you're sweet, helpful, kind, dependable. You're just awesome in general, and I think being a good father is the last thing you should worry about."

A smile touches his lips again. "What's the first thing I should be worried about?"

I smile too. "Being married!" We laugh, and I'm grateful the mood's been brightened a little bit.

We drive for a while more, and my stomach starts growling. "Do you think we can pull off somewhere and grab some food? Like go through a drive-through? We don't have to go in."

Jaylen stares at the road and the heavy traffic. We're in the middle lane, and the traffic is so heavy it makes shifting lanes difficult. I sigh. "Never mind. I'll just wait till we get there. I know your mom probably cooked up enough food to feed us ten times."

We laugh. We have easy conversation the rest of the ride, and I know in the back of my head I'm supposed to be breaking the news to Jaylen, but now that I think about it, I think it's dangerous to tell a man some news like this while he's driving. What if he gets emotional, and we get in an accident? What if he gets so distracted he doesn't hit his brakes in time? I'd rather not risk Jaslene's safety by telling her father the news while he's driving. I'll tell him once we arrive at Sheri's house.

We pull up to Sheri's house about two hours later. The neighborhood is quiet as always, with all the houses having plenty of space between one another. I try to keep my glance from next door, the house I used to live in with Grandma Mae, but of course my eyes go straight to it. The grass is brown, and the windows are boarded up. It's been in foreclosure for a while, and I guess no one is interested in buying it. I know when I lived in there it needed a lot of work. I don't care either way if it's sold or not. It's just going to be hard living next door to all the memories and the times we shared.

I take a deep breath and scoop up Jaslene in her car seat. Maybe being reminded of the memories isn't a bad thing. I'm going to use those memories to make me happy, not keep me sad.

I walk slowly to Sheri's front porch with Jaylen right beside me, but before we can even reach the porch Sheri swings the door open, releasing the scent of steaks and baked potatoes. My toes start curling in anticipation, and I want to run past her and into the kitchen. However, I know I won't eat for another thirty minutes. Sheri has never seen my baby before, and then we will have to "catch up," as she likes to put it.

"Oh, baby! I'm glad y'all made it! Come here, give me a kiss. And oh! Who do we have here?" Sheri says, leading us into the house.

"It's me. Your son Jaylen," Jaylen says to Sheri's question.

"Oh, shut up, boy," Sheri says, swatting him away. I laugh and take a seat on the couch.

Sheri takes Jaslene out of her car seat and cradles her. "Oh, Jessica. Your baby is so perfect. I bet she hardly cries."

"Nope. Not really," I say, grinning from ear to ear.

Jaylen pats his mother's shoulders and heads for the kitchen, but Sheri stops him in his tracks. "Boy, if you don't come in this living room and sit down. Those steaks ain't going nowhere."

Jaylen sighs dramatically and kicks his feet, coming back into the living room. He collapses close to me on the couch, so much so that our thighs are touching. I hate feeling this way, but I know my sudden heart-rate increase is because of him.

Sheri and I talk about everything I've been up to. She mentions Chris a lot and even brings up the paternity test, but I tell her that the results haven't come back yet. I know Jaylen is sitting right next to me and is hearing all this, and me telling Sheri this lie will hurt his understanding of Jaslene not really being Chris's baby but his instead. My chests starts to hurt, and I wish I had told Jaylen before I had even left Malcolm's house.

After what seems like forever and after Jaylen finished bringing all of my luggage in the house, we all head to the kitchen to eat. "What time do you have to be back, Jay?" I ask him.

"Whenever I get back. I'm still grown, remember?" He smiles at me as I sit beside him at the table. Sheri pulls the steaks out of the oven and lays them on the table.

Sheri rips off her apron. "Well, if you plan on getting married, you gon' have to tell your wife when you plan on coming home. Coming in at all hours of the night ain't right. I remember your father . . ."

I zone out. I stare at the food placed in front of me wishing she would just finish her story so we can eat. Of course I could reach over and just grab it, but I want to have a hand tomorrow. I know she'd pop my hand off if I tried to touch this food without saying grace.

". . . And that's why I kicked him out!" Sheri says with a nod of her head to make it official. "Now, let's say grace so we can eat before this food gets cold." She looks over at me. "Say grace, Jessica—'cause I know you got a lot to be thankful for."

I close my eyes and fold my hands together. After a deep breath I start. "Thank you for this blessed meal, that we have food to eat for another day. I thank you for keeping Jaylen, myself and my child safe as we traveled from Chicago to Aurora safely. Thank you for being ever-present in my life. I thank you for Sheri giving me a place to live and helping me raise my child. I thank you most of all for Jaslene. She is my little miracle. She came into my life and gave me a family. I know that I have to become a better person for her, and nothing as silly as a man or any relationship will come in between me and my daughter. I just want to thank you that I have my life, that I have Jaslene, and that I have friends who care about me. Thank you for all that you've done in all of our lives. Amen."

I open my eyes, and they fall to Jaslene lying in her cradle next to me. I smile at her, then focus all my attention on the food placed in front of me. From the corner of my eye I see Jaylen staring at me. Our eyes lock, and he's looking at me with soft eyes that are filled with patience, and understanding. There's also something else in his eyes that I can't put my finger on. I smile timidly at him, and he smiles back and gives me a wink. I blush and lower my head, and focus back on my plate, hoping to hide the redness growing in my face.

I'm halfway through the steak, when Sheri coughs. It's the kind of cough that requires your attention. I look up, and she tilts her head to the side like she's expecting something. I lean back in my chair and take my elbows off the table. I guess living here isn't going to be a free ride.

As fast as I feel I'm eating, Jaylen still finishes both his steak and potato before me and reaches for a second steak. I, on the other hand, put down my fork and knife satisfied. I hear soft whines and look down at Jaslene. Her mouth is opening and closing, and I know she wants to eat too. I bend over and pick her up. Deciding that the kitchen table is not the best place to breast-feed, I excuse myself to go to the living room.

"You could have at least put your plate in the sink," Sheri says, looking at my sauce-stained plate full of napkins and crumbs. "That's gonna be your responsibility here. Washing the dishes."

I nod. "Anything you say."

189

As I sit down to feed Jaslene, I notice for the first time how aggressive she is while eating. I wonder if she got that from her father. I turn my head to the kitchen and watch Jaylen as he finishes off his second steak. He's eating a lot slower now and starts talking to Sheri like she's his old friend. They laugh and I smile too.

After Jaslene finishes, I rock her in my arms and burp her. I know she's about to fall asleep soon, so I place her back into her cradle. Jaylen walks in the room rubbing his abs.

"You're going to really have to work that steak off," I say, nodding at his belly.

He shrugs. "Yeah, well . . . I better hit it. Give me a hug." He stretches his arms wide, and I'm in them in a second. I hug him tight, like I don't want him to go and be left alone with his child and his mom, but I push back the thought and release him. I never did tell him the truth about Jaslene. Well, I can't tell him now. He's about to leave. But what if I don't see him again soon? I can't have Malcolm tell him, which I know he'll do, and I know he'll be asking about the results from the hospital soon since we all knew they were coming this week.

I bite my lip.

"Take care, Jessica. Call me if you need anything. Anything. Just let me know. Either me, or Malcolm if you want. Okay?" I nod.

Jaylen bends over and kisses me on the check and then Jaslene on her forehead. I catch my breath every time the two of them are close just in case Jaylen recognizes her as his own. But he doesn't this time, and he kisses Sheri on the cheek before leaving out the door. I let out a loud sigh of relief even though I shouldn't be relieved at all. Why didn't I tell him?

"So . . ." Sheri says, standing up from her chair at the kitchen table. She just finished her second steak as well. "When exactly were you planning on telling Jaylen that this is his baby?"

I snap my head around to face her. My mouth's hanging open like an idiot. "How did you know? I mean, I never said that—"

She shakes her head sharply and stares at Jaslene in her cradle by the couch. "You know that Miller gene is the strongest gene pool I know." Her voice is calm and soft. Like she's telling a bedtime story.

She continues. "I took one look at Jaslene and thought, oh, now I know this baby is ours some which a way. I didn't know how exactly, but I knew. Let me show you something." She walks to the entertainment center and pulls out a book from the bottom cabinet.

Sheri sits down on the opposite end of the couch, and I sit next to her. She opens the book on her lap, and I see all the pictures of Jaylen and Malcolm when they were kids. She turns to the very beginning of the book to show baby pictures, and with the first picture I see, I understand her point. Jaslene looks just like Jaylen and Malcolm both when they were babies. "Now, I didn't know if she was Jaylen's or Malcolm's, but as soon as you and Jaylen got in this house and sat on that couch so close, I knew it was Jaylen's."

"I don't understand what you mean," I say.

"Y'all kept looking in each other's eyes, smiling, sitting all close. A blind person could see y'all had sex before."

I don't know what to say. I want to break down and bawl my eyes out, but I've done it so many times already over this that I just let out a tired breath. "It's true. She's his, but I can't tell him. I mean, I know I should, but I can't make myself say the words. I know the second I tell him his whole life is going to go downhill—"

"Girl, hush. A baby is a blessing, and he has every right to be a part of Jaslene's life as a father. Don't have her growing up in here not knowing who her daddy is."

"I mean, I'm going to tell him. I'm just not ready yet."

"Do you want me to tell him for you? Because one way or the other he's got to know," Sheri says, looking around the living room. "Now, where I put my cell phone at? That darn thing so small I'm always losing it."

"No, don't call him. I'll tell him. I just . . . I don't know."

"Well, I think you better call him now and tell him to come back here before he gets on that freeway. He just left, so he couldn't have gotten that far."

"How about I tell him next weekend? That's when he's bringing Jaslene's crib," I say, trying to reason with her.

"No. Now, while you still have the motivation."

"I don't have motivation. I'm scared out of my mind."

"What you scared for? He obviously loves Jaslene already."

"Yeah, because she's mine. He loves her like an uncle or a godfather or something."

Sheri rolls her eyes. "Here it is," she says, picking up her phone from underneath a magazine on the coffee table. She holds it close to her face. "Now let me dial his number."

"Okay! No, don't. I mean, I'll do it," I say, pulling out my phone. I sigh. I'm not sure how I'm going to do this, but I know it will hurt Jaylen's feelings coming from his mom rather than from me. Besides, if I don't, Malcolm will tell him for sure if Jaylen goes back without knowing the truth. And I don't want to hurt him any more than I have to.

"Hello?" Jaylen says, picking up on the second ring.

"Hey, Jay. We need to talk seriously before you leave. Are you on the freeway yet? Can you turn back around? It's really, really important." Sheri nods her head after every word I say to encourage me to keep talking.

There's a pause, then a moment later he says, "Sure," and we hang up. For the next ten minutes I can't sit down. I keep playing the words over and over in my head, but I still can't figure out how to start off our talk. Will he scream? Will he even believe it's his?

The door opens, and my heart rate increases. Jaylen's standing at the door with a worried look on his face. "Nothing's wrong," I say. "Let's just talk."

He nods, coming closer to me. "You know I was just here a while ago, right?"

"Yeah, but, um ... well Sheri was here, and I didn't want to talk in front of her. Then I was really hungry, so we had to eat. Then right after we ate you left, and—"

"I know what happened, Jess. I was here," he says, sounding irritated, and I regret calling him back here. I can't talk to him if he's in a bad mood.

Just then Sheri pops her head in from around the hallway. "Jessica, why don't you take Jaslene to her new room and lay her on the bed since she doesn't have a crib yet. Just put a bunch of pillows around her so she don't fall off."

I nod. I know she wants Jaylen to follow me into the room so we can talk in private. I think Sheri wants to clean up in the kitchen. "Wanna help?" I ask Jaylen. He shrugs.

When we get into Jaslene's room, which is Malcolm's old room cleaned out, I place Jaslene on the bed. I start to pull off her clothes to change her into pajamas. I work slowly.

"Are we going to talk about the really important thing? Because Angela's nagging the shit out of me right now, and it's annoying the hell out of me."

I realize he's in a rush. It takes everything in me not to say we can talk next weekend, but I know that if I don't do it now, I may never come this close to telling him, and this is something he needs to hear from me. I take a deep breath and face him.

"What do you think about Jaslene?" I say, and it comes out stupid. It sounded like a much more appealing conversation starter in my head.

He frowns. "What? Jaslene? Oh my God, Jess. She's perfect. Now, what do you need to talk about? I told you Ang is chewing my ass out."

I keep my composure. I feel the sadness creeping up in my throat at the news I'm about to tell him. I just don't know how to say it. "Isn't she pretty? She's a very good baby too."

He rolls his eyes. He doesn't say anything for a moment, but then he takes a deep breath and comes closer to me. My heart rate does that marathon run again. "I know you're using Jaslene to avoid talking about what you really want to talk about."

I shake my head. He is actually wrong this time. "No, I'm not. She is the subject."

His eyebrows raise, then he frowns and stares down at her. "What's wrong? Is she all right? What—you got the news from the hospital?"

"Um . . . yeah. Sort of." I shrug, staring at Jaslene too.

Jaylen looks at me. "What do you mean by sort of?"

I turn to face him. "She's yours."

Jaylen's face goes from frowning to complete shock with his mouth hung open wide. I stare at his face wondering what he's thinking then I look into his eyes.

Part Two:

Jaylen

Chapter Twelve

My heart stops. I look down at Jaslene for half a second, then back at Jessica. What did she just say? "She's mine?"

Jessica closes her eyes and nods. I stand up and start pacing the room. "How do you know? I never took the test. Chris did."

She opens her eyes but stares at the floor instead of me. "The results came back negative. He's not her father."

I rub a hand down my face. This is unbelievable. Should I even believe it? "When did you find this out?

How come all of a sudden you know this stuff?" I ask. I step closer to her, but she still doesn't look up. Look me in the eye, I say in my head. If you're telling me the truth, look me in the eye.

"I found out last week. I mean, that's when I got the call. And then they sent something in the mail confirming what the person said over the phone."

"Last week? You found out it wasn't Chris's last week?" I'm pissed. I can't believe she's been lying to me this whole time. I stare over at Jaslene, who's spread out across the bed. She's so tiny. So vulnerable. And she's mine? How could . . . ? "Were you on birth control when we had sex, Jess?" I ask as softy as I can muster.

"No," she says after a few moments. "I stopped right after I broke up with Chris. So by the time you and I did it, I had been off for days."

I close my mouth tightly. She was off the pill, but she still let me go in raw? If I had known she was off the pill, I never would have . . . God, what the fuck is going on here?

I shake my head and start pacing again. Okay. Think, Jaylen, think. You have a daughter. A daughter? Oh my God. Mom's gonna kill me. Angela is going to bury me. God. Angela.

I stare at Jessica. I need her to face me. "Look at me, Jess. Come here." Jessica stands up and comes

199

within two feet of me still looking down like a kid who got caught stealing. "Look me in the eye and tell me she's mine."

Slowly she looks up at me. She goes from staring at my feet to my chest to my neck and eventually my eyes. She straightens her shoulders. "Jaslene Mae Smith is your daughter. She was conceived ten months ago, and although we thought she was early, she was actually on time, if we look at the day you and I had sex. She has a lot of your features including your ears, hairline, and chin. She's smart and beautiful, and she is your daughter.

"After we had unprotected sex, I went back to Chris. And we also had unprotected sex because he was trying to get me pregnant. I thought he succeeded, but in fact I had been pregnant the day I walked back into his house. There was no gap in between my sleeping with you and Chris for there to be another man involved. Chris took the test, and it came back that Jaslene isn't his, and that's why I know without a shadow of a doubt that she is your child."

I close my eyes to try to slow my heart beat. Father. Not uncle, not godfather but father. I think about Jessica and our friendship over the years and how much I care about her. I know she's telling the truth. She loved Chris and hated him just as bad. She wanted to have a family with him, and she told me how happy she was when they had gotten engaged. That was before he hit her for the second time. She thought she was carrying his baby, but I guess I beat him to the punch.

All this information is playing in circles over and over in my head, but I can't get a grip on this.

I never planned to be a father this early in my life, but it seems like I have no choice. Deep down I know I'd gladly be Jaslene's father in place of Chris. He doesn't need to have a reason to ever come near Jessica another day in his life. Not if I can help it.

"I'm so sorry, Jay," Jessica says. I open my eyes, and tears are running down her face. I wrap my arms around her and hug her tight. I trace my fingers through her hair to calm her down. We're parents now, and we should treat it like a blessing instead of a curse.

I never thought the two of us would be parents. Growing up together and playing in this very house as kids, I never saw it coming, but it's not that bad. I shake my head softly. Malcolm is never going to believe this one.

"There's nothing to be sorry for. I know you're scared, but this whole thing isn't your fault. Neither of us meant for this to happen."

"But Angela—"

I let out a breath I forgot I was holding. "Let's not talk about that right now. But, Jess, that's my problem. Don't worry yourself about it."

She pulls back from me and looks down at the floor again. I still have my hands on her arms. "We don't have to tell her if you don't want to. She doesn't have to know. I don't care if you don't tell her. With me living in Aurora and you guys up north, there would be no way she would find out."

I raise my eyebrow at her. "I'm not about to lie to my fiancée about this, Jess. It's too important, and it doesn't matter where you live, Jess. I still have to tell her the truth."

She still stays looking down, and I pull her into my arms again. "I'll handle it," I tell her again.

"Aren't you mad at me? Don't you hate me for ruining your life? Your engagement will end because of this," she says, like I'm not aware of the consequences of telling Angela. Jessica and I had sex when Angela and I were still together. When she finds out I'm Jaslene's father, all hell will break loose.

I think about my engagement to Angela and how hurt she'll feel, but I shake my head. "I know, Jess. Look at me. There is nothing you can do that would make me hate you. I just can't hate you, Jess. You're too . . ." What is the word to describe Jessica? Special? Sweet? "Important in my life."

She stares at me blankly for a few seconds, and I think that I might have said the wrong thing. She smiles sweetly like she doesn't believe me, then continues. "But you're going to tell her? Look, Jay. I know what it's like to be cheated on. It's not a good feeling, and I just feel like the biggest hypocrite in the universe. I would hate for you to break her heart over this."

"Jessica, we laid together and . . . you know that what's done in the dark comes to the light. I have to tell her, and I don't know if I'll be able to fix my relationship because of this, but I'm going to try."

Jessica opens her mouth to say something, but closes it. I take a deep breath. "I don't hate you, Jess. I could never hate you." I hug her tighter so she knows I mean it.

"So what should I do now? Nothing?" she asks after a while.

"Um . . . I'll be back next weekend to drop off her crib. Just relax and look for some college around the area that you can transfer to or something."

She pulls back and looks at me with a scrunched-up face. "There's too much going on to focus on school."

"Just stay in school, Jess. I know you want to do the photography thing, and I'm not letting Jaslene or anything slow you down."

"But—"

"Look, we'll get past this, but you have to stay focused. I know getting pregnant by me wasn't part of your plan, but we're going to have to work something out and make the best of it."

She comes into my arms again and squeezes my midsection hard. "I'm glad I wasn't pregnant by Chris. I'm sad that this had to interrupt your life so badly, but I promise that Jaslene will be the best daughter you've ever had."

I smile and look over at Jaslene again. I notice her eyes staring up at me, and I feel both excitement and nervousness for the future we'll have together. I feel like I haven't known her that long yet, but we have the rest of our lives to have that perfect father-daughter bond. My chest rises in pride. "She already is."

Jessica and I walk out of room five minutes later but leave the door cracked open to make sure we'll hear Jaslene if she starts crying. When we reach the kitchen, Mom is staring up at up from her chair like she's waiting for a verdict. I guess I'm going to have to tell her she has a granddaughter. I think about the time and realize I've stayed here an extra hour, and Angela is gonna kill me twice tonight for coming home late. I look outside the window, and sure enough it's dark outside.

"Well, how was the talk?" Mom asks, brining my attention back to her.

"Well, um, actually—" I start, but Jessica cuts me off.

"It's fine now. I told him," she says.

Mom nods her head. "Good. Now you have to tell Angela, Jaylen."

Hold the fuck up. Wait a minute.

"You knew? When?" I ask, looking back and forth between her and Jessica.

"The second I laid eyes on that baby I knew. She looks like you when you was a baby. Too much alike. Your father had some strong genes, and they be passing on too."

I think about how much Jaslene looks like me and nod. "You're right. I mean, this is all too big of a shock to me right now, and it's a lot to take in. I need to go home and digest this a bit."

Mom nods and wraps her arms around me in a reassuring hug. "Come back soon, Jaylen. Jaslene's your responsibility now too."

My heart beats faster. I'm responsible for another human being. "Yes ma'am."

Jessica walks me outside, and I give her a hug while we lean against my car. "Do you need anything?" I ask her. She shakes her head.

"We'll be fine."

I dig into my wallet anyway and pull out two hundred dollars. "Are you sure? I feel like I'm supposed to give you money."

Her eyebrows frown as she stares at the money. "We don't need anything. Your mom has plenty of food, and I'm all stacked on toys and diapers for now.'

I roll my eyes at her stubbornness and thrust my money in her hand and close it tight. "Take it just in case. I probably won't be back to till next weekend."

She swallows deeply and looks at me with soft eyes, like she doesn't want me to go. I feel my feet are too heavy to move too, but I know I need to get back to Chicago before I give Angela another reason to kill me.

I hug Jess one more time before getting in the car. She waves at me until I pull off and find myself glancing at her in my rearview mirror until I can't see her anymore.

When I reach the highway, traffic is backed up as usual, and so far that's the only excuse I've come up with to tell Angela why I'm late. Why is she blowing up my phone anyway? She knows I left Chicago for the day to help Jessica move.

I can't get my mind off the fact that Jaslene is my daughter. I'm a father? I'm only twenty-five. I lean all the way back in my seat and try to focus. How am I going to tell Angela this? I can't even believe it myself. I wish Jess had told me as soon as she found out instead of waiting until after she moved to another city. What was she afraid of all this time? Me telling Angela? She's gonna find out one way or the other.

When I pull up to my apartment building, I hesitate before going inside. She's going to be in a rotten mood, and I have too much on my mind to deal with it. I've decided not to tell Angela about Jaslene tonight. I need to clear my thoughts and get my head together first.

I open the door to my place, and she's standing there with her pink-and-white PJs on looking sexy without any makeup or bra. I smile. "Traffic kept me longer than I thought. What did you eat?" I stroll past her and into the kitchen. I'm not hungry, but I open the fridge and pull out a beer.

I sit down at the table, she joins me with her arms folded underneath her small chest. "Are you still mad or something?" I ask.

She shrugs. "Not really, I guess. I ate some chicken earlier."

"Aw, okay. What else you do today other than work?" I ask, sipping my beer.

Her face lights up. "I ran into an old girlfriend, and you'll never guess what she told me."

"What?"

"She told me that she ran into Chris. Chris! Jessica's Chris. She told me that Chris is going around town saying that Jess's baby ain't his, and he got the paternity test to prove it."

I don't say anything. I just keep still.

She continues. "So I'm thinking to myself—not to bash on your friend or anything. But she must not know who the baby daddy is because my friend said that Chris is saying that his homie had fucked her." She stops to laugh. "OMG! Oh, I'm sorry. I mean, I do kind of like Jess. She's nice, and that baby is gorgeous. I guess that's why she left—or one of the main reasons."

I set my beer down. "Rumors could just be rumors, Ang."

"Yeah, I know. But this is a lot more interesting. What she say when you was down there?" she asks.

"Who? Jessica? Nothing. Mom made dinner and talked our asses off. Me and Malcolm are going down there next weekend to set up her crib," I say, changing the subject. There is no way in hell I'm telling her the truth tonight.

"I think she lying about not getting the paternity test results back. 'Cause how come Chris has a copy but she don't and she the mother? I think she's lying."

I blow out a slow breath. "I can ask her about it, but I don't want it to seem weird if it's not Chris's baby. You know?" Damn, I shouldn't be lying to Angela like this. I know damn well Chris is not the father.

"Naw, just be casual with it. Do you want me to talk to her? I can go down there next weekend with y'all and have a one-on-one girl talk."

My eyes bulge out. "No . . . I mean y'all ain't that close, and the last thing she'll want to do is confess something like this to you," I say, trying to keep Angela as far away from Jessica as possible.

"I guess, but damn! Can you believe her not knowing who her child's father is? I mean, she always seemed like a goody-two-shoes to me, and . . . OMG! I know who it is!" She stands and claps her hands. "It's Malcolm's!"

I spit out a stream of beer and cough. "No."

She laughs. "No, for real—think about it. They've been living together this whole time. For like seven or eight months, and that's around the time she got pregnant. And you know how Malcolm is. There ain't no way he could hold himself from fucking her. At least one time. Yeah, y'all grew up together, but Malcolm a freak and apparently Jessica is too."

"They ain't never fuck, Ang," I say calmly, looking at the top of my beer can. I don't know why, but

209

thoughts of Malcolm and Jessica doing it are playing in my head, and it's making my stomach turn.

"How do you know? Were you over there with them every night? You know she was probably walking around in cute PJs and Malcolm walking around without a shirt on. I bet money they freaked around, and even if they didn't fuck, somebody gave somebody some head."

She laughs again, but I don't say anything. Now my head is really spinning. What the fuck? No, Malcolm would have told me if he hit it. Then again, I never told him.

"Malcolm would have told me," I say anyway just to shut her up, but of course it doesn't work.

"He ain't got to tell you everything," she says, sitting back down. "Besides, he probably thought you would beat his ass for it." She laughs. I stand up and throw my beer can away. I'm done with this talk.

"Where are you going?" she asks, standing up too.

"To bed."

"Wait, I'll come too. All this freaky talk is making me horny."

"I'm not in the mood," I say, walking straight toward my room.

I hear her small footsteps behind me. "And why the hell not?" she asks in her tight edgy voice she uses when she's annoyed.

"'Cause I'm tired as hell. Driving, talking, and I just ate a fat-ass meal. I'm taking my ass to sleep," I say, turning around to face her in the hallway.

She blows out a heavy breath and follows me into our bedroom. "Fine, but I'm pleasuring myself right next to you, and if you care to help me, be my guest."

I let out a small laugh at her comment despite myself. Of course Angela would say some weird shit like that. I cut off the light, take off my clothes, and slide into bed beside her. The sounds of the night are entertaining.

Chapter Thirteen

I knock on Malcolm's door the next day wanting to get to the bottom of a couple things that had me up half the night. I want to ask him, did he or did he not ever in his life fuck Jessica or anything freaky. I know how he is sometimes, and I know how things can get carried away. I don't know what I'll do exactly if he tells me he has done things with her, but I just know I'm not okay with it. I stayed up the other half of the night figuring why I wasn't okay with him having something going on with Jessica.

He comes to the door a few seconds later all dressed, and I remember he's about to leave to open Miller House downtown. I haven't found a permanent manager yet, so me and Malcolm take turns opening and closing between that bar and my other bar Miller as well. Both of them bringing me in plenty of money.

"What's up?"

"Oh, you about to leave?" I ask, staring at him.

He nods. "Yeah, ain't you got to work today too?"

"I got someone else to open Miller for me. I wanted to talk to you."

"Oh, I know what it's about. Okay. Just come with me to Miller House and we'll talk there before everybody else comes in." I nod, but I can't get my mind off of him and Jessica. I never want to lay hands on my brother, but if he ever had sex with her, I know I won't be able to control my temper. If he never did, then I'll be more confident that Jaslene is mine. I also need to tell him about Jaslene being my daughter.

Twenty minutes later we pull up to my bar and go inside. All the chairs are still above the tables, so we start taking them down one by one. "So," he says. "What's up?"

"Did you and Jessica ever fuck?" I blurt out without any beating around the bush.

He gives me a shocked look. Then he frowns. "You seriously asking me that, bro?"

I put down a chair. "Just answer the question." The words come out stronger than I intended.

I see him tense in response. "No."

We stare each other down, forgetting about the chairs. I step closer and so does he. "How do I know that you haven't had sex with her?" I ask.

"You don't," he says plainly. What the fuck he mean, I don't? What the fuck he trying to say? We stare at each other for a while. My fists are balled, and his jaw is clenched as we stare eye to eye. "Are you really trying to deny that Jaslene is your baby?"

I back up when he says this. "You know?"

"Who the fuck you thought told Jess to tell you?"

I let out a breath. I start getting pissed off. "Everybody knew this fucking shit but me. What the fuck!"

"I was the first person she told, bro. I didn't want to tell you 'cause I knew it'd be better coming from her."

"Mom knows."

Malcolm doesn't say anything for a while. "I didn't tell Mom. How she know?"

"She said she took one look at Jaslene and knew. I don't know how though. I looked at Jaslene plenty of times and didn't see any resemblance."

"Then again, you wasn't looking for any resemblance either."

"True."

We don't say anything for a while. Then I speak up. "Do you think she's mine?"

He gives me a half smile. "Well, it ain't Chris's, and it sure as hell ain't mine, so I guess that leaves you."

"Y'all ain't never fuck?" I ask again with a calmer tone.

He rolls his eyes. "Nigga, if I fucked Jessica, I would have been telling everybody. But, naw, I don't see her like that. She was kinda always more interested in you for some reason. Which reminds me. Why the hell you ain't never told me y'all fucked!"

We laugh. "Man, I guess I don't know. That was always me and Jess's business and—"

"Wait up! What you mean by always? How long y'all been fucking?" he asks.

"We only fucked once . . . well, twice. But the first one don't count," I say.

"The first time? When was this?" he asks.

"What? You thought Chris took her virginity? Hell, naw."

His mouth drops, but I don't laugh. If I laughed he'd think I was lying, but I wasn't. "You lying, bro. You? Y'all? When? How long ago was this, and where was I?"

"Where were you? Nigga, what you was gon' do? Watch?" I say, putting down some more chairs.

"You know what I mean. So why didn't that time count? You didn't know what you was doing?"

"No, I did. It's not rocket science. We just got interrupted. It was just something we did. It had no sentimental meaning behind it."

"Oh, okay. So I guess when y'all made this baby, y'all was just finishing up where y'all left off, huh?"

I don't say anything. I don't think it will matter.

"What I'm gon' do about this baby, bro? You know I ain't ready. I mean, I'm ready financially, but damn. I'm not even with her. She don't even live here anymore, and what the hell am I gonna do about Angela?"

"Calm down, bro. We'll figure something out. Were you gon' tell Angela?"

I shrug. "I got to. She gon' find out even if I don't."

"How?"

I frown. "Oh, I don't know. Maybe when she sees a seven-year-old girl version of me walking beside me? I can't not tell her. I just don't know when or how."

He's quiet for a while. "Do you have any doubt that Jaslene is yours?"

"Why you say that?" I look at him again. I swear if he's about to confess that they fucked, I'm going to lose it.

"I'm just saying that you don't want to tell Angela that Jaslene is your baby if you're not 110 percent

216

sure." He's quiet for a while. "I mean—don't get me wrong, Jaylen. You know I love Jessica like a sister, and I believe her, but ... I mean, she was wrong before, and ... I don't know—I just think you should be 100 percent sure first. So—"

"So you think I should take the test?" I ask softly.

He nods.

By the time I leave the bar a half hour later, my head is spinning. On the one hand I know Jessica isn't lying to me that I'm the father, but on the other it doesn't hurt just to be sure. If that's the case, then I'm pretty much saying that I doubt Jaslene. I slide my hand down my face. I'm still sitting in my car outside the bar trying to get my thoughts together. One more test. The most important one. What will I do when I get the results? Should I tell Angela after I'm sure? That seems better, but I feel I already know what the results are going to be, and not telling her soon would mean I'm putting it off for later.

I lean back and close my eyes. Right away I see Jaslene's tiny fingers reaching out to me, and I sit up. I try to get myself together, but it's hard to concentrate. Jaslene. Angela. Another paternity test. What the hell am I going to do?

I think about Angela and how happy she was when I proposed to her. Her face had lit up. I swear I've never seen her smile that much. I take a deep breath. I hate to think about it in this way, but I know the main reason I proposed was because she kept nagging me about it. She wouldn't say propose exactly, but she did keep bringing up life after we're married and how she couldn't wait to walk down the aisle in a white cotton dress. I got the hint. There was no way I couldn't. So I just proposed. It wasn't like I planned to get married the next day, but now I feel like our commitment to each other is so deep that even a hint of this news will not only break her heart but her spirit too. Jessica's right about this. Telling Angela will be the hardest thing I ever do.

I put the car in gear and head to Miller. I still have some paperwork to do, and I'm not looking forward to it. I keep telling myself that everything is going to be all right, but I don't see how. Everything that I planned in my mind is going backward. Chris was supposed to be Jaslene's father. We were going to make sure he paid child support. Jessica would be fine and financially stable, and I would be planning to marry Angela guilt-free. For the most part anyway. I never told her that me and Jessica had sex. It was one time that I let things get out of hand. Jessica was just supposed to be staying over with me until Malcolm got back from Vegas. She had just broken up with Chris and needed a place to stay. I shouldn't have let it go as far as it went, but I can't take back what happened now. I just have to keep pushing myself forward, but if I had one minute to talk to myself in the past, I would tell myself to wear a condom.

I walk into the bar and see Tony, the opening employee, getting things set up for this afternoon. We open at twelve, so he only has an hour left. "What up, man?" I say without breaking my stride toward the back.

"Just good, boss," he says quickly to get his words out before I close my office door and shut out the world.

My office is longer than it is wide and holds just a desk, laptop, and a miniature filing cabinet. I sit down in the brown leather seat and lean back. I open the filing cabinet to get started on some paperwork, but after ten minutes of staring at one page I know I'm not going to get any work done today. I can't stop thinking about Jaslene. Is she really mine? Am I really her father? Shouldn't I be doing something for her right now?

I lean forward and put my head in my hands. This is not how I pictured being a father at all. I am supposed to at least be married to the woman. And I didn't think the mother of my child would be Jessica.

Not a knock against her, but in my mind this isn't how I pictured this happening. I take a deep breath and start fidgeting. Angela pops into my mind, and everything she said last night about Jessica not knowing who Jaslene's father is plays over in my head. How can I tell her I'm the daddy? She'll never ever let me live this one down.

Will we even still be together? I don't know why I'm thinking there's even a chance she'll stay with me. I wouldn't stay with me if I was her. I mean, it's one thing telling her I cheated on her, but ten times worse saying that I fathered someone else's child. That's just fucking dirty.

At twelve o'clock I get up and help Tony with a few last things. I didn't want to be alone anymore, and even though I don't tell Tony about everything going on with me, right now just talking to someone makes me feel better.

As soon as I get off work, I pick up Angela from her job. She's waiting for me in the parking lot with a huge smile on her face. "Let's go out to eat, baby. I'm starving," she says after giving me a kiss.

I shrug and pull out. "Where you want to go?"

"Someplace fancy."

We drive around for a while until I park outside Gardinno's, a little Italian restaurant we visited every so often. It takes us a while to get our seat, but eventually a table is cleared for us and we take our seats next to a window overlooking Lake Michigan. The menu is simple, classy, with no pictures, and we take our time looking over it. "Thanks for taking me here. We haven't done something like this in a while."

"I took you out when I proposed," I say. "That was only what? Last week?"

She looks down lovingly at her ring. "Yes, you're right, baby."

I don't know what she means by that, but I feel like she's buttering me up. She mostly doesn't easily agree with me.

After our waitress comes and goes, Angela and I stare lovingly at each other. "How was your day, baby?" she asks with her hands laced beneath her chin.

"Good."

"Oh, well that's boring. Ask me what happened to me today," she says, placing both hands flat on the table.

Okay, I'll buy it. "What?"

"I think I may be getting a promotion," she says. Her grin reaches her ears, and her smile is so bright I can't help but smile too.

"Congratulations, baby. I'm happy for you. So what happened today to make you think that?"

"Well, today I was just doing my work as usual, when all of a sudden the vice president of the company walks in and sees me going above and beyond my call of duty and tells my boss." She claps her hands together. "Can you believe it?"

I tilt my head to the side and go over in my head again what she just told me. It doesn't make sense. "I thought you was just doing your usual work. How could he have seen you going above and beyond? And how is him telling your boss you're doing a good job going to guarantee a promotion?" As soon as the words leave my mouth, I can tell they hurt her feelings. She really had her heart set on getting a promotion.

Her frown wavers. "I don't know. I'm just saying it might happen, you know. Everything else is going so good for me, I figured why not one more good thing? Look, I just want to keep an open mind, okay? I know at work we have a spot available, and I figure since the vice president said something good about me, then maybe I'll be a lot more noticeable to my boss. Is that dream so crazy?"

"No, baby. It's not. Dream on. I mean, you're going to get it. I know you are," I say, raising my glass at her in salute.

The food comes, and I dive into my steak. It doesn't taste like my mom's, but it's still pretty good. We eat in silence, but halfway through dinner my phone rings. I take it out of my pocket and check the caller ID. Jessica.

I hit Silence and continue eating, but I can feel Angela staring at me as if she's waiting for an update. "Why you didn't answer? Who was that?"

I put my fork down and try to think fast. "Baby, I'm having dinner with you. It doesn't matter who it was because the call would interrupt our time together. Let's just enjoy our meal. I can always call back."

She opens her mouth and then closes it. She can't debate the fact that I put our relationship above a call because she loves that special treatment. I, on the other hand, start to fidget beneath the table and wonder what Jessica wanted. What if something's wrong with Jaslene? What if she had to be rushed to the hospital?

When the check comes, I pay the woman before she has a chance to leave the table. "Are you okay, Jay?" Angela asks, getting her purse together.

"Yeah, I'm just ready to go home," I say with a shrug.

She smiles and leans over the table. "I can't wait to get home too," she says with a wink.

My eyebrows shoot up, and I know she's talking about sex. I can't get my mind off Jaslene and Jessica long enough to get an erection. I smile though, and just as my card comes back, I thank the waitress, give her ten bucks, and escort my fiancée out of the building.

As soon as I get home, I go to the bathroom. I pull out my phone and text Jessica asking what's up. It takes her two long minutes to reply, and I realize how desperate I am to know that both of them are safe. They better be safe.

She texts back that she just wanted to know what I was up to, and I let out a breath. Good. I tell her I've just gotten back from dinner with Angela, but it takes her a longer time to reply back. I ask her how's Jaslene, and she replies that she's fine.

There's a knock on the bathroom door, and I realize I've been in the bathroom a long time. I didn't use the toilet, but I flush it anyway to give my time in here some credibility. When I come out, she smiles. "Do you want me to shower first? I can," she says, trying to slide pass me and into the bathroom.

I forgot that she wanted sex tonight, but I think about her being in the shower long enough for me to finish texting Jessica, and I agree. I go into the bedroom and lie down on the bed. I feel like a no-good man cheating still, but deep down I know I just wanted to make sure Jessica didn't need anything. I feel like I'm responsible for her now for some reason. Like she's my wife or something when she's not.

Jessica texts me back saying that she's sorry for calling and interrupting our dinner. I text her that it's okay, but she doesn't text back. I was going to ask how my mom was doing, but I hear the shower go off in the bathroom. I put my phone to the side and take my clothes off.

Chapter Fourteen

I wake up at seven a.m. with a headache and roll over to find Angela spread out across the entire bed— one leg on me and one arm across my chest. I take a deep breath before sitting up and looking at the clock. It's my day off, but I still have to take Angela to work. I stroke her arm until her head shifts in my direction.

"What?" she groans, not opening her eyes.

"Time."

She groans again, turning her head the other way, back toward the sunlight coming through the blinds. I notice her eyes shut tighter, but she doesn't move, so I stand up and get out of bed, stripping the little bit of sheet left covering the lower half of her body.

"Jaylen."

"What?"

"Five more minutes, bae. I promise," she says, shoving her head under the closest pillow.

"It's your job, Ang. I'm just trying to—"

"It's five minutes. God. Go get dressed. I'll be up," she says under the pillow.

I roll my eyes and get dressed, tossing on a pair of jeans and a dark hoodie. I stand up and look outside at the falling snow. Angela is going to hate going outside in this weather 'cause she's never liked the snow. I can understand her distaste for winter since she complains about being limited to the clothes she wears, but I never minded the snow. My mom and Malcolm don't like the snow either, but for me and Jessica it's our favorite season.

Just as my mind shifts to Jessica, the dream I had last night comes to mind, but I push it back. It makes my headache worse, and I just need to get Angela to work so I can come back home and chill. I pick up my phone and dial Malcolm to ask him to come over. I need to talk to my brother right now.

About an hour and a half later I'm sitting on my couch, when Malcolm opens my door with his spare key. "What's good, bro?" he asks, coming in my living

227

room. He sits down next to me on the couch and we bump hands.

"I need to talk about Jessica." I say. "I feel like I'm pulling myself too thin. Like I have to take care of Jessica, Jaslene, and Angela."

"Why you feel like that, bro?" Malcolm says, going to the kitchen.

"I had this crazy-ass dream last night that Jessica and Angela were my two wives. Like some Africa-tribe-type shit. And we all was living here, but they were sleeping in two separate rooms. Jessica and Jaslene in one and Angela in the other, and every night they would fight about who's room I was going to sleep in."

"Sounds like heaven," Malcolm says, bringing over two beers from the fridge. He hands me one.

"Naw, it was kinda sad actually. I don't know why, but it felt like Jessica was not getting treated as fairly as Angela was. Like I'd come home and they both come to greet me, but Angela always managed to get the hugs and kisses while Jessica just stood in the background smiling at me. And whenever I tried to show Jessica some love, Angela would jump in the way and bring the attention back to her. It was so annoying."

"Oh."

"That ain't the worst part. Jessica did all the housework and all the cleaning and taking care of Jaslene, while Angela just laid around the house."

Malcolm stares at me for a while. "How long was this dream?"

"It felt like a couple of seconds, but I slept all night. I was glad when I woke up. It felt like Jessica was living in hell and she didn't even realize it."

He continues to stare at me, and he stares for so long that I get uncomfortable. "What?" I ask.

"Are you in love with Jessica?" he asks, softly examining my face.

I shake my head. "No, bro. Not like that. We just fucked one time. We're just friends. I mean, we're just friends now, like co-parents or something, but we don't feel that way for each other. It was just a dream. Just a stupid dream."

I close the back door and climb into the driver's side with Malcolm sitting beside me bobbing his head to the Tupac music I have blasting through the speakers. It's the weekend, and we're heading to Aurora to set up this crib for Jaslene. I haven't seen them in a week, and I find myself constantly worried about them. It's like that dream I told Malcolm about with Jessica being treated unfairly. I want to make sure she's okay. I haven't told Angela the truth yet, and I think I understand a little bit of why Jessica was hesitant to tell me. It's nerve-wracking.

After we get on the freeway, I turn the music down. Malcolm turns his head to me with expectancy in his eyes. "So you think I should ask for a paternity test?" I ask.

He rolls his eyes. "For the fifth time, nigga, yeah!" He laughs. "Why you keep asking me, bro? Look— you know she's yours. We'd just be doing it for technicality. To make it official. She ain't gonna have a problem with it because she knows Jaslene is yours too. So you good, bro."

I nod my head. "I just wanted to be sure. I just don't want to hurt her feelings or anything. She's been hurt so much, and some of it was my fault."

"What fault was that? Oh, you talking about that big fight y'all had? Man, that was so long ago. Like last year sometime."

"She was still hurt though, bro," I say with a shrug. "There's no going around it."

He nods and I focus on the road. We drive for almost two hours until we finally make it to our mom's house. I park the car and get out. I was half-expecting them to be standing by the door, because they know we're coming.

Malcolm grabs the crib that we had deconstructed and put back in the box, and hauls it up the walkway. I am about to knock, when the door swings open and Jessica stares at me like she hasn't seen me in years. "Hi, how are you?" she asks, stepping out of the way so we can come in.

"We're good," I say. I look around the room and notice how much things have changed. Not in a bad way but in a more "there's a baby here" way. There're toys lying on the couch and a few on the floor. Jaslene's high chair is standing tall and sturdy in the kitchen. The swing set I bought them is in the living room too, next to the couch. The house looks more lived in than before with a little mess. Like home.

"Hey, Jess," Malcolm says, giving her a hug.

"Hey, Malcolm! I missed you. How you been doing? You're not being bad, are you?" she says, smiling from ear to ear.

Malcolm shrugs and plops down on the couch. "Yeah, girl. You know I'm always good."

"Are you sure? Because I saw your status on Facebook, and it sounded like you're really enjoying having your own place back."

Malcolm shrugs, and the two of them keep going back and forth, but I take the crib and slide it back to Jessica's room. I wonder if she wants the crib in here or if she wants it in the other room. I'm standing in the hallway trying to figure it out, when Mom comes out of her room carrying Jaslene on her hip. "Oh, there you are," Mom says. She uses her free arm to give me a hug. I wrap my arm around them both.

"Yeah, I'm here. Malcolm's in the living room too. He's going to help me set up the crib so it'll go faster."

She nods. "Good. I haven't seen him in a long time. Here, take your daughter," she says, placing Jaslene into my arms.

I smile down at Jaslene and smell her hair. She smells so fresh, and she looks so happy that my heart swells for this little girl. My angel.

I keep holding and playing with Jaslene until Malcolm comes into the hallway. "We setting this sucker up or what?"

I nod. Then I remember something and shake my head. "Let me talk to Jessica about . . ." I nod down at Jaslene.

Malcolm shrugs. "I'll just get started. What room we putting it in?"

I shrug. "Maybe your old room. I don't know—ask Mom, and tell Jess to meet me in my room. I mean her room."

I go into her room and sit down on the bed with Jaslene in my lap. It doesn't take too long for Jessica to show up, but as soon as she closes the door and sits beside me, I freeze up about what I wanted to say. About what I wanted to ask for anyway.

"I missed you," she says softly, staring at Jaslene, but I know she's talking to me. I don't know why she won't look at me.

"Missed you too."

We stay silent for a while and listen to Jaslene babble. I like the noise and feel like I'm missing a lot of her growing up since she's down here and I'm in Chicago. "What did Angela say when you told her?" Jessica asks, still staring down at Jaslene.

I rearrange Jaslene in my arms so she's facing her mother better. "I haven't told her yet."

Jessica looks up at me now with a weird look on her face. "Oh, I thought you were going to. Not that I blame you. I know how hard it must be."

I nod. "I just want to be sure of a couple things first before I say anything."

"Like what?" she asks.

I realize I shouldn't have said that, but now I have no choice but to bring up the paternity test. "I wanted to . . . um . . . make sure she's mine before I tell Angela."

Jessica still looks confused. She looks down at Jaslene again and shakes her head. "But she is yours." She looks up at me with a stern face. "I'm not lying."

"I know."

"So why do you need to—"

"I just want to be sure. Without a doubt," I say with a shrug, hoping she'll realize how not a big deal this is. "If I know for sure, then telling Angela will be easier if I have concrete evidence."

Instead she looks hurt. Really hurt. She stands and moves to the other side of the room. I stand too. "Why do you need all this proof? How can you deny her? I thought you loved her." Her eyes are sparkling, and before I have time to respond, the tears start coming down.

That stabs my heart. Does she really think that? "Of course I love Jaslene. I loved her before I found out she was mine, and I'm not denying her. I just want to have no doubts. I mean, I just want it in writing that . . . look, I just have to do this."

She turns and faces the wall, and I roll my eyes. Damn, why is she acting this way? I lay Jaslene on the bed and walk over to Jessica. She pushes me away, but I come right back to her. "I'm not denying her."

"Yes, you are! First Chris. Now you! I just can't take it anymore. Why doesn't anyone want my daughter?" Her cries are coming out loud now, and I take her face in my hands and shove it in my face so she has no choice but to look me straight in the eyes.

"I love Jaslene. I want Jaslene. I believe the test will come back positive, and I don't know what you're thinking, but I do want it to come back that she's mine because I do love her, and I want to be her father."

She moves her head slightly in my hands. "No you don't. It'll mess up everything for you. Your engagement, your relationship. Your whole life will change. I don't want you to hope that she's not yours because I don't want you to be disappointed."

"I promise." I give her a soft kiss on the forehead. "I won't be."

She stares at me again, and her tears stop flowing. "Why? Why do you want her to be yours if you know that Angela is going to kill you?"

I sigh and let go of her face. I walk back to the bed and sit down. I watch Jaslene suck on her pacifier and kick her legs. "I don't know. It's like being told you're in charge of a difficult job, and even though you think you can't handle it, you find that you don't want to turn the job down, because of the benefits. If that makes sense."

"Not really," she says, coming to sit beside me again.

"I mean that I don't want to not be Jaslene's father because I can't picture myself not being her father anymore. It's like, if I'm not, who is? And it's like I want to be her father. I want to have this connection with you." The last sentence is a whisper.

Jessica smiles and gives me a hug. "I promise she'll be the best daughter you can ever imagine."

"How many times I got to tell you? You don't have to sell her to me. I'm already in love."

Jessica laughs. Then she gets serious. "So you still want the test?" I nod and she sighs deeply. "Okay. Whenever you want to do it, just let me know."

I go into Malcolm's old bedroom when I'm finished talking to Jess to check on his progress with the crib. Mom's in here too, and parts of the crib are laid out on the floor. "All right, I'm here, bro."

"All right, hand me that piece by your foot," Malcolm says without looking back. He has his hand stretched out, but before I can give it to him, Mom reaches down herself and hands it to him.

"Malcolm has this under control," Mom says, patting my back. "I want to talk to you and Jessica now."

Malcolm looks back at us, and I shrug as Mom and I exit the room. Man, I can tell it's gonna be a long night.

We walk back into Jessica's room, where she's changing Jaslene. She smiles when she looks up, but frowns when she notices the stern look on my mom's

236

face. "What's wrong?" Jessica asks, wrapping up Jaslene and pulling her back into her arms.

"We need to talk about you two sleeping together." Oh, God. I can tell by Jessica's face she feels the same way I do. How the hell do we get out of this one? "Let's go into the living room."

Jessica and I follow my mom into the living room, and she nods her head toward the couch. After Jessica and I sit down, Mom stares at us with narrowed eyes at me. "Do you guys have any idea how wrong . . . ? No, wait, how sinful it was for you guys to have sex?" She slides a hand down her face, shaking her head. "I don't even know where to begin."

Jessica remains silent, staring down at the floor, and I feel like I should come up with some defense on our behalf, but I come up with nothing.

"Jaylen," she says, and I turn back to face her. "You have a girlfriend. A lovely girlfriend that never deserved to be treated the way you treated her. How can you call yourself a man when you really ain't no better than all the other dogs on the street?"

She turns to Jessica. "Jessica. Now, not too long ago you were that girlfriend. You were the victim of a cheating boyfriend, and you should know what it feels like to have someone you love betray your trust, but here you are doing the same thing. Now tell me, how does that make sense?"

"It was a mistake," Jessica says, still staring down at the carpet. "I never planned—"

"Oh, I know you didn't plan it because if you did, you wouldn't be staying in my house."

"Mom."

Mom turns back to me. "Yeah, let me get back to you. Jessica was single at the time, but you had every reason to say no to the sex. Now, I'm not sure who came on to who, but I know, Jaylen—you should have never let it go as far as it went. Didn't you think about Angela? Don't you love her? How could you be helping out Jessica's relationship problems telling her how bad of a man Chris is when you go and do the same type of shit?"

I stand up and walk out the door. Mom took it too far when she said I was just like that man. I hate that piece of shit, and she wants to refer to me being like him. Hell naw.

As soon as the fresh air touches my face I feel better, but I don't stop walking. I walk past my car and continue down the street at a slower pace but still ignoring the screams from Mom as she continues to call my name.

I needed the fresh air, but I know the real reason I wanted to leave was because I couldn't stand how right my mom was. How could I do what I did to Angela?

How could I have hurt her in the same way that Chris hurt Jessica minus the beatings? I don't deserve her.

I cross the intersection and come across the small park I played in when I was a kid. I take a seat on one of the benches and stare into a pool of water made by the rain. I take a deep breath and lean my head back. How the hell can my life be in such shambles after having it be so good? And it's all my fault.

Yeah, Jessica came on to me, but I didn't have to accept. I should have told her no, but I couldn't. It felt like I had to make love to her. Like, if I didn't make love to her, she would never know how it felt to really be made love to. Not fuck but to make love. But that clearly wasn't my job.

I look around the small park past the two slides and swing sets and notice Malcolm coming toward me. I know he was told by Mom to find me. He has a great memory, knowing that this was my favorite hiding spot.

"Hey," Malcolm says, taking a seat next to me on the bench. I shrug. "I heard the argument or the yelling that was going on. You know how Mom is sometimes. She be saying some off-the-wall-type shit just to make someone else feel bad."

He pauses, waiting for me to respond. When I don't, he continues. "You remember that time when I got caught drinking alcohol? She called me a raging alcoholic that would amount to nothing but a bum. Need I remind you that I only had a can a beer?" He laughs. "I think Mom's extreme worries override her rational thinking. I know she didn't mean what she said."

I shake my head. "What she said about me, what she said about Jessica—it's true."

"Naw, bro. It's not. You're not like Chris."

I clench my fists. "I don't have to physically hurt women to be like Chris. That man's a piece of shit."

"I know."

"The same way he hurt Jessica is the same thing I did to Angela. I cheated on her."

Malcolm leans forward. "Okay, but there's a difference though. Chris doesn't have a heart or a conscience. He didn't care that he hurt Jessica, and he did it multiple times too, but he didn't care. You care, bro. You made a mistake, but at least you realize it's a mistake and don't think of it as something guys just do or whatever the hell Chris's mind-set was."

Malcolm continues when I don't respond. "If there ever come a time when you start cheating and you don't give a fuck and think you'll never get caught, then I'll call you Chris myself."

He pats my back and stands. He stretches a hand for me to grab. "Come on, bro. I know this one's gonna be a tough one, but I got your back. You know you need to tell Angela, so the sooner we fix this crib and get away from Mom, the sooner you can get that part over with."

I grab his hand, and he propels me to my feet.

As we walk back to the house I look over to Malcolm, who raises an eyebrow in question. "Can you go inside the house and tell Jessica to come with Jaslene? I want to talk to her in private." He nods.

When we get to the house I sit inside my car and wait. I want to have a talk with Jessica more about the sex we had last summer.

A few minutes later Jessica comes out with Jaslene bundled up in her arms. I watch her face and notice how sad and unsure she looks, and I can tell my mom's words got to her. Just like they got to me.

When she opens the door and sits down, I pat her knee. "Don't worry about my mom. I forgot how vocal she can be sometimes."

She smiles gently as she stares at my hand on her knee. I pull my hand away and focus my attention on Jaslene. "Can I hold her?"

Jessica's face lights up and she nods, holding her arms out so I can pick up our daughter.

I smile at Jaslene in my arms as I watch her drift off to sleep.

"You're a great dad," Jessica says, turning sideways in her seat facing me.

"Thanks," I say. "I wanted to talk to you."

"Is it about the paternity test?" she asks, watching my eyes.

"No, it's about the sex. Our sex. I want to talk about it again."

She looks down, probably remembering the night we went against our consciences and good sense and made love. "We don't have to talk about it."

"I want to."

We sit in silence for a while just listening to Jaslene's breathing. "I guess when it comes to the sex we had, the main question I have is, why?"

"Why what?" she asks, staring at me for half a second, then focusing her eyes on Jaslene.

"Why did you come in my room? I told you I wasn't going to go after Chris."

She doesn't say anything for a long time but continues to stare at Jaslene wrapped in my arms like she wants to snatch her up and run inside the house.

"It was a mistake," she says finally.

"That's not what I asked," I say softly.

"I wanted it. I don't know. I was horny. I just wanted it," she blurts out. She starts breathing hard, and I know she might burst into tears any second. "It was a mistake, and I hate thinking about it, let alone talking about it. I definitely don't want to talk about it with you. I thought we were going to pretend it never happened."

I nod toward Jaslene. "We can't pretend nothing now."

Jessica leans back into her seat and covers her eyes with her hand. I shake my head and use one arm to reach over to her. She flinches, but I take my hand and play with her hair to calm her down. "Don't cry, Jess. We'll figure this out. I mean, we're working this out. It'll be okay. Jaslene will be okay. Everything will be okay."

She takes her hand away and stares straight into my eyes. "Angela won't be okay."

As she says those words, it feels like she stabbed me with a knife.

I know she's right. I just don't want to admit it.

Chapter Fifteen

I walk through my door three hours later to find Angela waiting up for me. I smile, but she's so engulfed in the TV that she only mutters a soft "about time" and slides over on the couch so I can sit down. I sit down quietly and stare at the reality show unfolding in front of our eyes. I listen to their drama for a while and realize the real-life drama I'm going to have to face tonight. I decided tonight was going to be the night when I would tell Angela the truth. I was going to wait for a better night, but no night is better for telling bad news. I take a deep breath and cut off the TV with the remote.

"What the fuck you do that for?" she asks with her face scrunched up.

"We need to talk about something important, and I need all your attention," I say, turning my whole body around on the couch to face her. I think she notices how serious I am by my expression because she relaxes her face and turns her attention to me fully.

"You know how all this drama is going on with Jessica moving to Aurora and the whole Chris paternity thing?" I figure if I ramble for a while, the hard part will slide out of my mouth easier.

"Yeah," she says, leaning forward slightly. "Did you find some information out when you went down there?" Her voice sounds excited, and despite the bad news I'm about to tell her, I feel annoyed that she gets so much pleasure out of Jessica's pain.

"No." I look down for a few seconds before looking up and meeting her eye again. "It's not good news, Ang."

"Oh my God. Did something happen? Is everyone all right?" Now her face is full of concern.

"Yeah," I say, then I stand up. I stare down at Angela on the couch as she looks up at me with a confused face. "I found out a while ago who Jaslene's father is."

Her face immediately brightens. "Oh! Tell me— you got to tell me! I been telling everyone it's the guy from the supermarket that I saw her talking to one time! Is it him? How did you find this out? Why didn't you tell me sooner?" She was off the couch now and practically bouncing around with anticipation. "So who is it?"

"I'm Jaslene's father." That smacks the smile off her face.

Angela's mouth falls to the ground. Then she swallows hard. "What do you mean you're the father?" She stretches each word out.

I don't know what else to say so I just stand there looking at her with a sad face. When she doesn't respond, I nod my head.

"You . . . you sick son of a bitch!" Angela screams, kicking over the coffee table. She's staring at me like she wants to kill me or hunt me down like a sick hunter and then skin me alive. "I knew you was fucking her! I knew it!"

"No, Ang. I'm not fucking her. We had sex one time, and she just got pregnant." I shout loudly but I know she's not trying to hear me.

"You no-good bastard," she screams, continuing to destroy my furniture, but I'm not caring about that right now. All I'm caring about is her.

"Angela, will you just talk with me? I feel like shit for what I did."

"You damn right!"

"But I don't want to lose you."

"You have a month-old daughter with your so-called best friend. Fuck you."

I take a deep breath and step closer to her, but she steps back with her arms folded across her chest. "I hate you," she says, staring me right in the eyes, and it burns my heart.

"Angela—"

"No." She shakes her head, looking down at the floor, and I know she's about to cry. "I fucking hate you. I wish you would die."

"Don't say that."

She pulls my ring off her finger and throws it at my chest. Her tears all rain down her face, and I have the urge to wipe them away. "It's over, Jaylen," she says. She walks quickly back to our bedroom.

I follow her. I don't know what to say, and I know she'll never get back with me, but I have to try. I love Angela. I fell in love with her the first day I saw her, and I'd hate to see her walk out of my life forever especially over something that only happened one time.

"Please, Ang. Just listen to me."

"Why should I listen to you? You're nothing but a liar!" Angela opens drawers and tosses all her clothes on the bed. I stand in the doorway watching her.

"It only happened one time, Ang. It was a mistake, and I shouldn't have let it go as far as it went, but I'm not in love with her. It was just sex. I'm in love with you. You're the girl with the ring on your finger," I say, even though it hurt like hell when she threw it at me.

Angela wipes a few tears away, but they keep coming down. She keeps gathering her clothes, not even looking at me.

"Don't go, Ang. I can't picture my life without you."

"Too bad you don't love me enough not to cheat on me," she says, going to our closet. She pulls out a suitcase and hauls it onto the bed. I walk fully into the room and place a hand over the suitcase.

"Don't go," I say as firmly as I can.

"Who's gonna stop me?" she says, brushing past me to grab more clothes from the closet.

"You don't have anywhere to go. You also don't have a car to leave in."

"Have you forgotten that my sister just moved to Chicago? I'll go stay with her. She'll come pick me up," she says so quickly, it's like she's always had this Plan B.

"Your sister? The one with five kids and two baby daddies? You're going to go stay with her in that crowded three-bedroom apartment? You'd rather do that than stay here and freakin' talk to me?"

"What the hell do you got to say!" she shouts, throwing her cashmere sweater on the floor. "You've already said the main thing of the night. Now I know what type of man you really is, how much of a fool I've been, and how I can never trust your ass again. There you go. I said it for you. Mission accomplished. Talk over."

"Angela—"

"No, fuck you, Jay. For real." She shakes her head, and her voice cracks. "I mean, I thought you really loved me—"

"I do love you—"

"Cut the crap, Jay. I thought we were meant for each other. I thought you wanted me to be your wife for real, but now all of a sudden you telling me you had a baby on me. How the fuck am I suppose to feel?"

"I never said—"

"What? Do you want me to forgive you? Do you want me to say, hey okay, no big deal, we'll get through this as long as we love each other, huh? Do you think I'm a fuckin' idiot? Do you take me as a fool? I fuckin' hate you!"

I don't say anything but watch her pack up to leave me. I fucking screwed up big-time, and I hate this feeling. What the fuck am I supposed to say? I'm sorry?

I listen to her as she calls her sister in tears retelling her everything I told her. She curses me out some more to her sister, then hangs up. I'm leaning against the wall watching her wait for her sister to come pick her up, and I have nothing I can say. I know talking to her right now will only make things worse. The best thing I can hope for now is time for her to cool off and for her to think with a clearer mind. Because I do want to work this out with Angela. And I know that to make it work we'll literally have to start from square one.

It takes thirty minutes for her sister to get here, and I wonder how far away she lives. I help carry Angela's stuff to the door. She's stopped crying by now, but she won't speak to me. I sit the suitcases on the floor, and she and her sister make the back-and-forth trip from my door to the car. I look out my living room window down to the street and see Angela's sister's car filled with five kids looking like they're under the age of ten. I shake my head and realize how desperate Angela is to get away from me.

About an hour after Angela's left, I lie on top of my covers in a bedroom half empty. I've never felt this alone in my life, and I hate it. I never knew I much I'd miss Angela until she left me. I keep replaying tonight over and over again in my head, trying to think where I went wrong, but I already know where. I went wrong a year ago when I let Jessica into this room.

My thoughts go back to that night Jessica and I made love, and I think, why did I let her kiss me? Why did I let her take control over the situation when I should have been the one to say no? I should have been thinking of Angela, and now she's gone.

I run a hand over my face in frustration. My life is so fucked up right now, and I can't even find a way off this roller coaster. I just want Angela back.

Suddenly my phone starts ringing in my pocket, and I pull it out. It's Jessica calling, and for the first time in a very long time I don't want to answer her call. I put the phone down beside me and listen to it ring. It stops after a few more seconds and doesn't ring again. I let out a breath. I know I shouldn't be taking my anger out on Jessica, but I'm in such a state right now that I'm not thinking straight. I want to call her back, so I can make sure there's nothing wrong with Jaslene or anything, but I don't want to talk to anybody. I don't even want to see anybody. I just want Angela.

Why did I even let her walk out the door? I'd rather have her here chewing off my head than not have her here at all.

Chapter Sixteen

I maneuver around the kitchen early the next morning, trying to fix some breakfast before I leave for work, but I know I don't have enough time. Angela used to make my breakfast before I left, and now I have no choice but to grab some fast-food breakfast somewhere to tie me over till lunch.

I walk out of my apartment with the sun beaming down on me. Since I woke up Jessica has called me twice, but I haven't called back. Malcolm also called, but I'm not in the mood to talk to anyone right now unless its Angela, and that's probably not going to happen.

I don't know what it is, but I feel depressed. I feel like I just want to stay in my room or go over to Angela's sister's house and haul Angela back like her life depended on it.

As soon as I arrive in my back office at my bar, I collapse into my seat. I stare down at the paperwork I still needed to finish, not wanting to do anything. I lean back and place my hands behind my head and close my eyes. I must have dozed off because the next thing I hear is banging on my door. I look over at the clock and see it's nine thirty. I've been asleep for an hour and a half.

I get up and unlock my door, and Malcolm storms in. "What up with you, bro?" he asks, looking at me with his head tilted. I close the door behind him and go back to sit at my desk.

"Nothing, why?" I say with a shrug.

He eyes me like he knows I'm lying. "Jessica called me. She's worried about you."

"Why?"

"Because you're not answering her calls," he says, taking a seat in the chair in front of my desk. He leans forward. "Did y'all get in a fight or something?"

"Who?" I ask.

"You and Jessica."

"Nope," I answer, starting to do my paperwork.

I can feel Malcolm watching me. "Did you and Angela get into it?" When I don't say anything, he finally gets it. "Oh, I see. You told her the truth, didn't you?"

I don't say anything, and we both sit in silence. After two minutes he speaks again, "Where is she?"

"She went to stay with her sister."

"The one with five kids?" he asks, leaning forward with his mouth hung open.

"Yup."

"Damn." He shakes his head and leans back into his seat. "So you single?"

"No. I'm trying to get her back," I say.

"Oh."

"Why you say 'oh'?" I ask.

"No reason," he says, leaning forward again. "You should call Jessica back. She's worrying about you. I told her you probably told Angela everything."

"I will in a second." We make small talk about other things, and when he leaves I'm left in my office alone again thinking about Angela.

Around noon I leave the bar after taking longer than necessary on my paperwork. Twenty minutes later I'm in Angela's sister neighborhood. It's low-populated with only a small number of houses on the block. I can't get my mind off Angela, and as I'm in my car, I drive past her sister's house. Angela's sister runs a hair salon business from her home, so looking up her address was just a matter of Googling her.

The house has a gated metal fence and a wide blue porch filled with toys. I can't see Angela through the window from inside my car, and I drive off. I don't want to come off as a stalker.

I pull around the corner just as my phone rings again. I'm hoping it's Angela, thinking she might have seen me in my car, but it's Jessica. I pick up this time, remembering what Malcolm said about her being worried.

"Hey," she says once I answer. "How are you?" It's nice to hear her voice despite my mood.

"Been better," I say, continuing my drive home.

She's quiet for a few seconds for before she starts again. "You told her?" she says, referring to Angela.

"I had to tell her eventually."

"But now?" she asks, as if a later time would have been better.

"Yeah. I told her last night."

The line's quiet, and I wonder what she's thinking. "What is it, Jess?"

"Nothing."

"Not nothing. I know when something's wrong with you," I say.

"It's just that I wouldn't have minded if you wanted to keep it secret that you're Jaslene's father."

"Yes, you would have. It would have bothered you deep inside. I know it would. But listen, it doesn't matter now. I told Angela. The truth is out, and there's nothing we can do but hope that me and her can work things out. She would have found out eventually one way or another."

"Did you guys break up?" she asks.

"What do you think?" I say. There's a long pause again.

"I'm sorry."

"No, I'm sorry. I mean, it's cool. I'm just so frustrated right now."

"That she left?"

"More so about why she left." There's an even longer pause before I hear her whisper something. "What did you say?" I ask.

She sniffs and I know she's crying. "I said I'm sorry. I didn't mean for this to happen. I just wanted . . . I mean, it just happened. You didn't have to tell her!"

I shift my phone to my other ear. "Stop, Jess. Like I said before, you don't have to worry about this. Stop blaming yourself for something I consented to."

"Because I asked you to consent to it," she says.

"Actually that night we didn't do much talking," I say, and she's dead silent.

I know that was a soft spot, but it was the truth. She came in my room and we fucked. There was no asking, talking, debating. It was just me and her together.

I pull up to my apartment and get out. When I get inside, I'm disappointed to find that my house is still the same way I left it. Part of me was hoping that Angela would have changed her mind and come back, but that's a stupid thought.

Jessica's still on the phone with me. She's not saying anything, but I can hear her breathing. I can also hear a little of Jaslene in the background. "How's Jaslene?" I ask, trying to change the subject.

"She's right here," Jessica says, her voice perking up. "Do you want to talk to her?"

"Sure."

I hear shuffling over the phone, and I listen to Jaslene make goo-goo sounds and Jessica in the background saying, "Say, 'hi, Daddy.'" This moment right here puts me in the best mood I've had all day, and I realize that I should have called Jessica back sooner. Just because my life is in shambles, doesn't mean I have to shun my family and the people I care about.

I collapse on the sofa and listen to Jaslene. I swear I can listen to her all day and not get tired. Jessica's making her laugh, and I play along too, making funny noises over the phone. I feel the urge to see them both, and I contemplate making a trip down there to get my mind off things, but I push the idea to the side for now. Right now I needed to put my effort into saving my relationship.

"What do you think I should do about Angela, Jess?" I say after we've gotten all our laughs out.

"I think you should show up at her sister's house with roses and a letter written with how much you love her and can't live without her."

I smile. "That would be what you would want someone to do. Angela would throw those flowers back in my face."

She laughs. "I think you should try it. Or you could at least send her letters. Something romantic."

"Right now I'm just letting her cool off."

"What did Malcolm say you should do?" she asks.

"I didn't ask him yet. I wanted a woman's perspective."

"But I'm the woman you cheated with. That's kinda weird that you're asking me."

"I trust your opinion. Besides, you're still my friend." There's a silence on the other end before she speaks again.

"Yeah. We'll always stay friends."

Two days later I still haven't figured out what I'm going to do about Angela. I cracked yesterday and called her, but she didn't answer. I'm sitting on my couch in front of the Lakers game, when there's a knock at the door.

I look through the peephole and see Angela and her sister outside. I swing my door open, and both of them come in with their arms crossed beneath their breasts. Angela's sister is about half a foot taller than Angela and half a tone darker. I try not to stare, but I do notice the small scar line beneath her right eye.

"You remember Tammie," Angela says, nodding to her sister. Tammie doesn't say anything, and I don't say anything either. "I'm just here to get a few last things, and she's here to help me carry them out."

Angela starts heading back toward our bedroom. I'm not sure what's left for her to get, but I follow her. "Can we talk, Angela?" I ask. Her sister comes up behind me, and I feel the urge to turn around and tell her to step back, but I'm not trying to focus on her.

"No," she says quickly. "I'm just here to get my stuff." She walks around the room looking in drawers, but all her stuff she took two nights ago. She walks over to the closet and tries to find anything that looks remotely like it belonged to her, but she comes up with nothing.

Then she brushes past me and Tammie out of the room and into the bathroom. I follow her. "Just give me five minutes, Ang."

"Would you leave me alone!" Angela springs around holding her old toothbrush in her hand. She's had the toothbrush since the day she moved in here, and that was almost a year ago. Why does she want to take that?

"I'll never leave you alone. Look, I know we're not going to get back together. I just want to talk to you. I feel like you should know some things," I say as gently as I can. I know her sister is close by eavesdropping, and I'm starting to think that the reason's she here is to keep Angela from changing her mind about leaving me.

"No, thank you," she says, opening the medicine cabinet above the sink. She sticks her head inside, but I know she won't find anything that's hers only. The thing's mostly empty anyway.

I let out a breath and try again. "Don't you want some closure? I know there's some things you want to get off your chest."

She pauses for a while, and I know she's considering my idea. She turns and stares at me. "Tammie, come back in exactly five minutes."

Her sister nods and walks out. I try to think back to a time when I heard her talk and can't remember any. She must talk though. She has five kids.

"What?" Angela says, folding her arms across her chest.

I close the bathroom door and lean against it. This might be my one shot at getting Angela to change her mind, and I have to do it in under five minutes with a sister here to haul Angela away again. I don't want to see her walk out again. "I'm stupid. I know you know that already, so I'll just move on. I do love you, Angela, and after all that has happened to us over the time we've been together, I know our love is real. I was stupid to put that in jeopardy. I know a burning question you have is, why—"

"I know why you did it," she interrupts. "Because you're a no-good bastard that can't keep his dick in his pants."

"No," I say. "If that was true, I would have cheated on you with different women days after I met you, but I didn't. You know why I didn't? Because I fell in love with you, that's why."

"I can't tell that now."

"That's why I wanted to tell you why. It's not an excuse for me to cheat, but it's the only explanation I could come up with for my actions. I'm not in love with Jessica. It was not sex of love. It was sex of pleasure. There wasn't anything deeper there."

"I don't care if it was sex of pleasure, passion, love, hate—you shouldn't have fucked her! That's no excuse and that's no reason. Was that supposed to make me feel better? The thoughts going through your head while you were doing her don't matter. That fact that you even did it is what hurts," she says, then sits on the edge of the tub. "I mean, this wasn't how it was supposed to turn out with us."

I walk over and kneel down before her. I know saying I'm sorry won't ever place a smile on her face, but I place a hand on her knee, and she tries to shake me off. "Can't we start over?"

"No." She puts her head in her hands, and I wrap her in my arms. She tries to push me off, but I won't let go. She's going to hear me out.

"I'm not saying start over right now. I'm not asking you to move back in next week. I know we need some time apart, and I know it's not healthy for us to stay together after what happened. But after our break I want you to come back here, and I want to work this out with you as an adult. I'll do whatever you think we should do to save this relationship. We've both invested too much time and too much love just to say good-bye over this one big stupid thing. I know this is all my fault, and I know you'll never be able to trust me fully again, but I'm willing to take it one step at a time if you are. I want you, Angela. I need you."

She doesn't say anything for a while. I continue to hold her tight in my arms as I kneel down in front of her. I know she wants to say yes, and I know it's probably going to take many talks like this for her to even take me seriously, but I'm willing to try.

"I'll see," she says in her soft voice. I let go of her and stare into her eyes. She's stares back, and for the first time I feel a little hope that we can work this out. "But I'm still leaving, and I won't be back for a long time." She then walks around me and out of the bathroom.

Chapter Seventeen

I walk into my mom's house, and it smells like bacon. It's nine o' clock, and I came here bright and early this Saturday to spend all day with Jaslene. I haven't seen her in a week, and I missed her.

It's been four days since I last spoken to Angela and a full week since I've been back down here to Aurora. I'm excited to see Jaslene again. She's six weeks old now, and she's growing fast. Malcolm didn't come with me this time.

Mom comes out of the kitchen wearing a pink apron and holding a spatula in her hand. "Hey, baby," Mom says, pulling her face to the side for a kiss.

I kiss my mom and give her a tight hug. I haven't talked to her much since I stormed out of here last week. "Where's Jessica?" I ask, already walking back toward the room.

"Taking a shower. You can wait in here until she's done," Mom says quickly, but I don't stop walking.

"Where's my daughter?" I ask, going further down the hallway. I can hear the shower running and can smell the ivory soap fragrance seeping underneath the bathroom door. I inhale deeply, and for one split second I get the urge to open the door, but I shake my head and open the door to Jaslene's room. It's Malcolm's old bedroom, and the crib he set up looks nice. I never got the chance to see it after I stormed off, but he put it up fine.

Jaslene's staring up at me with her hands opening in closing. I scoop her up and hug her to my chest. "I missed you, Jas."

I walk out of the room with Jaslene in my arms, and as soon as I get into the hallway, Jessica opens the door to the bathroom. She's only wearing at a towel, and my hearts stops in my chest. I stare at her curves with my mouth open, but only for half a second. I turn and walk down the hallway and into the kitchen. I feel like I was holding my breath the whole time, because the second I get back to the table, I let out my breath. I can't get the image out of my head of Jessica only wearing a towel. Why did I look anyway? Why did I want to keep looking? I heard the door open. I should have never looked her way.

"What's wrong with you?" Mom asks. I sit down at the table and rest Jaslene on my shoulder, who sucks her pacifier loudly in my ear.

"Nothing," I answer.

After I finish eating some scrambled eggs, toast, bacon, and hash browns, Jessica walks into the room wearing blue jeans and a pink-and-white T-shirt. Her hair's still wet from the shower, and I look down at Jaslene trying my hardest not to be a pervert. Why am I looking at Jessica like this? We fucked one time almost a year ago. All the sexual tension between us, if there ever was any, should be gone.

"Hey, Jay," she says. She reaches over and rubs Jaslene's head.

"You look nice," I say despite myself.

She looks down at her clothes before smiling politely. "Thank you. I was hoping to get out of the house today."

I look up at her puzzled. She wants to go somewhere? Well, that's fine. I know she must have been cooped up in this house for the last two weeks. "Where do you want to go?" I ask.

Jessica glances over at my mom, who is still chewing her eggs. Then Jessica looks back at me.

"Maybe to the park. It's so nice outside. I figured we can push Jaslene around in the stroller and—"

"Sounds fine to me. Let's go," I say, standing and ready to get out of this house for real.

"Jessica," Mom says, wiping her mouth. "Don't you want to eat first?"

She looks down at the food, and I can tell by her widened eyes that she wants those hash browns, but she shakes her head. "I'll just eat something light on the way back."

"You can eat, Jess," I say, sitting back down. I lean Jaslene against my shoulder. "Me and Jaslene will wait. We got all day."

Jessica smiles and sits down beside me. I don't know what it is, but I don't like her sitting so close to me. It's not that I don't want her close; it's just that I want her even closer, and that's what's scaring me.

I sit quietly and wait till Jessica's finished eating. Mom stands and starts clearing the table. "How long y'all gon' be gone?" she asks, dropping the dishes into the soap-water-filled sink.

I shrug. "Not that long, I think."

As soon as Jessica finishes eating, we get Jaslene buckled in her stroller and start walking down the street in no particular direction with no particular destination. The weather is still a bit chilly, but not too cold. We have Jaslene dressed in winter clothes to be on the safe side though. Jessica's smiling the whole time, like it's her birthday again. She looks around the neighborhood and stores as if we didn't grow up in this town. "Jay, I know the reason you wanted to hang out all day," Jessica says as we reach the end of a block.

"Why?" I ask.

"Because you still want to do the paternity test," she says so firmly I think it was her idea.

I honestly haven't thought about the paternity test since I mentioned it last week. With all that was going on, making sure I was Jaslene's father didn't even cross my mind. "We don't really have to anymore. I know she's mine. She does look like me."

Her eyes get big. "You can see it now?" She's talking about Jaslene resembling me.

"Yes."

"Oh." We keep walking for a while down the next block before she says, "I just don't want you to have any doubts whatsoever in your mind that she's yours."

"I'm good."

"Let's take one anyway. Just in case Angela wants proof."

I pause at the mention of Angela, and my whole mood shifts. Here I am playing family when Angela is brokenhearted and stuck in her sister's house with her sister's kids. I feel like crap again, and Jessica steps closer to me and smiles lightly. "I know you miss her."

"You have no idea."

"I think I have an idea," she says with a finger pointed on her chin.

I shake my head and smile softly. "I can handle it, Jessica."

"Wait, just let me think. See, if I was her I would have to know that you really cared about me and loved me in order for me to even think about forgiving you."

"Jess . . ."

"You need to do something big. Something so meaningful that she can't ignore you and something she'll never forget."

I think about it for a while, but shrug eventually. "She's not that type of girl, Jess."

"Then what type of girl is she?" Jessica asks with her hands on her hips.

I think about it. "She's the type of girl that won't base a big decision like going back with someone on something as sweet as a grand apology. She needs time, and even then she might not come around. I don't know how to explain it, but tactics like what you're suggested are not going to work."

"They'd work for me." she says.

"She's not you."

We don't say anything for a while and just keep walking. I don't know how she took the fact that Angela is in no way like her, but for me it wasn't really an insult. It wasn't a compliment, but it wasn't an insult either. It's just a fact, and there're some things I like about Jessica and some things I like about Angela. The two of them are just different.

I know I shouldn't be comparing them, but I know Jessica would easily fall for a romantic gesture like showing up at her house with a dozen roses, music playing, and a poem written. It was easy for Chris and her other loser boyfriends to win Jessica back after they did something stupid. Jessica just wanted their love, and those men just wanted what they could get from her.

We make a circle and turn around, heading back to the house. I know it doesn't seem like it, but I did enjoy this walk. I don't want to go back inside the house just yet, so I suggest that we get in the car and drive around the town. When we reach the car, we drive around for a while, not really knowing where to go. We keep driving, but we don't talk too much. Eventually she starts feeding Jaslene, and I pull over. "Why do you want me and Angela to get back together so bad?" I ask, staring as she positions Jaslene under her breast. When I realize I'm staring, I look away just as quickly.

"Because you guys are in love, and I want to save your engagement," she says, then looks out the window. "I wish I could have saved mine."

I frown when I realize she's talking about her old engagement to Chris. "Don't wish that."

"Why?"

"Because you were engaged to Chris. I don't know why you're acting like you're sixty-five years old. You have plenty of time to find a husband. Don't rush it."

"I'm not trying to rush it. I just don't like feeling alone," she says, then goes quiet. We've had this same talk before about her family, and I've told her how much my family is like her own, but there's just something about it not being the real thing. "I just want a husband and kids to come home to at night. I want a big house with a big backyard. I want to build my own swing set for the kids to play on. I want to make my husband dinner and cuddle every night. I want that life, Jay."

"You can have that life if you want to, Jess. It just has to be with the right person, and that person wasn't Chris."

"I know that now."

"Good."

"Do you want a life like that?" she asks, looking back at me and into my eyes.

"I never thought about it, but I guess."

She laughs. "You must if you were planning to marry Angela."

"Yeah." We stop talking for a while and enjoy each other's silence.

"I really hope things work out with you and Angela, Jaylen," she says, looking me straight in the eye, and I know she's being honest.

"Thank you."

"If you think that me talking to her will help in any way—"

"No." I say, and we both laugh again. I haven't laughed this much since I left Chicago, and part of me doesn't want to go back anytime soon. The only reason would be for Angela. Her, and my business, but then again, I can always have Malcolm watch over that.

By the time we made it back to my mom's house I had forgotten all about the whole paternity test thing until Malcolm sent me a text. He asked me if Jessica and I had gone to the hospital yet to fill out the forms. I know I don't need the test, but my mind keeps going back to Angela and how she might need the test as proof in case she doubts Jessica had my baby.

I'm sitting on the couch with Jaslene asleep on my chest looking at the text message. Jessica is helping Mom fix lunch, and to be honest, I am more sleepy than hungry. I don't want to yell out to Jessica because Jaslene will wake up. Instead I replied back to

Malcolm's text and tell him that we might not do the whole paternity test. He replies by saying better safe than sorry, and I roll my eyes. I know he knows Jaslene is mine and is only covering my back by telling me to make sure first, but I know the test is a waste of time.

Jessica walks in the room and smiles down at me and Jaslene. "You guys look so cute," she says.

I smile back. "Hey listen, Jess. You want to just go ahead and do this paternity test? I know Angela's gonna want me to make sure." It's not really the truth since Angela and I aren't really talking right now, but I don't want to make my asking her sound like I'm doubting Jaslene is mine.

"Oh okay, sure. Do you want to go after we have lunch?" she says, smiling a little softer. I can tell I hurt her feelings by changing my mind again, but I'm glad she's cool with it.

The dirty plates clink together as Mom plants them in the sink to wash. I lean back in my seat and pat my stomach. Mom loves to cook, and she appreciates it when I clean my plate. Jaslene's sleeping inside her crib in the room. Jessica stands up to help my mom clear the table of our glasses, so I stay seated.

Mom turns her narrow eyes to my face, and I notice the dark shadows beneath them. She must not have been getting much sleep since Jaslene moved in. I know taking care of a newborn must involve a lot of loss of sleep, something that I'm experiencing a lot myself recently. "You tell Angela yet?" Mom asks. Her tone is cold enough to freeze the hot water she's washing the dishes in. In other words, to her my answer better be a yes.

I nod slowly. I don't want to share all the details of what happened with me and Angela to my mom, especially with Jessica standing right there. I also don't want Jessica feeling even more guilty about my situation. Even though I've told her over and over that what happened between me and Angela is mostly my fault because I had a choice, I know she won't let it go.

"Good," Mom says, handing a washed plate to Jessica to rinse off. "So what happened?"

"We broke up." What did she think was going to happen?

She doesn't say anything for a while and continues to wash dishes. Jessica gives me a few glances with a soft smile before looking back down again.

I stand up, ready to go home, but I know I might as well drive to the hospital and do the paternity test while I'm in town. "Where are you guys going now?" Mom asks as soon as she sees me and Jessica carry Jaslene into the living room in her car seat. All three of us are ready to go, and I just want to get this over with.

Jessica fiddles with the baby bag she has on her shoulder and looks at my mom with wary eyes as if she really needs her permission to leave the house. "We'll be right back."

"That didn't answer my question." Mom narrows her eyes from where she sits on the couch.

I grab Jessica's hand and usher her out the door without saying anything else to my mom. Damn, she's nosy, and I know Jessica would stand there and tell her every little detail of whatever my mom wanted to know.

I buckle Jaslene into the car safely. She's still sleeping with the pacifier dangling from her mouth. Jessica passes me the baby bag, which I put in the seat next to Jaslene. After my daughter's settled in, I take a seat behind the wheel and release a deep breath. "Sorry about my mom acting weird," I say to Jessica.

She shrugs. "She probably thought that you were the one acting weird."

"Do you think I'm acting weird?"

She looks me directly in the eye. "Yes."

"May I ask why?"

She looks back toward the front, and I know she sees nothing but our old neighborhood, since I haven't driven off yet. She doesn't say anything for a few moments, and I'm about to repeat my question, when she turns back to face me. I know she's trying to hide them, but I can still see the tears pricking on the sides of her eyes. "Why did you change your mind about the paternity test again? It's like you can't make up your mind. Do you believe that she's yours or not?"

I lean back in my seat and look straight ahead. I thought about giving a smart answer, but the look she's giving me tells me she's not in the mood for my sarcasm. "She's mine. I'm just getting it done in case Angela needs proof."

She stares at me for a long moment with her arms crossed. "Just in case she asks you or just in case you're not the father?"

I roll my eyes and put the car in Drive. I do not want to argue with her right now, and if she wants to keep pressing my buttons with this issue, I'm not going to respond.

We don't say anything on the ride to the hospital, and I don't even glance her way. I don't know why I'm mad, but I think she's overreacting about this paternity test. If she knows Jaslene is mine, why is she getting so upset? Just because I asked for the test? That's dumb to me.

We pull up to the hospital ten minutes later, and we both stomp out of the car in silence. She goes around and grabs both Jaslene and the baby bag, leaving me with nothing to carry. "You really gon' be tripping like this, Jess?" I ask, walking a few paces behind her. She doesn't turn around, neither does she respond.

The stench of Pine-Sol greets us when we enter the lobby. I look over to my right and notice a janitor mopping vigorously, like he was cleaning up blood. I turn my attention back to Jessica, who has walked up to the receptionist. Jessica schedules us an appointment to get the test done next weekend, but I kind of had my mind set on doing it now. "There're no openings today?" I ask the gray-haired woman. She pushes her glasses further up her nose and shakes her head before diving back to her computer.

Jessica turns away and starts walking back toward the exit. "At least we have an appointment to get it done, so you should be happy now," she says without looking back. I jog up to her and snatch the baby bag off her shoulder.

"I don't know why you're giving me the cold shoulder after you agreed to do this in the first place." I sling the baby bag over my own shoulder and continue to walk out the lobby. I need some fresh air.

"I agreed because I thought you had doubts," she says, stopping outside the doors to glare at me. "Then you told me you didn't have doubts and that you believed me and your mom."

"Yeah, but—"

"Now you're saying you want the test, and I know it's because you have doubts, and I want to know why." Her eyes narrow into slits, like she's staring a hole into my eyes. I would be lying if I said I didn't have doubts, but it's hard to explain. I look down at Jaslene inside the car seat dangling from Jessica's hand. I know Jaslene is mine, but I guess there's still a part of me that's shocked that she's not Chris's. There's a part of me that's shocked that I'm a father seemingly out of nowhere, and getting this paternity test will prove that all of this is real and that my life has truly changed forever.

I shake my head and shrug. "It's complicated," I say, and start walking toward the car.

Chapter Eighteen

I pull up to Angela's sister's house once I'm back from Aurora and spot Angela sitting alone on the porch. She's sitting with her chin in her hands looking down at the pavement beneath her feet. I've never seen her look so sad. She obviously didn't notice me pull up, so I get out of the car. When she hears my car door close, she glances up and immediately changes her expression to irritation.

I place my hands up as I walk up to her. She stands and starts to head back inside. "Wait, Ang. I just want to talk."

"I don't feel like talking to you right now," she says, avoiding my eyes.

"I figure that never is a good time, but I want to make things right between us." I look up toward the house and notice a few tiny shadows peering through the window. Her sister's kids couldn't be more than eight years old at the most, and I know Ang hates living in such an enclosed place with all of them. "Let me take you to dinner."

"No."

"We can talk here too, but I'd figure you'd want some time away from"—I nod toward the window, and a few of the kids duck when they see me look their way again—"the house."

Angela looks back quickly, then shrugs. "What do you have to say?"

"Wanna come sit in the car?"

"No."

I sigh and stand at the bottom of the porch. The porch is made of wood and painted a light green. The paint had been chipped off by what looks like years of weather and abuse. I stab my shoe on the edge of the first step, then look up at Angela's eyes. "I miss you."

She rolls her eyes, and I doubt she believes me. I won't be surprised if she doesn't believe a word I say.

"I want to work this out with you. I don't care how long it takes. I know you hate me, but I want to make this right."

"Try going back in time then."

I let out a breath. Angela and I been through a lot over the last year, and I don't want it all thrown away. "If I could I would."

She looks me in the eye again. "How do you know if that baby is even yours? She thought it was Chris's at first, and now she's switching it up?"

"I take the paternity test next week."

She lets out a breath. "Somehow that doesn't make me feel better about this situation."

"Well, what do you want me to do?" I ask, throwing my arms up. "The sooner we get the results back, the sooner we'll know what we're dealing with so that we can deal with this."

She doesn't say anything but stares at me like I'm a walking torch.

"I want to work this out with you and make this right. I know I shouldn't have lied about her, but that doesn't change how I feel about you."

She rolls her eyes again and stands. "I'm going back inside. Talk to me when you get the paternity test back and you show up not the father." With that she turns around and storms back into the house.

I can smell the scented candles burning even before I open the door to Malcolm's apartment around ten p.m. I shake my head and push the door open anyway.

The ceiling light is dimmed, and the only light is coming from the two candles sitting on a table next to dinner plates and a rose. Malcolm's standing in the middle of the room dressed in nothing but a red silk robe and black slippers. His face turns from smiling and inviting to disgust and irritation. "What are you doing here?" he asks puffing out a breath as he tightens the belt on his robe, "I got a honey coming over here in, like, five minutes."

I walk in and throw myself on the couch. He looks down at me like he wants to sling me out the window, but I don't care. "What should I do now that I've scheduled that paternity test, bro?"

"Who cares? I'm trying to get some pussy tonight." Malcolm groans. "Come over tomorrow and we'll talk about it then."

"The pussy or the paternity test?"

"Nigga, what?" He shakes his head. "What you want, man? Hurry up."

"I just feel weird with everything going on. It's like part of me knows that having a paternity test come back positive will mean the end of my relationship with Angela, if there's any hope for it. So part of me, just a tiny part, wonders what would happen if the test came back negative. If I wasn't Jaslene's father."

Malcolm breathes heavily and plops down in one of the two chairs he set out. "Do you want it to come back negative?"

"No, but ... I'm just wondering what would happen if it did. Like, what would I do from there?"

Malcolm leans all the way back. "Do you think it's going to come back negative?"

"No. I'm just planning for the worst, that's all. It'll break my heart if I'm not her father. After being told I was and after I set it in my mind that I was, it's impossible to think that I'm not anymore. I can't picture Jaslene with another father."

Malcolm rubs his chin. "I don't think you really have anything to worry about when it comes to the results of the test. You just doing it to be sure. When it comes to you and Angela, you're going to have to struggle to keep the relationship regardless, 'cause you cheated on her whether the baby is yours or not."

I nod and lean back. He's right. Angela is not going to forgive me easily no matter how this test comes out. "So what do I do?"

"You hold your head up, keep your shoulders back, and stand up and walk your ass out my apartment so I can finish getting ready for my date," he says with a smirk.

I smile anyway and stand. "All right, man. I'll catch you later." We bump-fist and I'm about to walk out, when he speaks again.

"Hey, remember—relationships come and go, but you always gon' have your daughter."

I nod, taking his words in. There is never gonna be a time when I walk out of my daughter's life. No matter what. I turn the doorknob to leave, and a woman with blond weave and a brown trench coat is leaning on the door frame. I can tell she was just about to knock before I opened the door because her hand is raised in a fist. She smiles at me, showing off her pearly white teeth. "Malcolm didn't tell me there would be someone else joining us." She winks at me, and I look back at Malcolm, who's straightening out his robe. Somehow I don't think this date is going to end with the two of them playing Scrabble on the living room floor.

"Come on in, baby. That's my brother Jaylen, and he was just leaving," Malcolm says, strolling over to the door and ushering the woman in. Does he even know her name?

"Aw," the woman moans, looking in my eyes as she walks past me. "That's a shame."

I shake my head and walk out.

The next week goes by slow with no calls from Angela and the ever-present tension of the blood test approaching. I feel like I'm going to throw up, and I just want to get this test over with so I can get the results and move forward. In what direction I'll go forward in, I don't know yet.

Malcolm decides to drive down with me to Aurora. Neither of us is on the closing shift for my bars—a rare occasion—so we decided to ride down together. He wants to see his niece again, and Mom is preparing a big dinner for all of us after we get done with the test. It's starting to feel like a momentous event, but it's just a paternity test. At first I wasn't sure how Mom was going to take it, but Jessica told me that she understands my wanting to be careful. I hope Jessica isn't too offended by my taking the test.

Malcolm's still going on about the hot date he had last night. Apparently it was a different girl from the one I ran into a few nights ago.

I turn my head slightly to look at him, and he smiles triumphantly as he concludes his story. I smile and shake my head. This man never has a boring day.

"Are you nervous?" he asks me after a few more minutes of silence. He had turned the radio down so I wouldn't miss a detail of his story.

"Nervous about what?" I ask.

"The test."

I shrug. "It is what it is, but I know she's mine, so I don't have nothing to worry about." I pause and think about Angela. "Nothing to worry about when it comes to that, anyway."

He nods. "You talked to Angela, lately?"

"Not since the day I came over to your house."

He pauses for a few moments. "Do you feel like you're choosing between Angela and Jaslene?"

"No," I say. "If that was the case, there would be no contest."

"Do you think you're choosing between Angela and Jessica?" he asks in a low tone, like he's trying not to hit a nerve.

That's one's a little tougher to answer, but I know I have to choose Angela. I'm the one that did her wrong. "Kinda. Mostly because they both need me. Jessica needs me to help provide for our daughter, and Angela needs me to . . . just be there for her and love her. Don't get me wrong. I love them both. I just need to figure out—"

"You love them both? You're in love with Jessica?" he asks, saying it more like a statement then a question. He rubs his hands together. "I knew it!"

I smile and shake my head and try to stay focused on the road. "No, man. Not like that."

"You can say that all you want, Jay, but I know deep down you be thinking about her and stuff."

I steal a glance at him. "She's the mother of my child. She's my best friend. Of course I . . . look—I know we had fucked, but that was just . . . we're just friends, is what I'm trying to say." I pause then add, "She knows how I feel about Angela anyway," for good measure.

Malcolm leans back and places his hands behind his head. "You can say whatever you want."

I roll my eyes despite myself and focus on the road for the rest of the trip. I turn the music up and blast my CD of Snoop Dogg all the way to Aurora.

Chapter Nineteen

Jessica's sitting on the porch with Jaslene in her arms when I pull up front. She smiles and waves with her free hand. Malcolm gets out first and I follow. I can smell the food cooking from out here, and I can't wait to taste my mom's cooking again. There will never be anything that tastes as good to me as a home-cooked meal.

Before we walk up to the porch, Jessica stands up with the baby and walks toward us. "We can go straight to the hospital. Sheri says dinner will be ready when we get back."

We both nod. "Where's her bag?" I ask, nodding toward Jaslene.

"Oh! It's in the house. Can you grab that for me, Malcolm?" Jessica asks, turning her sweet eyes on Malcolm. He nods and goes inside. "She missed you," she says, looking down at Jaslene, who's falling asleep to the sound of her sucking her pacifier.

I smile and reach out my arms to hold her. "How can you tell?" I ask, taking my daughter in my arms. This feels right.

"She cries less when she's around you."

"She's been crying a lot?"

Jessica shrugs. "Mostly at night." I can tell she wants to say something else, and I fear that Jaslene isn't the only one that's crying at night.

"Are you okay?" I ask, trying to make eye contact with her.

She nods, and I'm about to press her further, when Malcolm comes back out carrying Jaslene's bag. "Okay, everybody. Let's go!" he says, swinging the bag on his shoulder and jogging to the car.

"What took you so long?" I ask Malcolm while putting Jaslene in the backseat beside him. Jessica's sitting up front beside me and Jaslene, and Malcolm's in the back.

"Mom. She took one look at me and started talking about how soon I should get my hair rebraided," he says, sliding one palm from the front of his head to the back of his neck. "Jess, you know how to braid, right? Hook a nigga up."

"Twenty-five dollars," she says, and I burst out laughing.

"I taught you well," I say after securing Jaslene and taking my place behind the wheel.

"Aw, what—Jess, you was for real? I thought you was playing," Malcolm says, pretending to be shocked.

Jessica chuckles. "You know I need the money."

"What? Yo' baby daddy sitting right there next to you. You can ask him for all the money you need. I just need a touch-up," Malcolm says.

She laughs before she goes quiet, and I catch her glance at me. "He has too much to worry about."

I look at her. "You know you can always ask me for anything."

"I don't need anything. I mean, nothing I need costs anything," she says, staring down at her hands.

I keep glancing between her and the road, but I'm not sure what she meant when she said her needs don't cost anything. Maybe I'm just buggin' and can't wrap my head around it.

None of us says anything for the rest of the ride except for a few grunts from Malcolm about his last date messing up his hair.

We pull up to the hospital, and I find a parking spot in the visitors' section of the building. We walk inside and spot the same receptionist we spoke to last week, and after we have confirmed that we have an appointment, all three of us take seats in the waiting area for our names to be called.

Malcolm's playing peek-a-boo with Jaslene, and Jessica's sitting beside me fidgeting her leg. I would love to say I'm just sitting here cool, but I'm nervous about the results. I don't expect it to be negative; I'm just nervous about the process in general. I have to keep reminding myself that I'm doing this not to prove anything but to just . . .

I glance over at Jaslene, and her laugher tugs my heart. I would never want a day when someone else can take her away from me. With this paternity test coming back positive, it means no other man can claim he's her father.

After a few minutes Jessica stops fidgeting and leans her head on my shoulder. I stare down at her, and she has her eyes closed. I guess I never realized how tiring it is to have to take care of a baby 24/7. "Have you ever thought about letting me take Jaslene home for a while? Like for the weekend, so you can have a break?" I ask, and her eyes pop open.

Jessica sits up, and all signs of tiredness are gone. "No. I'm fine. I know you never babysat before, so—"

"It's not babysitting if it's my child. I'm just taking care of her. I want to help out more than just giving money. Money that you rarely accept."

She opens her mouth, then closes it firmly. She has to know I'm right about that. "Okay, but let's wait until she gets a little bigger and until you work things out with Angela. If you guys work things out, she may not like Jaslene spending the night there."

"Like I give a damn. It's my daughter and my house. I'm not about to compromise on spending time with my daughter," I say.

"Yeah, I agree with him on that one," Malcolm says, nodding his head and bouncing Jaslene and looking over at Jessica. "Ang ain't got that much power."

Jessica looks at him, then back at me. She stares into my eyes as if she's assessing my ability to take care of our daughter without her being there. I raise one eyebrow in anticipation of her response. She smiles. "I agree. I believe you." She looks over at our baby. "I just feel so attached to Jaslene that I probably wouldn't know what to do with myself if she wasn't with me."

Malcolm leans over to her ear. "Just relax, masturbate, or get some sleep. Or better yet—go out looking for a job or a place to go to school."

"I agree," I say.

Jessica has her mouth open to rebut, but the receptionist interrupts, telling us it's our turn. All three of us stand and follow the nurse, who directs us to the doctor's room. The hallway is wide and spotless and has the clean linoleum floors that are made for sliding around in your socks. Eventually, we reach a corner room, and she leads us in. "He'll be in shortly," the nurse says before closing the door with the three of us standing in a nearly empty room.

A nurse comes in wearing the typical long white coat, and we conduct the paternity test by her taking a swab of my cheeks cells as well as the baby's. It's over soon, and I leave the room holding Jaslene in my arms, who is fully awake after having a cotton swab against her cheek. I insert a pacifier in her mouth knowing she'd prefer that to a swab. Jessica's walking close beside me swinging her arms back and forth. "Are you glad it's over with?" I ask her.

"I know I am," Malcolm says, coming up on my other side. "I'm hungry as hell, and that took longer than I thought it would."

I laugh, but my stomach is growling too. "Let's get up out of this place then." We leave the hospital and get back to Mom's home with stomachs prepared to chow down.

As soon as we walk through her front door, my stomach does backflips.

"Mmm . . . I can't wait to eat. Here, I'll put Jaslene down in her crib," Jessica says, reaching to take Jaslene out of my hands. She's in the carrier seat, and I hand Jessica the handle. Jessica smiles and starts walking toward Jaslene's room.

Mom comes out of the hallway just as Jessica walks past her. Mom's got flour on her cheeks, and I know she was really throwing down. "Y'all ready to eat? Then go wash your hands. Ain't no telling what y'all was touching up in that hospital."

Malcolm laughs, and we all head to the kitchen sink like trained boys. I honestly just want to eat. I'm not sure what the plan is after we eat, but as long as I'm spending time with Jaslene, I'm good. I sit down at the table, where mom's laid out food fit for kings. The aroma has the effect of waving a steak in front of a starving lion, and Malcolm and I waste no time swallowing a plate of mom's food before Jessica even comes to the table.

Out of the corner of my eye I notice Mom staring at me, and I put down my fork to stare back at her. Her face looks like she's studying a math problem. "What?" I ask.

"How was the hospital?" She looks between Malcolm and me, and I want to ask if the question was meant for anyone, but I know she's fishing for details.

About what, I don't know, but I can tell she wants me to answer.

"Good. Fast. Simple." What did she expect it to be?

"Oh." Mom leans back in her seat, but her skeptical eyes remain fastened on me. "From the way Jessica described, your off-and-on about the paternity test made it seem like the visit would be a nightmare."

I took a deep breath and leaned back in my seat as well. "It was never the hospital. I just—"

"Couldn't make up your mind about taking the test?"

I shrug. "Doesn't matter. The test is done. Now we just got to wait."

Mom leans forward toward me and uses a soft tone. "Do you expect anything different from what me and Jessica told you?"

I shake my head.

Malcolm rises from the table and clears his plate just as Jessica appears in the door frame. She gives a tired smile, and I know she must have had a hard time putting Jaslene to sleep.

"You okay?" I ask her.

She nods. "Can we talk?"

"Come in; eat something thing first, sweetie," Mom says, waving Jessica over. "You didn't eat breakfast."

I look at Jessica's face, and then her stomach, then back at her eyes. Her mouth parts likes she wants to dispute Mom's claim, but she shrugs instead. "I was busy with Jaslene, and then you guys showed up. It's no big deal."

I see Malcolm raise his eyebrows, and I stand up and walk the few steps until I'm standing in front of Jessica. I stare down at her and give her a small smile. "Eat first, then we'll talk."

I peek inside Jaslene's room and spot her sleeping in her crib in the dark room. Jessica added glow-in-the-dark stars to the ceiling to help create an out-in-space feel. There's a rocking chair I hadn't noticed before placed in the corner of the room. Other than the chair, a changing table, and the crib, the room is fairly empty. I like the unclutteredness and find the open space a good play area for whenever Jaslene starts walking and wants to play with a dozen toys scattered out across her room. There's a pain in my chest when I realize I won't be here for most of her growing up. She's already seven weeks old. Will I even be here visiting when she takes her first steps? Or says her first words?

I walk fully into the room and close the door behind me. I walk close to the crib and notice the baby monitor inside so Jessica can tell when she wakes up and cries. I take a deep, low breath and scan the room again.

I'm about to walk out of the room, when the door opens and Jessica steps in. She smiles and I smile back. I want to ask if she finished her meal, so I nod toward the door. She turns around and we leave the room, closing the door softly behind us. "Did you eat?"

"Yeah. Just two of the quesadillas. I don't know how long you're staying in town, so I wanted make sure we had time to talk," she says, walking toward her room. I follow close behind. We slip into the room before Malcolm or Mom turn around from the kitchen to comment or wave us over.

Her room's just as clean and uncluttered as Jaslene's. This was my old room, and I look over to where I used to keep all my race car toys in the corner when I was a boy. I smile. Jessica turns around sharply and smiles when she catches me smile. "Yes ma'am?" I ask, leaning against the door with my arms folded.

She looks over toward the wall, then down at the floor before settling her eyes on my arms. "I overheard Sheri talking to you." She pauses and looks at my face. When I don't say anything she continues. "I know none of this is what you expected with your first child, and I know this messed up a lot of stuff for you, but I just wanted to say that despite all of that, I'm glad you're Jaslene's father. She truly is lucky."

I feel the urge to reach out and hug her, but I don't. Mostly because I'm sure I probably wouldn't let go. "Thank you." She smiles. "How do you feel about all this?"

She tilts her head to the side, like I asked her a foreign question. She shrugs. "About what?"

I push myself off the door and walk close to her. "Everyone keeps asking how I feel about the test and what I think the results will be, but this test affects both of us."

She sighs and nods. "I'm not worried about the test the same way you are. I'm more worried about how the results are going to affect your life. Sometimes I feel depressed when I think about you wanting it to come back negative—"

"I never said that."

"I know. But just the thought of that and how Angela left you because of all this makes me feel . . . heavily blamed." She wraps her arms around herself, and I stop myself from wrapping mine around her too. "I didn't want this to happen at first. You being her father, I mean. Not because of lack of parenting skills but because I didn't want me and Jas to be a burden."

"You guys are never a burden. With the way my situation with Angela is going right now, you two are the only ones that keep me smiling."

Jessica smiles for half a second. "But I'm the reason you're having this problem with Angela right now though."

I open my mouth to object, but I realize she had a point. She's not completely to blame, but the two of us did create a life together when we had no right to. "Everything will be fine," I say, to round up everything. It's nice to know what she's thinking regarding this whole thing, and I'm glad she's glad I'm the father. I just hope this test proves the same thing.

I give my little girl one final kiss before turning around and walking out of the house. It's dark outside, and the April weather is starting to warm up a bit. Only a few patches of snow remain in some areas of the lawn, and it makes me think back to earlier this year in February, when Jessica was still pregnant and the snow kept falling down in loads every few days.

I take a deep break and get inside the car. We stayed a lot longer than we'd planned to, but I don't mind.

"Bye, Jay," Jessica calls after me. "Come back soon."

Once Malcolm joins me, we start our trip to the freeway. Right as we enter the open ramp, I get a phone call from an employee at Miller House, and he sounds out of breath and petrified. "Jay, it's Mort! Come down to the bar now. You ain't gonna believe this shit!"

I grip the wheel tighter. Now what? "What happened?"

"Couple thugs came in and started throwing over tables, breaking bottles, fighting people. Took all our cash out the registers, and I—"

"Hold on, hold on, hold on. You say what! Aw, hell, naw." I pull the phone from my ear and retell the event to Malcolm, and he gives me the same what-the-fuck look I have on. "All right, man, I'm on my way. Did you call the cops? Was anyone hurt?"

"Yeah, I did. A few customers and I were able to catch, like, two of them, but I think one got away," Mort says, still sounding out of breath. "We tied them up, and we're keeping an eye on them until the police come. This just happened ten minutes ago."

I rub a hand down my face. I can't believe this shit. "Did they have guns?"

Malcolm reaches over and pulls the phone from my ear. I look at him, and he shakes his head. "Let me talk to Mort. You're dipping into other lanes and shit, and we just got on the freeway."

I glance back and forth from Malcolm to the road trying to figure out what Mort is saying according to Malcolm's responses. "Man, put him on Speaker. Tell him we on our way there."

I move over into the fast lane so I can get back to Chicago as fast as I can. Malcolm puts Mort on Speaker, but he's not saying too much that he hasn't already told me. The cops have been called and they're on their way, windows and tables are broken, two of the three guys who did it are caught. "You think it might be Chris?" Malcolm asks me.

I grip the wheel tighter. If he even had the slightest thing to do with this . . . "Can you get the other two guys to start talking?" Malcolm asks Mort.

"Man, these guys ain't saying shit." Mort's voice is loud, and I can picture him shaking his head. "Oh, but, Jay, they did have guns though. Well, one dude had a knife. None of them came in shooting though, so we were able to jump them before they pulled them out. So we were able to—"

"What did the other one look like?" I ask him. "The one who got away."

"Uh, tall. Medium skin tone, uh. He ran out fast, and a lot of commotion was going on. I'm sorry I didn't get a better look."

"All right. Just keep everything under control until the police come," I say.

Malcolm talks to him for a while longer before hanging up. I'm so mad it's hard for me to see straight. All I want to do is get to my bar. I'm speeding toward Chicago, but I have to slow down when the traffic gets heavier. We're closer to Chicago now, and I know I still have more than an hour of driving left.

Chapter Twenty

By the time we pull up in front of Miller House, I can tell all the customers have gone home. We get out the car and notice Mort, a short-built man with a balding head, talking to a police officer. Mort waves us over when we walk through the door. The bar is completely torn apart. Glasses are broken and tables are flipped just like Mort said, but there're also bloodstains on the floor, which are probably the result of a fight or the broken glass. Glass and broken furniture litter the entire floor, and I shake my head. I can't believe eight months of work just went down the toilet so fast. In just one night.

"There you go, Officer. He's the owner right there," he says to the blond officer in front of him, who is busy scribbling on a notepad.

The cop turns to me, and I read the name stated on his chest: Officer Seth. "Are you the owner of Miller House?"

"Yes."

He keeps writing, not even looking into my eyes. I clench my fists. I am already pissed off. "Do you have insurance?"

"Yes."

"Good," Officer Seth says, then looks at my eyes for the first time. "But we were unable to find the last guy; the other two are in our custody."

"Where are they?" I ask, looking around the shattered destruction of my bar. I don't see anyone other than Malcolm, Mort, and this cop.

"We took them down to the station for questioning about an hour ago," he says, giving me this "you would know if you guys had been here" look.

"I want to see them."

Officer Seth stares at my face and then notices my hands fisted up. His eyes turn back to mine. "We've got it under control. What I need you to do is fill out a statement of the incident—"

I zone out as he talks because all I can think about are those men who trashed my place. I want them. I think about all the jails in the area and try to calculate how long it would take to visit each one and find those two guys, especially when I don't know their names.

Officer Seth finishes talking and is looking at me like he's waiting for a response, but I don't even know the question he asked. I move around him and walk to the back toward my office. I twist the knob and am relieved to find it still locked. I'm the only one with a key. I open the door and go right to the fireproof safe sitting on the floor behind my desk. I punch in the combination and peek in. Everything, including statements, receipts, bookkeeping, and money, is still there untouched. I'm glad Mort and whoever else helped him had been able to block those men from coming in here. I look around the office one last time just to make sure nothing's been destroyed. I don't keep really valuable stuff here, like social security cards, titles, birth certificates.

I tap my desk and try to figure this shit out. I don't know the names of those bastards, I don't know if this was a random act or an attack specifically targeted at me, and I don't know who's behind this shit if they were targeting me.

My mind jumps to the guy that got away. We arrived at my bar an hour and a half after all this happened so he got away. Officer Seth walks into my office with narrowed eyes as if I'd disrespected him for walking away during our conversation, but I don't care about his feelings right now. "As I was saying, Mr. Miller, as soon as we get your statement, we can start the process. I assume you will be prosecuting?"

"Yes." I've still got my head on the guy who got away. How the hell did he get away when the other two guys didn't?

"Okay. I have the forms right here," Officer Seth says, waving a couple of papers in the air. He walks over to my desk and lays them on top. "As soon as you're ready. Um . . . the sooner the better."

"I'll get to it." I say, looking down at the papers, but my mind is elsewhere. I hear footsteps come in the office and look and see Malcolm staring a hole into me so deep I don't ask questions. I just follow him out of the room.

Officer Seth follows us, and Malcolm and I stop outside the office and stare at him. I know whatever Malcolm is about to tell me is not meant for the officer to hear. "Is everything all right?" Officer Seth asks anyway.

"Everything's cool," Malcolm says. "I was just about to ask him about the employees and where're they're going to work until the place gets fixed up."

"Oh." He still stands there as if he wants to be a part of the conversation.

I turn to him. "I'll drop off the report at the police station tomorrow morning. Thanks for coming."

He swings his arms back and forth a little bit, and I know he doesn't want to leave. After a few seconds, however, he nods. "You're welcome. Sorry again that this happened, and you fellows have a nice evening." He tips his head, and Malcolm and I wait until the door of the bar closes behind him.

"What?" I ask.

"I saw this note hanging out under the edge of one of the tables out there. It was right by the door, and I think it fell off the window during the commotion." He holds up a yellow sticky note with a sloppily written message.

I take it from his hands and think about where he found it. On a window is such a weird place to leave a note. The note is sticky due to liquor spills, and I can barely make out the words written in black ink.

I told you I was gon get you back nigga!!!! What, you thought I forgot?!!

The images of last summer flash past my eyes, and I see myself stomping Chris to the ground. I don't stop because I know what he did to Jessica. I know all about the tears, the screaming, the bruises he'd given her, and how broke and homeless he left her. I don't regret any of it.

I clench my fists, balling up the note. Malcolm stares at me and nods his head. I don't waste another second and storm out the bar heading to Chris' house. I don't need the cops to help me with this one.

We can't make our way to Chris's house fast enough. I know it was him that set this shit up. I think back to that note and remember what happened last summer when Malcolm and I molly-whopped his ass for beating Jessica.

I look to my right at Malcolm when we come to a red light, and his face looks stern and he's quiet. He's never quiet. I shake my head. If this nigga Chris thinks for one second that the shit he did tonight was just gonna be taken without repercussions . . . I shake my head and try to focus on the road. The traffic isn't as heavy right now, and I drive with a deadly calmness.

I turn down a narrow road that is lit only by a handful of streetlights. I tap my thumb against the steering wheel as I inch closer to his building. I can't wait to take that muthafucka by surprise.

"Stop!" Malcolm shouts, just as I'm about three houses down from Chris's apartment building. Malcolm's eyes are bulging, and then he narrows them into slits as he stares further down the road. "There's a cop there. Look over at the side of the building. There's three more over there."

I turn to look where he's pointing and can barely make out the figures moving in the shadows. I'm not sure if they're cops but . . .

Malcolm turns to face me again. "Turn your lights out and pull over."

I pull over to the curb and kill the engine. "What makes you think they're cops?" I ask him.

"Even if they're not cops, something is about to go down," Malcolm says with his eyes still on the shadows of the building.

"I don't even see a police car."

Malcolm doesn't say anything, and we both just sit there looking. A few long moments go by, and before another car comes down the street, Malcolm says, "Let your seat back!" Malcolm slides down flat in his seat. I do the same just as a police paddy wagon passes our car and stops right in front of Chris's apartment.

"Do you think this is the same police who were investigating my bar?" I ask.

"Somehow I don't think so," Malcolm says after letting his seat back up. I don't know why we're both being so cautious right now, but I know we can't get inside that building and take care of Chris with all these cops around. They probably got the building on lockdown. "The other two guys could have ratted

Chris out or . . . this could have nothing to do with your bar."

I rub a hand down my face to subdue my growing aggregation. "What now?" I ask him.

"Let's just wait," Malcolm says, scanning the area. No one is walking down the streets, and it feels like the calm before the storm. What the hell is going on?

A few more minutes pass, and we see the shadowy figures step from the darkness and enter the main doors of the apartment building one by one. Each figure has a semiautomatic gun strapped to his shoulder, as well as a bulletproof vest and the Chicago Police Department badge symbol.

"I think . . ." Malcolm starts but stops when we see the paddy wagon's doors fly open, and ten more cops swarm into the building. "This is a stakeout."

"You think it's a drug bust?"

"Damn. Just when we wanted to roll up on that nigga." Malcolm shakes his head and leans back in his seat.

"Let's wait it out then. These cops gon' leave at some point," I say, staying focused on the door of the building.

After a few moments there's a loud boom, and I duck my head instinctively. I look up a few seconds later and see five cops slide a man outside. He's kicking and screaming with no socks or T-shirt on.

"Holy shit," Malcolm says, leaning over to look out my window. "That's Chris!"

I stare hard but can't see his face with all the cops and hands blocking the view. The cops are grabbing him and throwing him in the paddy wagon, when I catch a glimpse of the contorted, pained face I hate so much. "Damn. They got his ass."

"What the fuck did he do?"

"Shh." I stare hard at the door as if I'm waiting for someone to hold up a reason-for-arrest sign. After a few more minutes, the wagon drives Chris away, and more cops come from the building holding duffle bags in each hand.

"Oh yeah, this is a drug bust." Malcolm nods. "That's probably weed."

"I don't remember Jess saying he smoked weed."

Malcolm looks at me with a "duh" look. "How would that even come up in conversation though? And you don't need to smoke it to sell it." He pauses. "We know Jess don't smoke. Right?"

"No, she doesn't," I say, still keeping my eye on the door. That's a lot of dope. He can't have done all that selling by himself.

A few more cops come out with bags. "We don't even know if it's weed. That shit could be crack or heroine or some shit," Malcolm says.

I lean back in my seat frustrated. "This nigga gon' go to jail and shit, and I didn't even get to whip his ass."

Malcolm shrugs. "That's what that nigga get though. Pussy-ass muthafucka. I hope he rot in jail—especially if he was behind your bar getting fucked up."

I clench my fists. "Let's go downtown. Bail him out and beat his ass."

Malcolm laughs.

"I'm serious."

Malcolm shakes his head, not even looking at my face. "You ain't paying nobody thousands of dollars to get them out of jail just to beat they ass. You especially ain't gonna do Chris the favor of bailing him out."

"If he got niggas, they can bail him out," I say, looking at the policemen standing around the area writing in notepads. "Then we get him."

"But how long will that take?"

I let out a breath. "I don't know."

After the cops pull off, I pull off as well. I don't follow them against my better instincts, but I go back to my bar. I can't leave it how it is right now. Inside the bar, Mort is still straightening things up. I give him a pat on the shoulder and tell him to go home and to come back early tomorrow to really get some cleaning

312

done. He thanks me, apologizes for what happened, and then leaves. I know he had a rough night dealing with the attack like this, and no one should have to go through that.

Malcolm and I set up bars on the window and take my safe out of my office and into my car to take home until I can fix my door and the few broken windows. Mort had swept up all the glass and straightened the tables, but the bar was no way near being ready to open tomorrow. There was still trash in the corners, and the floor needed a mop from the spilled liquor. All of which liquor needed to be replaced.

I shrug toward Malcolm after giving the area a final look. "I just need to start all this tomorrow. I'll call the insurance guy to come out and file that claim." I shake my head. "I just can't deal with all this shit tonight."

He nods. We take a bunch of the expensive bottles home just in case some wino wants to try his luck, but the cheap bottles we leave in there. Most of the glasses are broken anyway. I rub my temples and think about all the paperwork I'm going to have to do now and how I'm not feeling any of this.

I slam my brakes harder than I mean to when I drop Malcolm off, and he gives me a curious stare. He tells me to drive safe and I shrug, too irritated to think, let alone listen.

When I get home, it's no surprise that I can't sleep. I pace my entire house fifty times before I start seeing the sky break away to a soft blue. The blood test, Angela, and now this. I let out a frustrated breath and collapse on the couch. I rub my temples and let out a loud groan. I punch the sofa cushion beside me, and it sinks in deep. I shake my head and walk toward the shower. I'm going to have to get through another day, somehow.

Chapter Twenty-One

The next morning I'm sweeping up loose glass inside Miller House. I've already put up bars across the window and a window screen behind it until I purchase some more glass to put in. I'm still too fucking pissed that this shit happened though, and that I had not been able to take my frustrations out on the muthafuckas that did it.

Mort's here too, stacking up the new beer and liquor I brought to restock our supply. Those bastards shattered more than half of my supply, which cost me hundreds to replace. I shake my head. I swear this isn't my day.

The image of Chris getting arrested last night plays through my head like a video. He deserved it. I know he did. The most important thing is that he won't be coming anywhere near Jessica again. Whether he wanted to or not. I'm going to tell Jess what happened to him of course. Just not right now. I want to tell her face-to-face that the demon she's been having nightmares about is gone. I just wish I'd had the chance to beat his ass for what he did to my bar before he got locked up.

I hate the fact that I'm going to have to close the bar for tonight just to make sure everything can be up and running all clean and that there aren't any safety hazards to worry about. My employees are still gonna come in and help me clean up this mess and put on the final touches.

"Hey, Boss, you know what you could do?" Mort says from behind the bar. "You can have, like, another reopening and put up signs and shit. Or you can redecorate the place and make it even more of a sports bar."

I stare at him, then look at all the trash and shit I still have to clean up. "Maybe."

"I'm for real. You can add in cool new windows since you gotta get new ones anyway. Maybe some new wallpaper, some new tables, since some of them are broke. Think about it." Mort has a dreamy look in his eyes, like he has the desire to be an interior decorator. "I just think you should turn this tragedy into a new creation. You're a businessman. I know you can flip your investments." He shrugs and continues rubbing a damp rag across the bar, but the seed has already been planted in my head, and he knows it.

I look around the bar and start calculating how much it would cost to add a pool table or a foosball machine in the corner. I want to give this bar a sporty and chill vibe to it, and that's exactly what I'm going to do. The insurance should cover the costs of repairs, and I can invest some money of my own to make it even better. I set the broom down and head to my office. There's a lot of work and planning I need to do to rebuild my bar.

I nod my head to J Cole's song "Work Out" as I stand over all the paperwork and pictures on my kitchen table. I reach my hand into my bag of fries as I focus my eyes on some new table designs, new TVs, and new stereo surround-sound systems. I'm thinking about putting some stereos in the bathroom so people won't miss the game for a second. Just some rough ideas.

The sound of pounding on the door makes my head snap up. I narrow my eyes and look at the clock above the stove. It's still the early afternoon, but whoever it is at the door sure as hell wasn't invited. And Malcolm has a key, so he wouldn't bother to knock. I turn down the music on my iPhone and peek through the peephole. Oh, this should be interesting.

I swing the door open, and Angela struts into my apartment clutching her Victoria's Secret purse to her shoulder. She looks nice in her silk multicolored miniskirt and white high heels. I smile at her, but she frowns and looks at me as if I don't deserve to be in her presence or some shit, so I drop my smile and fold my arms. "What up?"

She shrugs and walks around my living room in a circle just looking at shit. "So you hear from your side chick yet about the paternity test?"

I let out a breath and let my arms fall. "She's not my side chick."

She raises one eyebrow. "What, she your main chick now? Is that how it is?"

I just stare her blankly. She cannot be serious. "Why are you here? To accuse me of more shit?"

"I just asked you if you got the paternity test back or not."

"No, I just did it yesterday."

"So you really think that baby's yours? I swear she got you fooled," Angela says, shaking her head and looking at me with pity.

I shove my hands in my pockets and remain calm. "Angela, you don't know Jessica like you think you know her."

"Oh, I know she's playing you. Look at the facts for a second here. First, she complains out the ass about Chris, but then gets engaged to him. Fact. Ends up pregnant and swears up and down its Chris's, then finds out it isn't. Fact. Now she's saying that it's yours, Chris got his niggas on the streets saying it's one of his homies', and now you feeling confident that it's yours, no questions asked? Now who sounds like the dumb ass?"

"Look—"

"Naw, Naw, let me finish," Angela says, raising a hand in the air. I raise an eyebrow at her, but she keeps talking. "All I'm saying is that I think she's playing you for a fool."

Angela lets her hand down and stares at me like she deserves an award. I shake my head and ignore everything she says. "What does this have to do with us? The main thing you should be worried about is working something out with me in our relationship. I can take care of what's going on with Jessica and my daughter."

"She's not your daughter! Bet money!"

"Shut the fuck up!" I don't mean to yell, but she's annoying the shit out of me. "You don't know shit

319

about Jessica, you don't know shit about what she did or didn't do, you don't know shit about what happened between me and her. Honestly, it all boils down to me and you. If you want to be with me, fine—we can work this out, do whatever. I'd be happy to do that, but don't you ever in your life disrespect Jessica when she's never a day in her life said anything bad about you.

"You know what she said to me after she told me I fathered Jaslene?" I continue stepping closer to her. "She said I could pretend that Jaslene wasn't mine. She said she didn't want to hurt you, and she didn't want us to break up. She's never tried to take me away from you—she freakin' liked you! You were always the one to fuckin' push her away and give her the cold shoulder from your own insecurities, and it's so fucking annoying. Get over it!"

"Get over it? You expect me to just get over what you did to me? You cheated on me, you lied to me, you had a baby on me, and you actually claiming that child and you expect me to just be like 'oh, okay, no big deal—this shit happens'? You fucking crazy for real."

"So what you want to do?" I ask, throwing my arms in the air. She doesn't say anything but stares at me. Not with hard eyes but with eyes taking in all the

ways she just listed of how I did her wrong. She looks
. . . disappointed.

I rub my hand over my face and take a deep breath.
"Look, Ang, I love you. You know I do. We been
through a lot of shit together, but at the same time this
whole paternity issue and hatred you have for her has
to stop if we're gonna work this out between us. And I
want to work this out between us. I want you to move
back in with me because frankly I'm lonely as fuck
without you. But you're gonna have to talk to me, not
yell. The shit me and you got to work out is between
me and you. Not Jessica, not your sister or your other
girlfriends, not anyone but us. So it don't matter what
the results of this test are 'cause at the end of the day
it's me and you anyway, so what you wanna do?"

She doesn't say anything for a while. But a few
moments later she shakes her head slowly. "I was
supposed to be the one to have your first child. I loved
you first, and now she fuckin' took that away from me.
I hate her!"

"I can understand that, Ang." I'm face-to-face with
her now, and I'm tempted to put my arms around her
but I don't. "But in that case you should hate me too."

She pushes me away. "I'm not supposed to hate
you! You're supposed to keep your dick in your pants
and not cheat on me! Why should I get back with
you?"

I don't know what to tell her, and it stings my chest. I hate myself for hurting her this bad especially when she didn't do anything against me to deserve this. "I would love for us to work this out, Ang. But I understand if you don't want to. What happened with us was completely my fault, and I'd love for us to eventually move past it because I love you. So at this point it's up to you."

Angela's quiet for a few moments. She's not staring at me but staring at the carpet beneath her. Suddenly she looks up at me, square in the eye. "You ain't shit. You don't deserve me, but I'll give you another chance for three reasons—"

"Wait, wait. We ain't working shit out if you're gonna be disrespectful."

"You was being disrespectful when you fucked her, so do you want to work this shit out or what?"

"Why do you want to?" I ask, brushing her comments off and trying to stay focused.

"If we don't get back together, then it'll be like she won and our relationship is destroyed—"

"She never wanted us to break up. I told you that."

"Two, I don't want you being single, and y'all two end up together playing family when it should be us—"

"What? Playing family? How would she and I even—"

322

"And three, I'm the only woman that's having your kids from now on, starting now—'cause I'm pregnant."

She smiles when says this, but all I can do is stare back.

"What. The. Fuck?"

Angela nods and rubs her stomach. "Yup, just found out last week. I think I'm about a month along," she says, smiling at her abdomen.

I raise an eyebrow in suspicion. "You're pregnant?"

"Yup."

"Right now as we speak?" I can't hide the skepticism in my voice, and she picks up on it and rolls her eyes.

"Yes, I am. Damn."

I keep staring at her face, waiting for the slightest hint that she could be lying, but a full minute passes and she doesn't. I close my eyes and take a moment to take in what all this means. She's pregnant with my second child, and I haven't even gotten over having my first one. When could she have gotten pregnant? We haven't been separated that long, maybe two weeks. Did she get pregnant before she left? She must have.

I open my eyes and shake my head slowly. Not only is my head spinning but I feel like my life in

323

general is getting out of control. How do I get back to normal? What is normal anymore?

"So what now?" I ask her, keeping my voice even and calm.

"I'll have to move back in with you, I guess," she says, shrugging, but her words sound too premeditated.

I fold my arms. "As a couple or as someone who needs a place to stay?"

"Why you being so cold?" she asks, giving an innocent smile.

"I'm not. Just trying to understand."

"Well, if you think me moving in is the best thing, then I should. That's the proper way to raise a baby anyway. Split homes never work out."

My jaw twitches. I know she's taking a jab at how Jessica and I are raising Jaslene with me going down there to see her and her eventually coming up here to stay with me sometimes when she gets older. Well, eventually she and Jaslene are going to have to get along. Angela's going to have to show as much love to her as she will to her own baby.

I shake off the comment for now and focus on Angela's pregnancy. I can't remember the last time we had sex, but I know she's on the pill. At least she was the last time we fucked. I narrow my eyes at her and remember way back when Jessica was still pregnant. Angela was all over her, trying to figure out everything she needed to know about babies. She's wanted to have this baby for a while now, and I guess she's finally succeeded. Too bad I don't remember making it happen.

"What happen with the pills, Ang?" I ask as casually as I can muster.

"Forgot to take a few. Had sex. Got pregnant. These things happen," she says. Perfectly again.

I let out a breath. "Whatever," I say. I'm not done questioning her yet, but I have a few other things I need to take care of first, including fixing my bar. "When you gonna move your things back in?"

She smiles triumphantly. "I'll be back here later tonight."

Chapter Twenty-Two

I'm in the passenger seat in Malcolm's car, driving over to see Jaslene in Aurora and to get the results of the paternity test. Jessica told me it came it the mail last night and that she wasn't going to touch it at all until I got there. It's been three days since Angela announced her pregnancy, and for some weird reason I don't feel good about it. After she announced her pregnancy, she insisted she move back in, and part of me is thinking she wants to be pregnant for the sole purpose of rubbing it in Jessica's face in a "ha-ha, you can't have him" sort of way. I don't know, maybe I'm wrong and just tripping, but her willingness to get back together seems . . . suspicious. Malcolm volunteered to drive to give my car a break traveling back and forth from Chicago and Aurora so much. I think he doesn't want me to drive, claiming I drive based on what my emotional level is.

I turn the radio down once we're deep in Chicago's rush-hour traffic. "Do you think it's mine, bro?"

"Angela's baby? I don't know. I guess." Malcolm shrugs, still keeping his eyes on the road. "Don't you want it to be yours?"

"Yes, but wanting something and getting something don't always coincide."

"That's true, but why you doubting this baby when you didn't really doubt Jessica's baby?" He laughs after thinking about it. "You're backward."

Hmmph. "Two different people."

He nods. "If I was you, I wouldn't worry about it too much. After all the shit that's been going on, you need to focus on what you know for sure. So when we see Jaslene's test today, you gon' know the truth. And if you want to eventually down the road somewhere test Angela's baby, then you can do that too. I mean shit—it ain't nothing but a test. Basically a simple yes or no answer: 'Is it yours or not,' right? It is what it is, so don't sweat it. Right now, anyway."

I nod. He's right. I don't want to be worrying about shit I don't need to be worrying about right now.

"So what happened with y'all? Did you and Angela work something out or—"

"She moved back in." I stare at a passing sign saying how many more miles to Aurora. "We're taking it slow."

"You miss her, don't you?" Malcolm asks, and I turn around to catch him staring at me.

"Who? Jaslene? Of course, I miss Jaslene."

"I mean Jessica, nigga."

I laugh then shrug. "I talked to her last night when Angela was in the shower. Just for a second though."

"Does Angela know you still be talking to Jess?"

"Yeah, she knows. She doesn't say anything because she knows I have to stay in communication with Jessica because of our daughter. So most of the time she just gives me evil stares while Jessica tells me about Jaslene over the phone."

"Oohhh. That sounds uncomfortable."

I laugh. "Get yo' feminine ass—"

"What? I'm just saying I wouldn't want to live like that." Malcolm smiles and shakes his head.

"Me neither. That's why it's taking so long for our relationship to get back where it was."

Malcolm just shakes his head again. "I don't get why you putting up with her."

"I love her despite a lot of shit. I ain't perfect either."

"Naw, no one is. Except me." Malcolm gives a brilliant smile, showing his pearly whites.

I shake my head and stare at the road again. I start fidgeting in my seat in anticipation for the traffic to move faster again. That's what I try telling myself, but I know that's not the real reason. I know it's because I can't wait to see Jessica.

"Let me tell you what I found out about Chris though," Malcolm says, dragging me out of my daydream.

"I ran into my nigga Rorrell at the shop where I was getting my hair braided since somebody's baby momma didn't want to do it, but never mind. Anyway, Rorrell told me that he heard something from his guy that Chris caught some heavy time for heavy drug possession with intent to sell. I think he got like five-to-ten-something years. Something like that. That nigga fucked," Malcolm says with a smile on his face.

I smile too. In all honesty, it's what that nigga deserves.

Jessica's sitting on the porch with her hair draped over one shoulder. She smiles brighter when she notices us pull up in front of the house and she starts walking toward the car. I climb out and spring my arms open, and she collapses in my arms. We hold each other tight, and I take in the smell of her strawberry mango fragrance.

After a few seconds of this I peek up and catch Malcolm smiling at me before wiggling his eyebrows. "What?" I mouth, but he doesn't respond and goes into the house.

Jessica, oblivious to Malcolm's facial expression, looks up at me. "I have something to show you."

I nod and we head into Mom's house. The smell of cinnamon smacks me in the face the second I come through the door. I look around and spot Mom sitting at the kitchen table wearing just a dress and an apron around her waist. "Hey, boy!" she shouts over, smiling. "Your girl been crying for you."

Malcolm laughs. "Which one?" Malcolm says, nodding at Jessica and then nodding down the hallway where Jaslene was probably sleeping in her room.

I roll my eyes, and Jessica looks confused but leans me toward the hallway. I give my mom a kiss on the cheek and peek in the kitchen long enough to see a whole tray of homemade cinnabons on top of the stove. My stomach growls in response, and I remember I haven't eaten anything since last night. I was up picking out new decorations and equipment to redo my bar, and Angela wanting to "talk about things" didn't add to my sleep hours either.

Once I'm inside Jaslene's room, Jessica shuts the door. The room is halfway dark because the light is off and halfway lit because of the window with the low shade in the corner of the room. Jaslene's in the crib, and I can tell she just woke up by the fluttering of her eyes. I reach in and scoop her up and kiss her repeatedly. I know Jessica is about to show the test results she didn't open yet, and somehow I feel like snatching Jaslene up and running off with her—just in case my worst fear comes true.

"I have the envelope right here," Jessica says, walking over to the bed. She pulls the gold envelope from beneath a pillow and sits down. She pats the seat next to her, and I sit down too. "I didn't touch it or anything. I don't want you thinking I did anything with it."

"I know. You told me. I believe you," I say. For a split second I see a weird look on her face, but she quickly changes it to a smile. I think about what I said and realize that if I really believed her, we wouldn't be opening a letter about a paternity test in the first place.

Jessica lays the envelope on the bed in the space between us. She reaches out her arms for Jaslene, and I slide her over to her mother. I pick up the envelope and examine it. The tape doesn't look broken or reattached. I slide my finger under it and rip open the letter. I pull out the contents to see the words for myself in black and white.

My eyes roam the page quickly, and I find what I'm looking for. I let out a slow, steady breath when I realize the truth. I toss the envelope in the air and wrap my arms around Jessica. Before she can say anything, I kiss her deeply. I kiss her like she's given me the greatest gift of my life. Because she has. She's given me a daughter.

Part Three:

Jessica

Chapter Twenty-Three

I'm lost in Jaylen's kiss and am unable to think clearly or rationally. I just sit there and let him kiss me while I hold our daughter in my arms. I don't try to stop him even though I know I should. What's worse is after a few more seconds I start returning his kiss with a lot more urgency in my lip movements. I don't know if he notices, but I do want him and I do miss him.

The bedroom door creaks open, and Jaylen and I pull apart and stare at Malcolm's bulging eyes. "Oh my bad, y'all! Y'all keep going," Malcolm says, closing the door behind him, but Jaylen jumps up and follows him out of the room. The door's closed but I can still hear them talking. I stand and walk closer to the door to listen.

"Aw, you can go back in there, Jay. You know I ain't trying to cock-block shit," Malcolm says.

"Naw, naw, we was doing nothing. We were just—"

"Bro, you ain't got to explain shit to me," Malcolm says, and I can hear him laughing now. "I understand."

Suddenly the bedroom door opens up again, and I step back. Malcolm smiles at me, then smiles at Jaylen. He nudges Jaylen toward the room. "Y'all can go back in the room. I'll leave y'all alone." He winks and I roll my eyes.

"We good, bro," Jaylen says, shaking his head but not looking in my direction. It wasn't as if I was going to give him a look to agree with Malcolm's suggestion.

"Yeah, whatever you say," Malcolm says, still smiling in my direction.

I needed a distraction. "Don't you want to see your niece while you're here?" I ask, already passing Jaslene to his arms.

"Oh yeah, sure," he stutters, and scoops her close to his chest. "So the test is positive. I mean, she's yours?" He's looking at Jaylen, who just smiles and nods.

I'm staring up at Jaylen, lost in his sparkling eyes as he admires Jaslene in her uncle's arms. Oh my God. I love that man so much.

I gasp and look down at the carpet. I can feel both sets of eyes on me, but I don't meet them. "Let's go eat those cinnabons," I suggest, walking back down the hallway toward the kitchen. "I'm starving for this snack."

Sheri's standing in front of the tray of cinnabons with a spatula in her hand. "Yeah, y'all come over and eat. I put my feet up in this one."

She takes the spatula and scrapes up a bon. It's already dripping with frosting, and for a second I'm just staring at it like I've never seen one before. The truth is, I've never seen one look so good.

I feel a hand press on my lower back, and I look over my shoulder. Jaylen smiles at me, and my heart catches in my throat. "You gon' get one or you just gon' stare at one?" he teases as he continues to press his palm into my lower back. He's nudging me forward, but the touch is so gentle and feels so nice, I hesitate moving just so I can feel his hands on me a second longer.

"Hey, yo, Jess," Malcolm says, coming up on my other side holding a crying Jaslene in his hands. "I think she hungry."

I sigh. Not because I don't feel like breast-feeding but because it forces me to leave Jaylen's touch. I grasp Jaslene in my arms and take a seat at the kitchen table.

"Wrap your titties up if you gon' feed her in front of the guys," Sheri says, placing treat after treat onto a plate.

Jaylen stands behind the chair I'm seated in, and I fight the urge to look up at him and plant a kiss on his lips. I can't believe I have such intense feelings for him like this. Maybe because he's single now after breaking up with Angela, it makes me feel more comfortable with my letting my feelings surface in my consciousness.

I unbutton my blouse with my free hand and try to keep my breast concealed as I position Jaslene beneath me. She latches quickly, and I'm thankful. Malcolm looks from me to the plate of cinnabons on the table. "Do you want Jaylen to feed you one while you're breast-feeding Jaslene?"

I start blushing super hard, not believing he said that right in front of his mom. "No thank you, I'm fine." I can't see Jaylen's face from behind me, but I hope he's giving Malcolm a nasty look. Just because he caught us kissing doesn't mean we're gonna end up together. Not that I would really mind it.

Sheri gives Jaylen a raised eyebrow but doesn't say anything, which is a lot to be thankful for. Jaylen goes around the chair and eats a cinnabon on his own. He, Malcolm, and their mom make small talk for a while, and I catch Jaylen watching me more than once. I want to say something to him. I want to say something cool, but I really don't know where to start. Do I ask him about Angela? Did they get back together?

Soon Jaslene is finished with my milk, and I'm grateful. Of course, by this time everyone else is done eating, but we're all still just sitting around the table like one big family. I smile when I think of us as that. One big family sitting around the kitchen table talking about nothing.

"What you smiling for?" Malcolm asks, bringing all eyes on me again.

"Nothing," I say, looking down at Jaslene. "I'm just happy." I look up and see Jaylen staring intensely at me, then smile.

"That's good. Yes, we got a lot to be thankful for this year. We got a lot of blessings, with Jaslene being the main one," Sheri says.

"She's my everything," I say.

Jaylen rises from his seat, and my eyes follow him automatically. "You want to go for a walk?" he asks, nodding toward the front door. I nod and stand up with Jaslene in my arms. "We'll be right back," Jaylen calls from over his shoulder. He grabs Jaslene's baby bag by the door and holds the door open for us as we walk out. I feel like I'm forgetting something, but one look into Jaylen's eyes, I even forget where I am. This man should not have this strong effect on me.

When we get outside, however, we walk to the car. I think nothing of it and buckle Jaslene into the baby seat in the back. We drive about two blocks to the park Jaylen and I used to play at when we were kids. He kills the engine, but he doesn't get out. He just looks at me with such sweet gentle eyes, I collapse my fingers together to resist stroking his cheeks. He's so handsome to me. "Yes?" I ask.

"There's some stuff I got to tell you. Some stuff you should know, and it's not right to keep it hidden from you."

"Oh." Is he about to tell me how he feels about me? Is that okay? How does he feel? Should I tell him I love him? Should I tell him I dream about him? He is single now, technically, so it should be okay. But what if he doesn't want to say those thoughts? What if he doesn't even feel those thoughts?

He gives me this weird look, and I know he was trying to read my facial expression—the one I make when I'm thinking too much. He shakes his head and doesn't say anything about my thoughts. Instead, he leans back in the seat and says, "Chris and about two other dudes came up in Miller and started vandalizing shit. They had weapons, but no one was hurt too bad. They caught two of the guys, but Chris got away. We figured it was Chris and went to his house, only to see him get caught up in a drug bust."

I don't say anything as a bunch of emotions and thoughts wash over me. Chris? He brings up Chris, of all things, of all people. Then I think about the bar, and I hate that man even more. How dare he even attempt to pull off some shit like that? I shake my head and look Jaylen in the eye. "I am so sorry about what Chris did, Jaylen. I don't know what to tell you. I feel like it's my fault that he wanted to take revenge on you. You beat his ass because he was beating on me. Then he goes and destroys your bar. I'll come up there and help you rebuild the bar as soon as I can."

Jaylen laughs softly despite the mood the news brought on. "You don't have to help me, Jess. I just wanted to keep you informed about what's going on. You don't have to worry about that man anymore and he's not going to be interfering in your life again. I'm fixing up the bar, making it better than it ever was. Using the insurance money on the claim I'm filing."

"Oh. I mean, cool, great." Okay, so he wasn't going to say I love you. Maybe if I say it, it will brighten the mood or at least make him feel better. I think. I don't know what telling him my feelings will actually do for us both. I know he still loves Angela. In all honesty, I think he will keep loving her whether he loves me or not. I shake my head. As much as I think I know the truth, it doesn't make dealing with it any easier. I take a deep breath and decide to tell him anyway.

"Angela moved back in," he says.

I let the air in my mouth deflate. Move in? She moved back in? Then that means they must have . . . worked things out.

"Oh. Great. I'm so happy for you," I say, looking down at my hands. I wish Jaslene was in my arms so I could use her as an excuse to avoid his eyes. I have a thousand butterflies trying to break out of my stomach, and I catch myself fidgeting. Don't cry, Jess. Don't cry.

"Are you okay?" he asks, wrapping his arm around my shoulder. He uses his hand to move my face toward him, and I can't avoid his eyes anymore. "What's wrong?"

I think about lying or changing the subject, but I know he'll see right through it, so I just sigh and speak my mind. "That was . . . fast."

Jaylen nods. "It's really weird actually. Well, she was acting weird. She says she's pregnant, but I'm not sure."

Someone just ran up to me with a knife and stabbed my stomach. Pregnant? Her? Oh my God. Why? An image of Angela's evil smile flashes in front of me. She's having his child. Their own family. A real one. I suck in a breath and hold it tight as if it would hold the pieces of my heart together, but I know it won't.

"Congratulations," I say, releasing my breath, hoping my voice sounds sincere for his sake.

"Thanks," he mumbles, as if he doesn't feel like being congratulated. Then I remember what he just said about him doubting the pregnancy.

"Why don't you think she's pregnant?"

"Part of me thinks she's saying it just to get back with me."

"Why would she want to get back with you?" I ask. He gives me a weird look, and I gasp. "No! Not like that. I mean, why would she be willing to go back with you if she's still upset about Jaslene being your baby."

Jaylen removes his arms, puts his hands behind his head, and leans back in his seat. "At the time she didn't know for sure if Jaslene was mine. She also didn't want you . . . I mean she didn't want us to break up over this, basically. I think." I tilt my head in confusion, but he just shrugs. "Just know I think it's suspicious."

"I don't think you have anything to worry about. I don't think she'd lie about being pregnant," I say honestly.

"Have you met this woman?" Jaylen says with a hint of a smile on his lips.

"Then why are you with her?" I ask before I can stop myself.

He looks at the street ahead of us and the park to our left. After a while he turns to me to give an answer, and it sounds like the kind of answer you give by default. "I love her."

"Does she still love you? Even after all this?" I ask, sounding slightly more determined to figure out his mind and why he likes her so much.

He thinks about his answer before replying. "She's willing to give us another chance, so I guess she's still got some love there somewhere for me."

But I love you too, I cry out in my mind, but I won't bring myself to admit it. At least not right now anyway. Nothing would come of it, and because he's already back in a relationship. I feel the urge to cry again, but I hate crying in front of people. I don't speak or respond in any way to this statement because I don't want to start the waterworks. I don't know if he really intended to tell me all this stuff when we headed out for this "walk," but somehow, right now, it feels more like I'm getting dumped.

"What, Jessica?" I don't say anything. He sits up straight and pulls me into his arms and cradles me like a baby. "Tell me."

How can I say how I feel right now? After all the things he said to me about starting over again with Angela? I can't tell him how I feel. Not now, but I do want him to know I'm okay. Or for him to at least think I'm okay.

I press my lips against his neck while in his arms, and right away I can feel his whole body stiffen beneath me. I don't know if I did a safe thing, but he doesn't move, and I know 100 percent that he felt it. I pull back just a little and kiss him once, softly, on the lips. He's left staring so rigid and sexy at my lips, and then at my eyes, that I just want to push the seats down and take him right now. I mentally shake the thought off though.

"Congratulations on becoming a father again, Jay. I really mean that. I want you to be happy—no matter who you're with. And I, um . . . you're a great father, and any child is lucky to . . . any woman, for that matter, is lucky to have you. Angela is the luckiest woman in the world." I smile, but I think it's coming off as a sad smile because he doesn't smile back.

He nods though, and for some reason—maybe it's the long friendship we've had or the amount of time we've spent together—I think he can tell what I was trying to say by the words I didn't say. If that makes sense. I don't know what would have happened if he came back to Aurora single. I would have definitely told him my feelings, but I think he knows. I'm not sure, but I think he does.

He doesn't say his thoughts out loud, whatever they may be, but he pulls me tight into his arms again, and I breathe a lot better than when I wasn't in them. It's weird, but it feels like the closer I am to him—the person I'm not supposed to be close to—the more I want be close to him, because he's the only person in this whole wide world who understands me, and I know deep down in my heart that I can never really truly be happy with somebody else because I love him. He's Jaylen. He's my Jaylen.

Chapter Twenty-Four

Sheri bursts into my room the next morning just as I hear the sound of Jaslene's cry echoing down the hallway. "Time to get up. Your baby's crying."

I'm not even sitting up fully when twenty pounds falls on my chest. "Hold her while I warm up one of her breast-milk bottles."

The sound of the door closing gives me a headache. Jaslene's drooling, and I wipe the spit off her mouth. I don't know what it is, but I'm just not feeling it today. I feel like crap.

I press a finger against Jaslene's balled-up fist until she grabs my finger in her grip. I kiss her good morning, and she smiles back as if I told her a funny secret. "I wish your father was here," I say, even though she doesn't understand me.

I shake my head and stand up slowly. I feel weak, like I've been crying the whole night. Probably because I have. I couldn't get my mind off Jaylen and how much I want to be with him. I also feel horrible that a part me wishes he never got back with his girlfriend. I don't know if it's too much to ask, but deep down I kind of picture me and Jaylen and Jaslene as a family.

After our conversation in the car yesterday we drove back to his mom's house, and we went in and sat down like nothing happened. Like nothing was discussed, but it was different around him. It wasn't exactly like we were avoiding looking at each other, but we didn't hold eye contact, and the vibe in the room just felt sad. It was hard watching him leave again knowing that he was going back home to Angela, but I kept a strong face and smiled when I said good-bye.

I blow out a breath and go into the kitchen and see Sheri standing behind the bottle warmer on the counter. I take a seat at the table and try not to look as tired as I am. "Long night?" she asks, taking out a skillet from the cabinet.

I just nod.

"What you and Jaylen talk about when y'all went for that walk yesterday?"

My head snapped up. "What do you mean?"

Sheri shrugs as she opens the fridge. "Y'all came back looking all depressed. Not in the face, but in the eyes. I saw it. Y'all can't get nothing past me."

I wasn't surprised that she saw me look sad but Jaylen looked sad? I mean, disappointed? Oh my God. Does he regret his decision to go back to Angela?

Before I let myself get too excited, I remind myself that Angela is pregnant and of the fact that Jaylen's been dying to get back with her. Maybe his disappointed eyes were disappointment for me. Like an "I feel sorry for you" disappointment.

I sink lower in my chair, and Sheri gives me her narrowed eyes, and I sit straight up again. "We just talked about him and Angela. The two of them . . . um. They worked things out."

"Well, that's good." Sheri hands me Jaslene's bottle, which I take quickly. I rub Jaslene's lips with the nipple until she opens her mouth to suck. For a few minutes I just watch her eat and avoid looks from Sheri as she cooks.

Just as she starts to say something, I hear my cell phone ringing from the bedroom. My heart rate immediately speeds up, and I can't get to the phone soon enough, but I have no choice but to move slowly and carefully with Jaslene in my arms. I stand and take slow, gradual steps back to my room ignoring Sheri's mumbles.

My phone is silent again by the time I enter my room, but I quickly pick it up, press Redial, and cradle the phone between my ear and my shoulder. I don't take the time to look at the caller ID, but as soon as I hear the voice over the phone, I'm immediately disappointed.

"Girl, you will not believe the grade I got on my exam," Kayla says when she picks up the phone. "I got a freakin' C! I'm like, what the fuck? I studied too hard for that test, and now all that hard work was for nothing. Can you believe this? This is the worst thing that can happen in my life."

"I think you're being overdramatic. There're a lot of things that can go wrong in your life, and getting a lower grade than you expected is not the worst." I hate that I'm coming off with an attitude, but it makes no sense for her to be complaining about that when I'm dealing with something a lot more serious, and worse—a lot of stuff out of my control. And somehow that feels worse.

"Yeah. I know, but at the same time I had goals. I wanted all A's, and now this is going to affect my final score for the class. I know you've got a lot going on too, and I don't want to seem like a spoiled brat, but I mean . . . school is important too, you know."

I take a deep breath and look down at Jaslene as she continues to suck. "Yeah, I know it's important."

"When are you going back again? You know you've been saying you're goin' back over and over again, but I still don't hear nothing about you being enrolled in anything down there."

"I'm going to go to school. I just need some things to be a little more stable first."

"Stable? Like what? Jaslene? Your baby daddy's mom can watch her while you're at school. I bet she won't have a problem with that." She has a point there. Sheri has been nagging me about school ever since I moved down here.

"I mean, stable in my life overall. Things just keep getting more complicated for me."

I can hear her take a breath. "Look—things are always going to stay complicated. If they don't, then life would be boring. What I'm saying is, girl, you have to take the leap and just go back to school. There's never going to be a perfect time, so you waiting is not going to help anyone."

"Well . . ."

"Think about it. It would be better to go to school now then when Jaslene has to go to school too, and you'll have to worry about transportation and all that other stuff, so if you get your degree while she's still young, you can go on to bigger and better things. Like getting an apartment down there."

I laugh despite my mood. "I'll need a job first."

"Well then, find a job. Damn, girl—it's not rocket science. Get your goals in order. Okay, see—I'll help you. First, get in school. Second, find a job. Third, get an apartment. Fourth, find a man. If you can find a man at school or at work, then you'll already be ahead," she says, and I laugh again.

"Well, that's a thought, I guess."

"Yes, and it's something that you can do too. I'm telling you, Jess. You just need to take it one step at a time. Don't let shit with this whole baby daddy drama hold you down. This is still your life—remember that."

"I will."

"Okay. Well, let me talk to you later. I have to bang my head over my desk a few times over this grade I got. Love you!" She hangs up, and I lean over the phone chuckling again. I feel a lot better after talking to her, and my mood has shifted. I look down at Jaslene and realize she finished her bottle, and I set it aside. I pick her up and keep patting her back until she lets out a satisfying burp, and once again I smile.

Sheri comes into my room telling me that breakfast is ready, and I follow her back into the kitchen. As we eat she talks about her plans of going to the grocery store, and I nod my head to feign interest. It's not that I think she's boring; my mind is just on other things right now.

"You should get out the house today, girl," Sheri says, leaning back and patting her round belly. "You been stuck in this house too much."

I shrug and plop another piece of bacon into my mouth.

"What you need to do is go down to that college I was telling you about yesterday. That nice community college, where you can enroll yourself in for next fall. They have some great programs you can get into about art and taking pictures, I think."

She flicks her hand as she says the last sentence as if my love for photography was just some hobby or toy. I stand and place Jaslene into her arms. "Sure," I say, more ready to leave the room than continue the conversation. "Let me just shower first."

I unlock the door to Sheri's house and stomp my wet shoes inside. I reach up and ring the water out of my hair like a mop. That's April's rains for you.

"Was it raining outside?" Sheri says, peeking over her newspaper while Jaslene naps in her swing at Sheri's foot.

I let out a puff of breath and raise my arms from my sides. Heavy drops of rain fall from my coat and onto the brown-and-black carpet. "What gave it away?"

She shakes her head and looks back down at her paper. I roll my eyes when she's not looking and take off my shoes. I just want to take a hot bath filled to the brim with pink-and-white bubbles and listen to some R&B.

I start walking toward the bathroom, when my phone rings. I pull the phone out of my pocket and immediately my mood shifts, and I smile from ear to ear. "Hi," I say, opening the bathroom door and flicking on the light. The bathroom is pretty small and only fits a tub with a connecting shower overhead, a toilet, and a sink right beside it. The room's one solid rectangle, just like a motel room bathroom.

"How are you?" His voice is deep and smooth, and my stomach catches butterflies again. How can I feel this way with him just asking a simple question?

"I'm good, Jaylen. How are you?" I say, probably not sounding half as sexy as I want to sound.

"Hi, Jess!" Another man's voice sounds over the phone. His voice is just as deep with a bit of huskiness to it. "We just called to see how you was doing."

I smile anyway. "Hello, Malcolm."

"So what you up to?" Malcolm asks, starting off the conversation.

"Just got home. I was at the community college here and went there to complete the enrollment application. I also walked around to look to see if they were hiring in the area," I say, cutting the hot water on full blast. I take a seat on the tub.

"Aw, cool, cool, cool. I see you trying to get your life together. That's what's up," Malcolm says.

"How's Jaslene?" Jaylen asks, and I'm happily reminded that he's on the phone too.

"She's awesome. She's taking a nap next to her grandmother in the living room. I'm about to take a bath and relax for a while. I got caught in a flash rain. So random," I say, reaching underneath the sink to grab the bubble bath. I twist open the top, and bubble gum flavor floods out. Ooh, I cannot wait for this bath.

I hear Jaylen laugh softly over the phone, and I get that fluttery feeling in my chest again. I shake my head and smile while pouring the soap into the waterfall. "So, Malcolm, are you over Jaylen's house or is he over at yours?"

"I'm over at his," Jaylen says. "I needed to get out of the house for a while."

I cut on some of the cold water into the tub so I won't cook. "Because of Angela?" I ask, even though I can already guess his answer.

"Yup," Jaylen says.

"She was annoying his ass off with baby names, and these regulations she's come up with about you," Malcolm adds.

"What. . .regulations? What does that mean?" I ask, ignoring the wariness of my voice.

"Who knows what that shit means, man," Malcolm says.

"I'll explain it to you when I come see you this weekend," Jaylen says in a slow, trailing voice. I get the hint that the topic isn't his favorite, but I can't get it out of my mind. What does she mean by regulations?"

I cut the cold water off and let the water blast hot till the tub is three quarters of the way full before shutting if off completely. "Can't you come sooner? To talk about this, I mean?"

"Damn, girl. You gon' see yo' baby daddy soon. He wanna see your ass too, I know."

"Shut up, Malcolm," Jaylen says while my cheeks warm. Why did Malcolm have to say exactly what I was thinking and hoping?

"I'll talk to you guys later. I'm about to get in this tub and relax," I say, already starting to flick my socks off.

"Okay, have a good night," Jaylen says.

"You too."

"Oh, you guys suck," Malcolm says. "Jaylen, say your feelings when you get off the phone. Never mind, he's shy. I'll say it. Love you, Jessica!"

Now I'm blushing for real. "Okay, good night," I say quickly before I can hear Jaylen object or yell at Malcolm.

"You forced it on that one, bro," I hear Jaylen say softly right before I hang up.

I shake my head and bite back a smile. I've never pictured Jaylen as the shy one or the one who can be embarrassed. He's never come off that way. I'm not even sure if what Malcolm says is how Jaylen feels. If he loves me or not. I mean, love me in a romantic, "let's be a family" way. Probably not, since he's just gotten back with his girlfriend that he's madly in love with. The same girlfriend that has apparently come up with regulations for Jaylen coming down here to see me and Jaslene. I hope it ain't anything stupid. But I know Jaylen wouldn't agree to anything stupid or anything that would lessen his time with Jaslene, so there's nothing to worry about there at least. It has to be about seeing less of me, which is understandable since I did get pregnant by her man.

I finish getting undressed and stand up in the tub. I sit down slowly, letting all the stress and excitement from the week soak away. I had placed my cell phone right on top of the sink for easy access. I keep the bathroom door cracked so I could hear if Jaslene wakes up and starts crying. Sheri's in there watching her, but I don't want her to feel too overwhelmed since I was gone for four hours. Eventually I shake my head and lean back, but right before I'm about to close my eyes, my cell phone starts ringing again.

I groan, reaching up and drying my hands on the towel that is on bar above the tub. "Hello," I say, letting my irritation show in my voice.

"Hey, girl, what's wrong with you?" Kayla asks, smacking over the phone.

"I was just relaxing in the bathtub when you called. What's up?"

Kayla stops smacking, pauses, then starts smacking again. I don't know what she's eating, but she has to be one of the most disgusting eaters I know. Maybe even worse than Malcolm. "We need to hang out," she says. "I'm bored as hell, and I know you're bored too. I haven't seen you since you moved away, and you're not even that far."

I think about this. I do miss Kayla a lot, and I know it was random of me to drop out of school and move to a different city with hardly any warning. That wasn't really cool. "Sure. Absolutely, Kayla. Whatever you want to do."

I'm sitting up in the bathtub, no longer lying against the rim. I rest my arms on the edge of the tub just to ensure I don't accidently drop my phone in the water. "Let's hang out this weekend," Kayla shouts excitedly.

I groan, knowing we can't because of Jaylen's planned visit. I can't, nor do I have any desire to, cancel that, especially since he has to tell me something important. "How about some time this week instead?"

"I work and have school during the week. Why can't we do it this weekend?"

"Jaylen comes to see Jaslene over the weekend."

"Oh. Well, how about he comes to see Jaslene and he brings you here to Chicago on his way back? We hang out, and then I'll drop you back off. Unless you want to sleep over."

"Huh? I mean, um, okay. Go back to Chicago? I don't know. I haven't been there since the whole paternity case incident. The first one anyway."

"Ohmygod. Who the fuck cares? There's plenty women out there getting paternity tests on people that ain't the father. You ain't the first, and you certainly ain't the last, so get over it. When you think about it, nobody really cares. They got they own drama to deal with."

A laugh escapes my lips. "Okay. Yeah, you right." It isn't like I'm going to run into Chris. He's in jail now.

"Good. So whenever Jaylen leaves your house, ride back with him and have him drop you off at my house. You can bring the baby if Sheri doesn't want to babysit."

"Okay."

"Love you. I'm about to finish eating this prime steak I got from the corner store."

I laugh. "What corner store sells prime steak?"

She smacks her lips at me. "Girl, bye."

I set the phone back on the sink and lean back in the tub. I can no longer have a thoughtless bath, but I like the thoughts that are filling my mind. I can't wait to spend some quality time with Kayla. It's like she's the only one outside of my situation looking in that can really give me a good perspective of what's going on.

Of course, Jaylen stays a constant presence in my thoughts no matter what I do. I take a deep breath and just enjoy the scent of the bubbles. I'm glad I chose this scent. It's my favorite fragrance next to . . . him. Dang it. He still can't leave my thoughts.

I get out of the tub a half hour later and go back to my room. I get dressed and then play with Jaslene until she falls asleep as we watch Teletubbies reruns in the living room.

Chapter Twenty-Five

I snuggle with Jaslene on my lap while sitting in the living room waiting for her father to pull up. Saturday could not have come fast enough, and it feels like the more I wished it was Saturday, the slower the week passed.

I look at my leg and frown. I can tell most of Jaslene's bouncing has to do with my fidgeting leg and not due to me manually causing the shakes. But Jaslene's smiling with her mouth open anyway, having the time of her life. I'm holding her underneath her armpits to keep her balance, and I swear she's the only person keeping me sane while I'm waiting.

I keep stealing glances from her to watch the door, waiting for Jaylen to come through any second. He called and said he was less than ten minutes away, but fifteen minutes has already gone by.

I'm fully dressed, ready to spend the day or night with Kayla whenever Jaylen leaves here. My heart starts racing when I hear the doorknob turn. I stop bouncing Jaslene and stand up, a huge smile on my face already.

Jaylen comes through the door, and a smile tugs his lips when he sees us standing in his mother's toy-scattered living room. "You look . . . good," he says, walking over and wrapping his arms around me and Jaslene.

I'm not wearing anything out of the ordinary—just some pink sweatpants and a bubblegum-pink T-shirt. Since I'm going to be staying overnight at Kayla's, I figure I don't really need to dress up.

"Thanks," I say, still not able to hide my blush. "I just put something on for the trip back."

"You straightened your hair."

"Oh." I forgot I had washed and pressed my hair last night. So that's what he meant. "Thank you."

Jaylen reaches up and twirls a finger around a strand that falls past my shoulders. "I love your hair."

I'm grinning now, and I would have stayed like that, grinning like an idiot in his face, if it wasn't for

Sheri walking into the living room. She's holding a little black radio with a long antenna sticking out. "Hey, baby!" she says, walking over to Jaylen and giving him a hug. "My radio is broken, and I can't fix the darn thing. Come over to the kitchen table and take a look at it for me."

I follow the two of them into the kitchen and watch Jaylen tinkle with her old radio. I don't want to seem like I don't give a crap about her broken radio and only want to spend time with Jaylen and Jaslene, so I take a seat at the kitchen table too. After a few minutes Jaylen figures out the problem, and Sheri turns on some jazz music that echoes throughout the whole house.

Jaylen's holding Jaslene now, and my favorite part is watching the two of them interact. I don't know what it is really, but it makes me feel happy. Like I made the two of them happy by bringing them together.

After about an hour of listening to jazz and Sheri and Jaylen catching up for the week, I'm ready to go. I get Jaylen's attention with a little cough and a nod toward the door. His eyes flicker, and he nods and stands.

"You guys leaving already? I didn't even get a chance to make some treats. I was thinking of chocolate chip brownies. The ones I used to make for you, Jay, when you were seven years old."

I smile. "Oh. I remember those," I say, standing up too. "They were good."

"Why don't you two stay for about another forty-five minutes while I make some? Oh, I do need to run to the store to buy the chocolate chips, though, so maybe an hour and fifteen minutes?" Sheri says, standing up too and wiping her hands on her pants.

"No, thank you," Jaylen and I say. We start heading for the door, and I toss Jaslene's overnight bag on my shoulder. "Bye," I say over my shoulder.

"Wait. Let me say good-bye to my granddaughter," Sheri says, walking over to Jaylen, who's holding Jaslene. She picks Jaslene up and bounces her a little. Then she kisses her face all over, and I'm left hanging out by the door tapping my foot. I know Jaylen needs to talk to me, and I know it's not anything good, so I don't know why I'm excited to be alone with him. Maybe it's because I'll be alone with him.

Finally, inside Jaylen's car I buckle up my seat belt for the long trip. I decide to keep Jaslene up front with me instead of in the back since this is going to be a longer car ride than usual. I place her on the floor in the car seat between my legs and glance over at Jaylen as he starts the car and pulls away. He looks over and smiles at me, and my heartbeat does that thing again when it stops and then starts beating again superfast. "You wanted to talk?" I say before we even make it off the block.

"Yeah," he says, shrugging and looking at the road ahead. It's still light out, but barely, and the sky has turned bluish purple with the sun's orange peeking out in the west. I get the urge to kick off my shoes and relax for the ride, but I don't. Not right now anyway. I want to focus and be attentive to what Jaylen says, not get too comfortable and get sleepy. "But let's talk about you first. How's the whole school thing going?"

I blink a few times. He wants to talk about me? Um . . . okay. "Well, I just applied for school there, but I was thinking about taking online classes so I don't have to leave Jaslene with your mom to babysit every day. I can also stay home and not have to worry about transportation, since the school is a bus ride away."

He nods as he listens. "That's a good idea."

"Really? I mean yeah. I thought a lot about it. I think I told you before, but I'm thinking about getting a job somewhere around campus. Or is that stupid? I mean, if I'm going to campus to work, I might as well go there for class, right?"

He's quiet before he looks over at me, and I'm proud of myself for not blushing this time. I hold his gaze and give him a face to let him know I'm serious.

"Eh. It's up to you, but I think you'll be fine just focusing on school for now. Just wait until you get back into your groove of classes, studying and taking care of Jaslene at the same time, before taking on a job too."

I nod. "Thanks. I mean, yeah, that makes a lot of sense. I know I shouldn't take on more than I can handle, but I feel like I'm so far behind in my life that I'm trying to play catch-up."

"You're just fine, Jess. You're already doing something a lot of people just talk about doing. You need to start being a lot more proud of your accomplishments."

I look down, blushing again. I watch Jaslene sleep and smile. As long as I'm making Jaslene proud and able to keep a roof over her head, I'm fine. I look up again, and we're finally climbing the freeway ramp. I settle more into my seat and look out into the black and gray buildings in the now-dark sky. I turn to Jaylen again. "What did Angela say? I remember you saying something about her making . . . regulations. What does that mean?"

I hear him take a deep breath. "Yeah, me and Angela been arguing about that lately."

"Arguing?" I shift in my seat. "It's not . . . I mean, is it about you seeing me? Or Jaslene?"

"Yes. She was basically trying to tell me when I can come see y'all, how long I can stay, and to take Malcolm with me. I got so pissed off. I mean, I'm working things out with her because I love her and all we've been through, but you ain't about to tell me how much time I can spend with my daughter. I don't care who you are. That's the part that pissed me off." He pauses to look at me. "That's like me saying to you, you can only see Jaslene for three hours a day. You'll cuss me the fuck out."

I laugh and stare at Jaslene. Yeah, I would be mad if anyone tried to limit or put a cap on how long a time I can spend with my own child.

"So we was arguing about that. I told her if she don't trust me, she don't trust me and we're at a standstill. She told me she wanted all my attention on her baby. Our baby, but I told her that's not fair to Jaslene." Jaylen shakes his head like he doesn't want to get stressed out over it. "It's like, she likes that you live far away and that I can't see you two as much. I don't know what her problem is with you—other than the obvious reasons. It's like she wants to move on and fix our relationship, but then she'll say stuff that sets us two steps back, and that's the frustrating part about it."

I nod. I wish I wasn't the problem in his relationship, but I guess, because of that one night we shared, I'll always be a thorn in Angela's life. "Since I'm staying with Kayla tonight, do you think me talking to her would help? Or all three of us talking to reach an agreement?"

Jaylen gives me his best nigga-please look and shakes his head.

"Okay, maybe simply talking to her won't help, but I feel like I should do something." I look at him and try to get him to understand. "I can't do nothing."

"There's nothing to do. I'll work things out with her. For now, I'll just keep coming to see you guys every weekend, giving you money, and spending time with Jaslene. I'm not about to force Malcolm to come every week just to babysit me."

I laugh softly. "So you're sure you won't pick me up in the air like a raging animal and make love to me on the top of your car?"

It was a joke, of course, but Jaylen remains quiet for a long time, and after a few minutes I think that either he didn't hear me or doesn't care to respond. I'm about to say something again to fill in the silence, when he says something so softly I barely hear him. "Maybe I should bring Malcolm every once in a while just in case."

An hour and a half later we pull up to Kayla's apartment building planted near the corner of a busy intersection. The area is dark because of the late hour, but I can spot a few tall men loitering around a few buildings as if they had no choice. I take a deep breath and a place a hand on Jaylen's arm right before he opens his door to get out. He raises his eyebrows and tilts his head to the side.

"Wait, Jay. Before you get out I want to talk to you." He releases his other hand off the door handle and turns toward me and looks in my eyes. "I just wanted to say that I am truly happy for you and Angela." I shake my head and look down at Jaslene. "I guess deep down inside I just want you to be happy because . . . I mean, you're my best friend, and I would never want to come between you and her or whoever makes you happy."

I look at him again. "I feel like Jaslene being your daughter made things difficult for you and Angela, but I guess somehow you found a way to win her back. I guess that means you really love her. It's amazing what love can do. Anyway, my point is, I just want to let you know that I will do anything to help your relationship, whether it's agreeing to Angela's stipulations or regulations or whatever. She wasn't the one in the wrong here. Whatever I can do to help you out and make things easier for you guys, I will."

He doesn't say anything for a few seconds, but then flicks a finger under his chin as he looks at me. "Anything?"

"Yes."

"Move back to Chicago."

I blink a few times. Move back? I can't move back. I've already started to rebuild my life in Aurora. Besides, too many bad memories live here. Not to mention my lack of a place to live. I shake my head slowly. "I can't do that."

Jaylen leans closer to me, and I catch my breath. He's about a foot away leaning over the cup holders. "Just listen to my reasons for a second. For one thing, if you moved back it'll be easier for me to see Jaslene. I can see her every day instead of just a few hours every week. I honestly feel like I'm missing out on her growth and life because you guys live too far away."

My whole body gets cold as I let his words sink in. I never knew he felt this way, and I never realized how much stuff he was going to miss since Jaslene is growing so fast. Soon she'll be walking and talking. Will Jaylen be visiting when she says her first words? Will she recognize him if she only sees him once or twice a week?

I suddenly feel like a horrible parent, and I look down at Jaslene and then back up at Jaylen. "I . . ." I swallow. "You're right. You're absolutely right. I think we need to even things out. She should spend the night with you sometimes. Two or three times a week she can stay up here with you, if you want to do it like that. She'll stay overnight. That way when classes start this fall I'll have days to myself to do homework and sleep and stuff."

I smile, and he smiles back softly. "It's still uses a lot of gas going back and forth from Chicago to Aurora though, Jess."

I nod. "I know, but, Jay, I have to stay down there. I really like it, and I think I'm going to like the school, and I think I might be able to find a job on campus somewhere. I'm really doing it. I'm really rebuilding my life and getting back on track."

Jaylen nods, and I let out a breath I didn't even know I was holding. Suddenly, he reaches over and plants a hand on my leg right between my thigh and my knee. He looks deep in my eyes, and I stare back at him. "But I'll miss you too much."

My heart starts pounding, and a smile appears on my face as I realize his last attempt to keep me involves saying something so sweet. I want to wrap my arms around him and tell him I love him and that I miss him too. That I miss him every day I'm not with him and that I think about him every time I look at Jaslene and every time I wake up and fall asleep. I open my mouth, but then I bite my tongue and close my mouth shut. He is not my man, and I am not going to live my life as the other woman. Somehow I know I deserve more than that. I have to aim higher than that.

I lower my eyes and shake my head. "I'm just a phone call away." I look back at him and keep my eyes and face firm. "Before I can do anything else, I have to get my life in order. I need to be the woman I know I can be, and I have to learn to depend on myself and take care of myself. In Aurora I have school and work and someone to help me take care of Jaslene 24/7. I wish I was at that point where I could drop everything and move to whatever city I wanted to because I have money, time, and resources, but I'm not there yet. I'm not saying I'll never move back to Chicago, but I know right now I need to step away and get back to the basics. It starts with me, and I have to make sure I'm stable enough for myself and my daughter. I'm never going to give this up."

Not three seconds after I finish, Jaylen grabs me and pulls me into his arms and holds me close. I neither have the strength, the attention span, nor the need to push him away. I let myself indulge in his warmth, his love, and right now I feel like I never want to move. That the outside world is too cold and that I'm in the safest place in the world with him.

All too soon he lets go but stays close. There's a sparkle in his eyes, and he's smiling. "I am so proud of you, Jessica."

I blush. He's proud. The man who created a business for himself after dropping out of business school. The man who takes control of his life every time he wakes up is proud. Everyone should be proud of him. And he's proud of me. "Thank you."

"Listen," Jaylen says, leaning back into his seat and putting his hands behind his head. Immediately I feel colder with him not close, and I get the urge to ask him to stay close, but I don't. "You're right about you needing to take care of yourself first. I don't want to come off as selfish, and you know I got your back no matter what. So you stay with my mom until you finish school or until you save up enough money or until you feel comfortable coming back. You left because you believed you'd have a better life in Aurora to start over, and I think you're right."

I nod and get a warm feeling in my chest just knowing that he believes in me.

"We can do whatever pickup and drop-off schedule you want to do with Jaslene. We can keep doing this once-a-week thing until your school starts, and then she'll start staying overnight with me to give you more days off and time for school. It doesn't have to be that concrete, but I'm saying I'm willing to work with you and help you any way possible."

I laugh, and he gives me a confused look. "No, no. I'm laughing because I started off the conversation telling you I'll do anything to help you out in your relationship, and now we're ending the conversation with you telling me you'll do anything for me."

"Hmmph," he says, then chuckles. "You're corny but you're cool."

I laugh again. "Thanks."

We sit in silence for a while, chuckling and smiling every so often. When my phone beeps with a text from Kayla asking where I am, I know it's time for me to go. I climb out of the car slowly, and Jaylen comes around to help me carry Jaslene and her bag while I grab my stuff from the backseat.

Jaylen follows me up to the door, and I ring the buzzer to Kayla's apartment, and after a few seconds I'm buzzed in. I've been here maybe once or twice before to study for homework or a quiz or to just hang out, but that was long ago, so I'm thankful when she pops into the hallway. I need the reminder of where her door is, and conveniently she's on the first floor. She smiles when she sees us, and she gladly takes the baby from Jaylen's hand.

We follow her into her apartment, and I can see both the living room and the kitchen in one glance. She only has one bedroom, so I guess it's big enough for just her.

"Would you guys like a drink?" Kayla says, walking toward the fridge and pulling out a bottle of red vodka.

"No thanks," Jaylen and I say. We look at each other and smile. I'm about to take a seat on the couch, when Jaylen taps me on the shoulder and nods toward the door.

"I'll be right back, Kayla," I say, following Jaylen out the door.

When we reach the hallway, we take a few steps from the door. Jaylen smiles at me. "I'm about to head out before Angela starts calling. But like I said, if you need anything from me, Jess—money, time, a listening ear—just text me or call me. Don't feel like just because I'm with Angela that our friendship has to be put on hold."

"Do you think we can be friends? Since everything that's happened with us, I mean."

He stares at me, and I wonder if he's thinking about my question or if he's thinking about being more than friends with me. I know I've thought about it, but I doubt he has. He probably just doesn't see me that way.

He rubs his chin and studies me like he's trying to figure me out. "I'm very sexually attracted to you. To be honest, one of the main reasons I'm more comfortable with you living in Aurora is I won't be as tempted to . . . um, yeah. Anyway, to answer your question: yes." We laugh, and he comes and wraps me in my arms. I inhale my favorite cologne and feel right at home. I rest my head against his chest. "Best friends."

I nod, still listening to his heartbeat. My fingers lace together behind his back, and even though I know he can't possibly be any closer to me, I want him closer. "Forever."

I know I want to be with him for the rest of my life. I honestly can't picture myself with anyone but him. However, the timing's not right. He has someone else, and I need to get things sorted out in my life, myself. I don't want anyone else though, and no matter what happens or how long it takes, I think I'll wait. I'll wait for him. For the first time in my life, I'm not going to settle on someone else because I can't have the person I really want. Patience, Jessica. Patience.

Chapter Twenty-Six

I walk back into Kayla's apartment and notice all
the clothes and dirty dishes lying on the couch and
floor. My nose wrinkles to the smell of onion dip left
out on her kitchen counter. Kayla is standing over
Jaslene making funny faces by puffing up her cheeks
and bulging her eyes. She turns around when she hears
me close the door. "What did y'all talk about?" she
asks, wiping her hands on her pants.

I shrug and turn my attention to the room. "What
happened in here?"

She blushes, then shrugs. "I was in a rush this
morning and couldn't clean up for you. I figured we
could do it now. Besides, I wasn't sure if I would have

to drive to Aurora to pick you up. You know, just in case Jaylen bailed on you." She tilts her head to the side. "Which brings back the topic. What was y'all talking about?"

I roll my eyes and pick up the jar of onion dip and screw the top back on. I don't want to talk about Jaylen anymore. Not because it's sad but because I want to just enjoy my time with Kayla. She was right about me needing some time away from that house. Even though I don't mind living there, there is never anything to do but stay in the house. "We were just clearing some things up."

"Oh, whatever," Kayla says, rolling her own eyes and starting to pick up clothes off the floor. "You'll tell me at some point."

I don't agree or disagree, but I really don't feel like talking right now. I can't get my mind off Jaylen, and I feel like we broke up and just had our "we'll stay friends" ending to it.

"Do you want me to put in some pizza? I brought two frozen sausage-and-pepperoni pizzas and buttered popcorn just for tonight."

I look around the small apartment in one glance and wonder what she wants to do tonight. It's just us. "Sure, go ahead."

We finish cleaning the entire living room and kitchen by the time the pizzas are done. We sit on the couch to eat, and she puts on a movie. I feel too tired from traveling to pay close attention to the movie, and I keep glancing down at Jaslene to make sure she stays asleep. She's still in the car seat, which will also serve as her bed for tonight.

"I think I'm going to head to bed," I say, standing up and stretching just as the ending credits of the movie play.

"Why?" Kayla asks, her eyes widening and watching me pick up Jaslene's cradle with one hand and my overnight bag with the other. "I was just about to pop in another movie."

"We can watch it tomorrow. I'm just so tired."

"I thought we was going to the mall and out to eat tomorrow before I take you home. How can we have a movie marathon then?" Her face is flushed, and she's pouting her lips like a spoiled kid.

I sigh. "We can wake up around noon and eat lunch, then we can go to the mall and out to eat and stuff. You'll have plenty of time to drop me off and make it back here to get some sleep for work."

She nods and flicks the TV off, and the room falls silent. It's an eerie silence that makes it perfect for a door to creak open or for someone to jump out and yell "boo." She stands up. "Okay, you win. I'm pretty tired too, after cleaning up. But can you please tell me something?" She pauses right before we enter her bedroom with one hand on the door frame and looking back at me with a wicked smile. "Are you in love with Jaylen?"

I blush and shrug, but I can tell by her face she isn't buying it. "Yes, but it doesn't matter. He's in love with his girlfriend. Who is pregnant, by the way."

She raises an eyebrow when I say this, but she shrugs and continues into the room. Her room is small and hosts a gigantic queen-size bed that takes up the majority of the limited space, leaving only a small walkway from the door, her closet, and the bed. "Well, I know one thing," she says, plopping onto the bed and kicking out of her pants. "He's sure as hell is in love with you."

I let out a breath when she says that, and it sounds almost like a laugh. Not that I think the idea of him being in love with me is funny, but the thought of him actually right now being in love with me seems . . . not likely. I mean, I know he must feel something for me, but I doubt if it's anything more than friendship or heavy sexual attraction. "What makes you think that?"

She rolls her eyes as she puts on her PJ pants. "The way he looks at you, for one thing. It looked like he didn't want to leave."

"Oh, well. We're just friends, so it really doesn't matter," I say, climbing onto the other side of the bed and kicking off my shoes. "That's the only way this whole thing will work between us. With Jaslene and me living with his mom in Aurora. It's weird, I know, but . . . I guess at this point being just friends is all we can be."

I look over, and Kayla's staring at me like I've got the information all wrong or missed some bright neon sign. "He loves you. That's all I know."

"He never told me," I say, turning back around to face the wall while I slide off my pants. "How can he? He's not with me and he's with—"

"It doesn't matter who he's with, Jess. You can't control how you feel about a person. I can tell, and I'm telling you. He loves you."

I look at Kayla over my shoulder, and she has a fist balled up and planted on top of the bed. She's staring at me with so much intensity that I can only nod in response. For a while we sit in silence as we both change into PJs, but after a few more minutes I feel that I have to say something.

"What's the point of him telling me he loves me, if he feels that way, that is? If we can't be together anyway. And even if he does love me, he must love Angela more. I mean, she was his girlfriend way before he and I had sex. I don't think I have anything on her."

"That's a lie."

"Come on. She's gorgeous and smart. She even has a college degree. She has no blemishes on her face, and she's in excellent physical shape. The two of them have so much in common, and I think they can talk forever. How can I beat that? I don't even have a job."

Kayla shakes her head and slides under the covers. I move Jaslene a little closer to my side of the bed on the floor so I can reach her when she wakes up. Before I climb under the covers myself, I catch Kayla's eye.

"Don't try to 'beat her.' Jess, you're beautiful too, and you need to stop worrying about beating anyone and just be yourself. Look, I know he loves you. I don't know how much he does, but I can tell by the way he looks at you and talks to you that he feels something strongly about you. And I don't think you have to worry about Angela. She'll do her thing, and you can do yours. If it's meant for you to be with Jaylen, then you will. But for now, don't sweat over him. Focus on yourself for now."

She turns over and flicks off the light, leaving only the glow of the moon shining through the corner of the room where a small window is perched. "Besides, I know Angela doesn't have shit on you." And with that she flips over to her side, and the next thing I know, it's morning.

I hold a baby-sized peal dress up to Jaslene's neck. Kayla and I are at the mall inside a baby store. Kayla is standing next to me texting as I pick out some clothes with the money Jaylen gave me. I rarely use it, but I figure I might as well treat Jaslene to a new set of clothes since she's growing so fast.

The store's smaller than I thought it was, but it does have a nice variety of baby girl selections. I move along, looking through the bundles of clothes, touching and feeling the fabrics, trying to find a nice outfit for my baby girl. I pick up a yellow dress with black polka dots and a scruffy collar, and frown. This is a harder choice than I thought.

We exit the store twenty minutes later, and I leave with a lot of baby shoes and only one dress I was able to find for a good price—a black-and-white one. I have my mind set on getting something to eat, when Kayla stops suddenly and points ahead toward a Macy's door entrance. "Let's go there real quick," she says.

I make a face and roll my eyes. "Girl, I'm starving."

"I just want to check out their jewelry selection," she says, then flicks her hair. "Then maybe I can get one of my suga daddies to buy me one."

I laugh. "Okay, whatever. I'm staying out here though, so just text me when—"

My mouth hangs open at my last words when I spot someone I know walking on the lower level of the mall. Kayla and I are upstairs standing near the railing and close enough that I can look over. That's when I notice Angela.

I move closer to the railing, gripping my hands tightly around it and trying hard not to shake. I haven't' seen Angela since I moved away from Chicago, and I doubt if Jaylen told her I was back. But I know that's her. She has that weave in down to her back, but I can still make out the sharp edges of her face.

Angela's looking around, but thankfully she's not looking up. I can spot her baby bump, and a tinge of jealousy flares up in my throat when I remember Jaylen telling me about her pregnancy.

I'm about to turn back around, when a man approaches Angela. I freeze watching them, and my mouth falls open again.

"Jessica? Jessica, what's wrong?" Kayla's shaking me, trying to revert my attention back to her, but I can't. My eyes are glued to the scene as I witness Angela and the tall, dark-skinned balding man lock hands and entangle themselves in the most engrossing kiss I've ever witnessed.

"Jess?"

I turn back to face Kayla, shaking my head. "Angela's cheating on Jaylen."

"What!"

I narrow my eyes and watch as Angela and her other man continue their public display of affection. Then my thoughts jump to Jaylen, who's most likely at work right now.

I turn back to face Kayla with my mouth gaping open. "Oh. My. God."

About the Author

Shaquanda Dalton was born and raised in Milwaukee, Wisconsin where she is currently pursuing a degree in Creative Writing. She has been writing stories since the age of nine and her debut novel "When Love Hurts" became an Amazon best seller.

In her free time, she blogs about her writing process and also encourages other writers to keep their dream alive. For more information on her blog visit learnasyouwrite.com

Connect with Shaquanda

Twitter- @Learnasyouwrite

Facebook- Jaylen and Jessica series

Did you enjoy I Won't Cry?

Please consider leaving an honest review on the amazon sales page.

Book 3 "I'll Make It Through" will be available late 2013.

Made in the USA
Monee, IL
01 February 2021